P9-CRZ-664

Ex-Library: Friends of
Lake County Public Library

the tension of opposites

the tension of opposites

KRISTINA McBRIDE

EGMONT
USA
NEW YORK

LAKE COUNTY PUBLIC LIBRARY

3 3113 02913 8346

EGMONT

We bring stories to life

First published by Egmont USA, 2010
443 Park Avenue South, Suite 806
New York, NY 10016

Copyright © Kristina McBride Purnhagen, 2010
All rights reserved

1 3 5 7 9 8 6 4 2

www.egmontusa.com
www.kristinamcbride.com

Library of Congress Cataloging-in-Publication Data is available
LCCN number: 2010009447
ISBN 978-1-60684-085-6

Book design by Greg Stadnyk

Printed in the United States of America

CPSIA tracking label information:
Random House Production • 1745 Broadway • New York, NY 10019

All rights reserved. No part of this publication may be reproduced, stored in a retrieval
system, or transmitted, in any form or by any means, electronic, mechanical, photocopying,
or otherwise, without the prior permission of the publisher and copyright owner.

LAKE COUNTY PUBLIC LIBRARY

To my loving husband, Eric, for helping me
make my dreams come true.
Love.
Always.

CONTENTS

A Rock-and-Roll Return

"You're taller than me," I said as I approached the thin figure standing in front of the green bench. A few hundred feet away, several kids playing soccer screamed, "Goaaal!" shattering the first moment of our reunion. Shaded by the leafy arms of the sweet gum tree, Coop turned to watch the boys jump in the air. I caught only a flash, but it was enough. His eyes reminded me of her.

I gently placed my oversize purse on the bench and stepped toward him. My eyes locked on his. "I'm surprised you called, Pooper."

"Hey, none of that." He chuckled. "It's *Cooper*."

My hand flew to my throat. "I can't get over your voice."

He smiled. Tilted his head so his bangs hung down the side of his face. "It'll happen."

I leaned forward and pulled him into a hug, squeezing a little too tight, smelling the familiar scent of the Pendeltons' fabric softener. As I pulled away, I noticed the freckles on his cheeks, darkened by the sun, and, in spite of his square shoulders, caught a flash of a boy I'd once known very well.

In the last two years, I'd seen him only on anniversaries, in the midst of large groups of people. I couldn't ever get close enough to talk. Not that I'd have had any idea what to say. And now, surrounded by the vast openness of our neighborhood park, with nothing between us, it was time for me to figure it out. Fast.

"Starting high school next week, aren't you?" I smiled but figured it came off a little weird, because he flinched.

He nodded. "You'll have to fill me in on everything, you being a mature sophomore and all."

I pressed my lips together, not wanting to tell him how it really was for me. That Tessa McMullen had gone and made herself invisible. "So, how's it going?"

"Could be better." Coop shrugged. "Could be worse."

I glanced down, taking in the huge size of his tennis shoes. The laces were loose. I wanted to lean down and tie them.

"You have your schedule yet?" I asked.

"No. I missed orientation. My parents had this . . ." He trailed off. Somehow, I knew he was about to lie but caught himself, remembering he didn't have to with me.

"How are they?"

His blue-gray eyes darted past me. "Pretty much the same."

I nodded, envisioning one of my favorite pictures of my oldest friend, an extreme close-up, which was tacked to the center of the bulletin board in my bedroom. I studied it often, recalling the day that she leaped barefoot through the long grass of the backyard toward the lens of my camera, pretending to be a shooting star. I was terrified of forgetting the details. The triangle of freckles that tilts to the left under her right eye. Or the dimple in her left cheek that forms only when she's truly smiling.

"I think of her every single day." My voice was a whisper, the words nearly carried away by the steady rush of the fountain centered in the pond behind me.

"Me, too." Coop slid onto the green bench. I waited a moment and sat next to him. "I wonder what she looks like."

I bit at the inside of my cheek. All kinds of statistics would argue that Noelle probably didn't look like much of anything right now. But I wondered stuff like that, too. Every time I saw her face on one of the faded posters still strewn about the town's businesses, I pictured her somewhere new.

Sometimes I saw Noelle sunning herself on a tropical beach, away on an endless vacation. But like my old therapist had told me, it wasn't healthy to ignore reality. Most of the time, I envisioned Noelle in a dark basement, chained to a moldy wall. But that went directly against the information I had found online the day the crisis-intervention speaker came to our middle school and tried to soften the blow of Noelle's absence. In my worst moments, I pictured Noelle's clean bones peeking up from a pile of damp leaves deep in the woods.

"You're probably wondering why I asked you to meet me here," Coop said. He had stubble all over his chin. Actual man stubble. It was white-blond, almost invisible, but it was there.

I shrugged and looked toward the tall plume of the fountain, using all my strength to keep from searching the sidewalk, from focusing on the one square that boiled to the surface of every one of my nightmares.

"She called," he said, his voice steady and sure.

I looked back to his eyes. He blinked. My heart stuttered.

"What?" I croaked.

"She called."

"Noelle?" This time, my voice was overtaken by the rushing fountain, pulled down into the dark, bubbling water. "I don't under—When? You're sure it was her?" My head felt heavy, suddenly strangled with a million questions. The acidic taste of bile tinged my dry mouth.

"Just let me talk, okay? It'll be easier that way."

I swallowed hard, trying to keep it down, then turned quickly, bending over the side of the bench just in time. My body heaved as I threw up all over thick tufts of grass.

Coop put his hand on my shoulder. "I'm fine," I said, wiping my mouth with the back of my hand. "Just tell me what's going on."

Coop squinted in the sunlight that flickered through the leaves above us. "A few weeks ago, someone called, and when I answered the phone, they didn't say anything. But I could tell the person hadn't hung up because there was this muffled sound in the background. Then, after like ten seconds, the line went dead. I didn't think much about it. Wrong number, right?" Coop bit his lip so hard it turned from pink to white.

"But it wasn't?"

"The number came up as a pay phone on the caller ID. With a two-one-six area code. I looked it up online, and that's Cleveland. You know how close that is?"

"It's up north, a few hours."

"Yeah. Lake Erie. It's only, like, three and a half hours away."

I sucked in a breath. "Are you telling me—"

"Lemme finish. Yesterday, the same number came up on the caller ID again. I answered, and it was a girl. She said my name and then hung up again."

"So you just *hope* it's her?"

"She called back about fifteen minutes later." Coop grabbed my hand. His knuckles were peppered with tiny freckles. "It *was* Noelle. She talked so fast, Tess. The first thing she said was 'It's me, Coop. We used to have a dog named Noodles.' It was like some secret code or something, and I can't believe it but I burst out laughing. So she yelled at me. That's when I knew it was her for sure, when she said, 'Shut up, Pooper, this is serious.'"

"What'd you say to that?"

"I apologized. What else?"

"Then what?" I leaned forward.

"It was fast. She said she'd be at the Rock and Roll Hall of Fame in two days at four o'clock, and for us to make sure a plain-clothes officer meets her in the bathroom nearest the entrance. She wants them to arrest the guy, but she has to be hiding from him. The guy who has had her all this time."

"So we're talking about . . . tomorrow?" I opened my mouth, then shut it, not sure I could ask the question in my mind. But I had to. "Noelle's going to be home tomorrow?"

"Well, not home, but safe." Coop tapped his thumb on my hand. "After giving me all the instructions, she said she missed me and hung up."

"Oh. My. God." I squeezed Coop's hand, the heat of his skin grounding me. "Is it for real?"

"It was definitely Noelle. Pooper? Who else but you and her know about that?"

"I can't believe this." I shook my head.

Coop pulled his hand away from mine and ran his fingers through his hair. "I can't, either. After all this time."

"What'd your parents say?"

"My mom fainted. My dad was real quiet, and then he started crying. Like, the heaving, sobbing kind of crying, you know? Then he told me to call the cops and ask for the detective who was on her case a couple years ago. The guy came over, and I gave him the whole story."

"And?"

"They've contacted cops in Cleveland." Coop nodded. "They'll be ready."

"Are your parents there?"

"We're all leaving in a few hours."

"Unbelievable."

"I know." Coop sighed. "You were her best friend. I thought I should tell you."

"Thanks, Coop. I can't believe this."

"It's crazy," he said. "After two years . . ."

"And sixteen days."

Coop ducked his head. "I'm scared."

"It'll be okay." I wrapped my arms around his shoulders. I felt his body tense up a little as I rubbed his back. "She's gonna be safe now."

Those words did it. Released all kinds of feelings that I couldn't control. My body started to shake against Coop's, and he squeezed me tight, holding on like that for a few minutes. I pressed back the tears, wanting to wait until I was alone. When I pulled away, I clasped my hands together to keep them steady.

"I'm a mess!"

"No worse than me," he said. "I'm scared about what to say to her."

"You'll know. You don't need to be scared." I smiled then. But the worried lines around his eyes told me that my smile didn't accomplish much. "You're like my little brother, Pooper-Cooper. If you need me, for anything, I'll be here."

Coop nodded. "Yeah. Okay." He looked to the fountain and took in a deep breath. "I better go. My parents are kind of schitzed out, making phone calls, packing, and stuff."

"Thanks," I said. "For thinking of me."

"Sure," Coop said, standing. "See ya."

As he turned and started walking back to his house, I reached into my oversize purse and wrapped my fingers around my grandpa Lou's old Nikon. My hands were steady by the time I pressed the viewfinder against my eye and watched Coop walk across a flat field of grass that bordered the park. I focused and snapped a shot of him. Then I sat back and stared at the crystal water springing from the fountain's base, racing toward the sky. The sound was soothing, a constant thrum that vibrated my body.

I ran my fingers along the cool underside of the camera, feeling the slight chip from when Grandpa Lou had dropped it on a rock while trying to get a shot of me climbing a tree in the woods.

As a breeze skated across my arms, my attention was pulled toward a line of quacking ducklings that waddled behind their mother in a crooked line, over the grass, into the water. I wondered if Noelle would remember how we used to watch the babies. We'd count them and give them names each season.

I tried to calm the emotions that had overtaken me. My tensed body and mind teetered and tottered between excitement and dread, confidence and fear, doubt and belief. Slowly, I lowered my shoulders, so tight they seemed determined to attach to my ears. I focused on my breathing, counting each deep inhalation, trying to prepare.

I looked around the park, surroundings nearly as familiar to me as my own bedroom. My eyes were drawn to the sidewalk, to the one square of concrete where time had stopped for Noelle two years ago. I had been riding my bike to Carrie's, pedaling fast as I wondered why Noelle wasn't answering my texts, when I found the only known clue. Noelle's red Schwinn was impossible to miss, lying on its side like it had been torn from her clinging hands and spit from the mouth of a monster.

It should look more malevolent, I thought, staring at the thin plane of concrete. *Maybe even flicker, like the mouth of a wormhole, threatening to suck the beauty out of life.*

Coop was probably home by now. I wondered what items the Pendeltons were tucking into their suitcases for the reunion with Noelle.

I stood quickly and grabbed my camera. As I focused on the fountain, which after everything, still churned water toward an empty blue sky, I realized how perfect my timing was. A momma duck followed by several ducklings swam into the picture just before I snapped the shot.

Walking back to my house, I was certain that Noelle and I had watched that momma duck waddling around the pond as a baby. I wondered what we had named her. Petunia? Or maybe Ruby?

She could be one from the spring when we were inspired by the days of the week. *How many weeks have passed,* I wondered, *since Noelle was taken? How many Mondays, Tuesdays, and Wednesdays?* I pictured that duck, her spiky tail feathers shaking back and forth with each careful step, and thought how crazy it would be if she was the one we'd called Friday, the very day that, after all this time, Noelle would turn from lost to found.

2

The Screaming Skull

The deep thrum of the drum line followed me as I made my way down the dirt trail, the echoing voice of the announcer sweeping through the air. "Touchdown by number seventy-two!" The sounds were faint, ghostlike, floating over the tops of the trees surrounding me, snaking through the leaves, puffing into my ears.

It was a muggy night. To keep my hair from sticking to my face, I'd braided it earlier, and the two thick ropes slapped against my back, keeping time with my steps.

I was violating some kind of high-school code by skipping the season's first Friday-night football game. Especially in Centerville, Ohio, where the football team's success or failure seemed to set the mood of the whole town. I was probably the only one not cheering the mighty Elks to victory. But I didn't care.

As I made my way to the Three Sisters, the tug of my grandfather's camera case, its strap slung over one shoulder and across my chest, comforted me. More reassuring than the sway of the camera, though, was the can of pepper spray weighing down my front right pocket as I walked deeper into the woods.

I wondered if Noelle was safe, if her plan had actually worked, and tried to picture her wrapped in the arms of her parents. It was hard to believe, but the last twenty-four hours of not knowing seemed longer than the entire two years Noelle had been missing.

Focus, I told myself, *on what you do know.*

Focus on what you have.

On the surface, my life was pretty great. The previous week, I'd passed my driving test on the first try. The picture on my license showed off the highlights that the summer sun had sizzled into my sandy-blonde hair. And with the help of my parents and grand-parents, not to mention years of accumulated babysitting money, I'd just purchased my dream car. A Jeep. Used, but yellow.

Just yesterday I'd snapped a brand-new parking pass onto the neck of my rearview mirror, and thanks to having been held back in kindergarten for "social reasons" (if I hadn't been so painfully shy, I might never have met Noelle), I was one of the few sopho-mores with the freedom to drive to school. Soon, I hoped to have my best friend sitting next to me as I cruised around town. With her auburn hair blowing loosely around her face, Noelle would flip through songs on my iPod until she found one of our old favorites, then turn up the volume and belt out all the words, which she would, no doubt, remember.

Stepping into the clearing, I felt a rush. The lighting couldn't have been better if I'd been handed a giant paintbrush and streaked the sky myself. Behind the Three Sisters, the orange-red glow of the setting sun gave the impression of a looming fire, somehow making the heat of the night even heavier. Standing back, I snapped a shot of all three trees; their intertwining branches and leaves caused them to seem like a single entity. They were truly stunning, the three 550-year-old oak trees proudly stretching toward the sky.

A roar erupted from the nearby stadium, and I imagined Chip Knowles, the star quarterback, jumping up and down on the field, his helmet reflecting bright flashes of light toward the crowd. I wondered how many cameras were poised to take a picture of his hopping into the air to bump chests with the other players.

Lying on my back, I found a spot to shoot from the ground up, showcasing the immense trunks, the reaching arms. I'd taken five or six pictures, so engrossed in the moment that I didn't notice anything but the trees.

I tried to sharpen the focus, concentrated on bracing my elbows to hold the Nikon steady. That was when I heard it, a familiar click that had not originated from the nature surrounding me. A click that wasn't my own.

I'd just taken a picture—the shutter had flashed before my eye, capturing the moment—yet my ears told me that a camera was in use. Another camera.

My breathing quickened, and I lay unmoving for a few interminable seconds, staring through my viewfinder at the still leaves above me, listening. Four mosquitoes feasted on my blood, attacking my leg, shoulder, and wrist, but I didn't move. And then I heard the click once again. No mistaking it this time. I hadn't imagined the sound.

I was not alone.

Gripping the canister of pepper spray in my pocket, I sat up and looked around. At first, I glanced past him, but I backtracked and found myself staring at a guy in cargo shorts and a green T-shirt. He was holding a camera to his face, focusing on the three enormous trees. His black hair was messy, limp curls framing his face in the oppressive heat.

I heard the sound of the shutter again and watched as he lowered his camera and met my stare. The guy's face was tanned, and he needed to shave. He was probably old enough for college. I tried to keep from noticing how beautiful he was, because thoughts like those can make you vulnerable, leave you open for attack. Having a squared jaw, smooth skin, and full lips certainly didn't make him safe. I rubbed my fingers along the smooth cylinder in my pocket.

Finally, he spoke. "You scared me."

"*I* scared *you*?" I asked with a shaky voice.

"Sorry. I figured everyone was at the game. It's like the town shut down or something. Kind of creepy." He gently placed the camera against his stomach, letting it hang from a thick strap around his neck. Awkward seconds of silence stretched into a minute. Then he spoke again. "They're amazing, aren't they?" He looked past me, sliding his eyes along the trunks of the Three Sisters until his gaze rested up high.

I pushed myself up from the ground and brushed dirt and grass off the butt of my shorts. Studying my exit, I realized that I would be forced to walk past him, within arm's reach, to get back to my Jeep.

I glanced at his arms. They were thick and looked strong

enough to keep me from leaving if that was what he wanted.

"You get some good shots?" he asked.

"I hope so." I had no desire to be pulled into a conversation by this guy, but short of running, I had no idea how to extricate myself from the situation.

"That was a good idea." He pointed to where the Three Sisters erupted from the ground. "Lying on your back and shooting up. Pretty cool."

"Saw it in a book." He couldn't be all bad, could he? He was a photographer, he had an old-school camera, and he knew about the Three Sisters. Still, I clutched the pepper spray.

He smiled, which scared me more than anything up to this point. I moved forward a few steps to give the impression that I was not afraid.

He tilted his head to the side. "Am I freaking you out or something?"

"No," I said, pulling my shoulders back. "Why?"

"Nothing, I guess." He walked backward a few steps toward the path. "Gonna be dark soon. I'm heading back to my car."

I looked to the sky as if his comment about darkness clued me in on something. From the stadium, the announcer's voice boomed, and the band started playing the fight song.

"Wanna walk back with me?" he asked.

"Think I'll take a few more shots before I go," I said.

"I can wait." He nodded, and a loose curl slumped into his eye. His lips pulled back again, just a hint of a smile this time. He splayed his hands in the air. "I'm harmless, really."

"I work better when I'm alone." I raised my camera to my face and turned, noticing the shadows that were crowding the tree-tops. It hurt a little somewhere in my stomach, having my back to this stranger. My insides screamed for me to turn, to watch his hands, to make sure he didn't get too close. But I couldn't. Not if I wanted him to leave.

"Hope they turn out," he said. "Your light's not going to last more than a few minutes."

I lowered the camera and noticed that he'd taken a few steps up the path. "I'm experimenting with the aperture and shutter speed," I said. "I know what I'm doing."

"I'm sure you do." He shot me another one of those smiles. This time it didn't creep me out. It just pissed me off.

He left and I stayed, waiting longer than necessary before making my way to the parking lot. *He should be long gone*, I told myself as I walked that last stretch of wooded trail.

But he wasn't. He was leaning against a black Mustang with his arms crossed over his chest. "Just wanted to make sure you got out okay," he said, a hint of velvety softness creeping into his words. Part of me wanted to believe him. But the always-guarded part of me had the urge to scrape that smile off his face with my fingernails.

"I'm fine." I waved my camera in the air and speed-walked to my Jeep, not wanting him to see me run. I unlocked the door quickly, slid into the driver's seat, and slammed the door before engaging the locks. I felt kind of silly. The top was off. He could jump in through the back if he really wanted to. But he just stood there, leaning against his car. When I turned the key in the ignition, the air-conditioning blasted warm air into my face, and the clock in the dashboard told me I was late checking in with my parents. But I needed to get out of there before digging through the camera case to find my phone.

As I pulled out of the parking space, I noticed a rusty orange Camaro that hadn't been in the parking lot when I arrived. For a second, I just sat there with the Jeep in reverse and stared at the rear window of the old car. Centered at the bottom of the window was a sticker of a screaming skull with flames shooting out the back of its head. It made my skin creep, spooked me even more than I already was. It was that silent scream. Lost forever.

Noelle was always in my mind. The trick was to push away any thoughts of what might have happened after the last time I saw her pedaling away on her red Schwinn. If I thought about it too hard, the little things got to me. Like not remembering if she turned back and waved over her shoulder that very last day, or just rode away without a glance.

It wasn't enough, just knowing that Noelle was alive and on her way back to us. So I sat there wondering if Noelle had screamed when she was taken. And if she had, why hadn't anyone heard?

I shivered in spite of the heat and put the car in drive.

She'll tell you everything soon, I told myself. *She's almost home.*

It was the guy who got me going, his offer to wait and walk with me through the woods. I tried not to think about the deep tan that must run along the smooth skin covered by his shirt. But that didn't work so well. And even though I promised myself I wouldn't look, the last thing I saw when I passed the black Mustang was that guy with all those dark curls, waving one hand in a silent good-bye.

Opposites

"Did you see the news?" a girl behind me asked.

"No," said another. "Something juicy?"

It was the first day of school, and I was standing in front of my open locker, staring at the looping *L* on the spine of my new literature textbook, listening to people nearby.

"Noelle Pendelton is alive."

"Get out!"

"Seriously. You've got to see the picture of the kidnapper guy. *So* creepy. His eyes make me feel like I have bugs crawling all over my skin."

"I'll have to get online during my free period."

The story of Noelle's return had been splashed all over the TV since the day she'd been found. My parents and I had eagerly awaited Friday's evening news, our nerves taut as we read and reread the Breaking News banner that ran along the bottom of our screen.

LOST OHIO TEEN FOUND AFTER TWO YEARS OF CAPTIVITY.

My mom and dad sat on the couch, pressed against each other, not even trying to hold back their tears. I was balled up on the recliner, rocking slowly back and forth.

When the news began, a quick clip ran, and I caught my first glimpse of Noelle as she was shuffled into the police station. It wasn't a good view, and I strained my eyes trying to see around the crowd, but of course, it didn't work; I was looking at a television. Trying to offer her some privacy, the officers held up folders and jackets so the media couldn't catch a good shot. The attempt to shield her helped, but from between two men, I saw a flash of her. Noelle's hair wasn't auburn anymore; it was jet-black and really long and stringy. She looked pale, and her face was kind of puffy. I felt the first glimmer of the fear Coop had been talking about.

I sat there in the leather seat holding on to a pillow, scratching my fingernails over its embroidered flowers. Suddenly, it seemed like a lot more than two years had passed since that last day with Noelle.

Then the screen flipped to a shot of a police car, and through what seemed like an electrical storm of camera flashes, I saw Charlie Croft.

I felt really cold, but also hot and tingly at the same time.

After everything, I finally knew what he looked like, the man who had taken Noelle. He was very tall and large; his round stomach pushed against the fabric of the orange coveralls he wore. Cuffs bound his hands and ankles. His scruffy face was covered with deep, craggy lines, and his dark hair was flattened against his head. The news camera caught him head-on as he shuffled from the car toward an open door in the rear of the police station. When he glanced up, I saw a flash of his eyes. They were an opaque black and made my head feel suddenly afloat. I gripped the arm of the leather chair, not wanting to lose control.

As the newscaster reported that Noelle's kidnapper had never been arrested before, my brain whirred, repeating the one question that over the last two years had been totally and completely, under all circumstances, off-limits. Only this time, it was worse, because for some reason, seeing Charlie Croft made everything terrifyingly real.

What, exactly, did that man do to my Noelle?

"Tessa," my mother said, stretching out a thin arm, waving me to the couch with her long fingers, "come over here."

My father scooted over and patted the tan fabric with his bear-size hand. Then he rubbed his eyes with his knuckles, smearing tears along his upper cheeks.

When I sat between them, their arms encircled me. The soft flannel of my mother's pajama top brushed my jaw, and the heat from my father's body melted me into a younger version of myself.

I breathed in the vanilla scent of my mother's lotion and waited to see the video of Noelle again. As reporters spewed the statistical unlikelihood of a missing child's being found after such a long period of time, all of them speaking with heavy voices as they deemed this homecoming a miracle, my father's hand gripped my arm.

I watched an interview with our seventh-grade social-studies teacher, who claimed that Noelle was "a little on the wild side, but in a fun way." And another with an old family friend of the Pendeltons' whose house we used to go to for barbecues every summer. He claimed Noelle could beat anyone at Ping-Pong. I'd forgotten about that.

The clip of Noelle played several more times. After I had every detail cataloged in my memory, I stood and looked at my parents. They were both wet-faced. Soggy and limp. I reached for a tissue on the end table and handed it to my mother.

"It is a miracle," she said, her words muffled by the thin paper that covered her leaking nose.

I smoothed down the fuzzy brown hairs sticking up from the top of her head.

My father stood and hugged me too tight, the zipper of his fleece biting into my cheek.

"We love you," he said, his voice catching.

"Love you, too," I answered, feeling robotic, like a mechanical me. I left them there staring after me, and climbed the steps toward my room. After crawling into bed, I stared at the clock on my nightstand, watching the numbers tick away as I wondered how many more hours it would be before I could talk to her again.

Four days later, as someone's shoulder bumped against mine while I walked down the crowded hall on the first day of my sophomore year, I realized that since Noelle wasn't there, I was her substitute.

Almost everyone I passed stared at me, but no one made eye contact.

"I heard there were a bunch of reporters at the park yesterday," someone said as they passed me.

"Did you see the house she lived in?"

"What about that interview with the old lady who lived next door?"

I hoped that Noelle would be as strong as I remembered so she could face all these people. But if the old lady they were talking about was right, numerous people had seen Noelle in public over the years. I wanted to know why she had never told anyone who she really was. And I wondered if it was possible that Charlie Croft had actually broken her.

After ditching lunch to hang out in the library, I made my way through the crowded halls and slowly walked into the photography classroom. I was freaking out a little because I knew life photography, a yearlong class for upperclassmen (and me), would be different than any other photography class I had ever taken.

My breath was all shaky, and I felt a little off balance as I walked through the doorway. A few people stared at me as I sat down, but I didn't hear anyone whispering about Noelle. If nothing else, that made me feel better.

I was looking at my desk, rubbing my finger along a message carved into the wood that said *Run, baby, run*, when I felt a tap on my arm. Darcy Granger plopped into the seat to my left, her face and arms deeply tanned from summer break. I felt my shoulders relax, falling several inches.

"I thought you dropped this class," I said.

"I talked my dad into letting me ax French four instead. Convinced him I won't use it ever again." She shrugged. "College will have nothing to do with French and everything to do with fashion photography." She swept her dark brown hair over her shoulder and leaned back in her seat, snapping a bubble of pink gum. She was always chewing gum, and she always smelled like strawberries.

"Isn't Paris the fashion capital of the world?" I asked.

Darcy flipped her hand in the air. Flopped her sandal against the bottom of her foot. "I did what I had to do."

"I'm glad you're here," I said.

"How many times do I have to tell you?" Darcy crossed her long legs under her desk and smoothed her short skirt along the tops of her thighs. "You don't need me."

"Whatever." I opened the blue folder in front of me and pulled out several pictures, placing them on my desk. "If it wasn't for you, I wouldn't even be in this room, all tied up in knots."

"You're not still mad at me, are you?" Darcy turned sideways in her seat so she was facing me. Her little nose twitched with each chomp of the gum. "Maybe I didn't do it the right way, but I know I did the right thing."

"You were trying to be nice," I said. "So I forgive you."

"Good. Enough of that." Darcy took a deep breath. "Did you see all the counselors in the atrium?"

I nodded. "Like they can say anything to help."

"I thought maybe you'd . . . I dunno, need to talk to someone. With everything they're saying on TV about—"

"Nope." I shook my head and looked down at the glossy

black-and-whites, glad that this girl who had decided to take me on as her pet project last year knew when to push and when to back off.

I was about to pass Darcy my favorite pictures of the Three Sisters when he walked into the room.

With one hand tucked in the front pocket of his jeans, he drifted through the door. I knew who it was immediately: all that messy black hair gave him up before he even looked at me. I tried to look away, but I was still staring when his eyes found me. He paused, and then smiled. That same smile he'd flashed me in the woods. He nodded and walked to the empty desk to my right, sliding into the seat as I shoved my pictures back into the blue folder.

"Hey," he said. "It's you."

I tipped my head toward him, trying not to grin or do anything stupid that might give away how shocked I was that he had recognized me.

"I didn't catch your name." He dropped a pen and notebook on his desk. "The other night, I mean. When you crept up and scared the crap out of me." He was smiling again. His teeth were almost perfect, except for one that turned in a little on the side of his top row.

"Tess," I said quietly. "And I remember the other night a little . . . differently."

"I'm Max." He pulled at a strand of his hair and tucked it behind his ear.

"Hey," I said, and then looked at Darcy.

She raised her perfectly plucked eyebrows, popped her gum, and mouthed the word *hot*.

I rolled my eyes, trying to act like I hadn't noticed. But really, all it took was one glance. Every girl in our school would want a piece of him. Except, of course, me. I wasn't interested in guys. Not that I liked girls or anything. I just preferred to be alone.

A minute later, the bell rang, and Mr. Hollon, one of the school's youngest teachers, walked to the front of the classroom. He was wearing a navy blazer and a teal tie-dye T-shirt. His hair was pulled back into a ponytail that brushed his shoulders as he patted his pockets, looking for something. I had to force myself to focus on all this. To keep my eyes from darting to the dark boy seated next to me.

"Lose something?" someone from behind me asked.

A few people chuckled.

"My blue pen," Mr. Hollon said.

More chuckles filled the room. The pen was clearly visible to all of us, tucked neatly behind Mr. Hollon's right ear.

Darcy ahemmed loudly and gestured toward the side of her face.

"One moment it is lost"—Mr. Hollon smiled and slowly reached for the item—"and the next it is found. And that, my friends, is our first lesson."

I heard low chatter around me.

"This simple demonstration is the foundation for a yearlong project that I expect you to begin thinking about immediately."

"Lost and found?" someone asked.

"Well," Mr. Hollon said, "what those two words represent."

I sucked in my breath. Knowing.

"Just like Noelle Pendelton."

The whisper slammed into my back, and I stiffened. In my peripheral vision, I saw Max look at me. I ignored him.

"Maybe this wasn't the best idea, considering the recent news. . . ." Mr. Hollon bent forward a bit and put the pen on the desk in front of him. "Let's try this another way. I'll say a word, and you say the first thing that comes to your mind. Ready?" He put his hands in the air. "Fast."

"Slow." Several voices spoke together.

"Hot."

"Cold." More voices joined in.

"Up."

"Down." This time almost the entire class answered together.

"We could go on all day, right?" Mr. Hollon nodded. "What are we listing?"

"Antonyms."

"Ooh, fancy." Mr. Hollon laughed. "Very good. And . . . antonyms are?"

"Opposites," Darcy said.

"Right!" Mr. Hollon touched his finger to the side of his nose. Then he quickly walked to the door and flipped off the light. After stepping to his desk, he hit a few buttons on his keyboard, and the image of an eagle soaring over a mountain peak flashed on the whiteboard behind him. "What's this?" he asked.

"A bird."

"An *eagle*."

"Okay." Mr. Hollon nodded. "But what does it represent?"

"Flight."

"Freedom."

"The United States."

"Now we're getting somewhere." Mr. Hollon looked at all of us. "Take out a pen and piece of paper."

There was shuffling all around as I opened my notebook and pulled a pen from my purse. I couldn't help looking at Max, this new guy who, with his slouching posture and legs stretching into the aisle, seemed more at ease with my classmates after a few hours than I did after my entire life.

"Write down what this picture represents to you."

I wrote *freedom*, not caring that I had stolen the word from the classmate who had shouted it out a few moments earlier.

"Now comes the tricky part. I want you to write down three things you could photograph that would oppose that thought, feeling, or idea."

I stared at my teacher.

Tricky?

Not so much.

I looked down at my paper and wrote one word three times.

Noelle

Noelle

Noelle

"Now," said Mr. Hollon. "Write three more words. What thought, feeling, or idea would your picture represent?"

I looked around the room, several words echoing through my head.

Kidnapped, abducted, snatched

Enslaved, imprisoned, restrained

Most people were hunched over their papers, writing. A few

others stared at the drop ceiling, squinting into the fluorescent light, or studied the rows of pictures that plastered the walls like patchwork wallpaper. I twisted in my seat, wanting to walk to the row of computers that ran along the back of the room, needing an update on Noelle and the guy who had taken her. Instead, I watched an orange-breasted robin land on a swaying branch of the tree right outside the classroom window. Counted the flowers Darcy doodled along the side of her paper.

Mr. Hollon walked past my desk, tapping his finger on my paper. I swiveled around to find Max facing me, one elbow balanced on his desktop and the other on the back of his seat. His fingers were intertwined, his hands resting on his chest.

"Whatcha got?" he asked, his whisper nearly scalding me.

I covered my paper with one hand. "You wouldn't understand."

Max leaned forward, and I breathed in his clean scent. My brain rode a wave of laundry detergent, shampoo, and bar soap. I fought to keep from being pulled under. If I allowed myself, I might sit here for the rest of my life, breathing him in.

Max propped his elbows on his knees and crossed his forearms over his legs. "Try me."

My hands started shaking, so I clasped them together. All those words were still shouting through my head, jumbling everything so that nothing made any sense. Least of all my desire to reach out and rub my thumb along Max's smooth lips. "I'm not even finished," I said.

Max stared at me, his smile pulling inward a bit. "Better get to it, then."

I ducked my head toward my notebook, scratching my pen

across the paper several inches from my eyes. Max leaned back into his seat. He swung his knees lazily in the aisle. Darcy flipped and flopped her sandal. She popped another bubble of her gum.

Finally, I wrote the three words represented by Noelle, thinking about how she and the idea of freedom opposed each other.

Captive

Prisoner

Hostage

Mr. Hollon finished his round through the desks and parked himself in front of the classroom, blocking my view of his prize-winning close-up of a praying mantis. "Anyone care to share?"

Max raised his hand.

Mr. Hollon's eyes scrunched closed. "Mr. . . . Kinsley, right?"

"Yeah." Max nodded. "I immediately pictured myself in the backseat of my parents' car." Several people laughed. "I was their prisoner as we drove from Montana to Ohio, away from all my friends and family, miserable about spending my junior and senior years with a bunch of strangers."

As Max spoke this long string of words, I was surprised to remember that his voice was velvety soft. Somehow my memory of the previous Friday in the woods had been distorted, the sound of his voice turning more abrasive with each passing day. I had expected his words to be gruff and crackly—scratchy to my ears, the way the stubble on his face would feel against my hand.

Mr. Hollon moved on, allowing several other people to share, and I tried to catch another glance of Max without being obvious. It didn't work. When he caught me looking, his face broke out into another one of those smiles from the woods. A smile that I found myself starting to like. Maybe a little too much. Just before I looked away, a few loose curls dipped forward onto his forehead, and he swiped them back with his hand.

"So there we have it. Your portfolio theme is the Tension of Opposites. We will learn many different techniques during the first three quarters of the year, and by the end of March, you will put together a portfolio demonstrating your mastery of each lesson. Fourth quarter will be an intensive on style. We'll talk about that later."

Everyone got quiet. I glanced at Max's brown leather shoes. He was tapping his foot, and I wondered what kind of music he liked. Then I squeezed my eyes shut. Since when did I care anything about a random guy sitting next to me?

"What about the Tension of Opposites?" Darcy asked.

"In addition to fulfilling a variety of requirements, while also taking the best pictures you can take, you'll infuse your work with emotion by showing the opposition that is evident in every aspect of life." Mr. Hollon looked around the room. "Put plainly, each photograph in your portfolio must have an opposing image."

I thought that maybe my first photograph could be of Max. The next, a self-portrait. He was so confident. And I was so . . . not.

"I know a few of you prefer to use thirty-five-millimeter cameras. I expect you to find some way to incorporate a digital trick or two into your final project. And I might suggest that you hoard all the film you can get your hands on. It's going out of style. Fast," Mr. Hollon said as he passed out the classroom rules and syllabus for the first quarter. "For the remainder of the period, I'd like for you to make a list of all the antonyms you can think of. Hopefully this exercise will jump-start your creative process."

I put my pen to the paper in front of me.

Right and wrong

Easy and difficult

Big and small

Concrete and imagined

Max leaned in to me again. "How'd your pictures turn out?"

His scent infiltrated my nose. Scrambled my brain all over again. "What?"

"The Three Sisters?" He tilted his head, his eyes soft and sincere.

"Oh." I took in a deep breath. Through my mouth. "Pretty good."

"I'd love to see them."

"Yeah, right," Darcy said. Then she snapped her hand to her mouth, hiding a smile.

I turned to her and widened my eyes.

"Oh. Did I say that out loud?" Darcy slid forward and looked past me, speaking directly to Max. "Tessa is a bit shy," she said, like I wasn't even there.

Max's brown eyes locked on mine. I looked away.

"Shy?" he asked Darcy.

"She only shows her pictures to two people. Mr. Hollon"— Darcy pointed at our teacher, now seated behind the mess piled on his desk, and then turned her finger toward herself—"and me."

"Really?" Max crossed his arms over his chest and looked at me. "Didn't you have to turn in some kind of portfolio to get accepted into this class? I thought the whole Art Department evaluated the applicants, deciding who's in and who's out."

"Yeah," I sighed. "Not my idea."

"Last year," Darcy said, "I was Mr. Hollon's teacher aide the same period Tessa had photography. When I saw how good her pictures were, I talked him into letting her apply early. Tessa, however, wasn't so easy to sway. She chickened out at the last minute." Darcy shrugged. "So I broke into her locker and turned the portfolio in for her."

Max sat back in his seat. "Classic."

"She's lucky it worked." I tapped my pen on my paper. Wrote two more words. *Friend* and *enemy*.

"All I did was get you in." Darcy pointed her finger at me. "You could've taken it off your schedule."

"I know," I said, looking from Darcy to Max. "I had this crazy *whatever* moment when I was in the counselor's office going over my classes. I just let it go."

"It was a good decision," Darcy said. "You'll see."

"Hey, Darcy," someone called from the back row. "Come back here for a minute. I gotta ask you something." Darcy popped out of her seat, rushing back to talk for the last five minutes of class.

"Just so you know," Max said, rapping his knuckles on my desk, "I like a challenge."

"Don't bother," I said. "Darcy's right. I don't show my stuff to anyone. Ever."

Max shook his head. "That right there. That was a challenge if I ever heard one."

"No," I said, wondering if Max could feel the vibrations of my pounding heart. "It totally wasn't."

"I'll have my pictures later this week," Max said. "I'll show you mine"—he smiled again, lowered his voice to a near whisper— "when you're ready to show me yours."

Part of me started to hate him. Wanted to scream for him to leave me alone. It was the side of me that did everything possible to keep people—all people—away. But another part of me, the side that was dying for a friend (or maybe a little more), the side that I wanted to tear out and mash into the carpet, felt a little excited.

"I don't think so," I said, bending over the lines of my notebook, pressing my mind toward the next pairing of opposites. Trying, trying, trying not to smile.

4

Special Delivery

Noelle and I are at our neighborhood park, sitting at the grassy edge of the pond. Thirty feet away, a fountain splashes water toward our bare feet, which dangle in the cool water. We're both laughing hysterically at something. Noelle's head is thrown back, her face tipped to the sky. Her eyes are squeezed tightly against the sun, and the fingers of both hands curl around long green grass that sprouts from under her legs. And me, I'm looking right at her, my mouth open wide as laughter pours from me. This is one of my favorite pictures from the summer I turned fourteen. Sitting there next to her, I had no idea it would be our last summer together.

Noelle had never seen the image, which had been taken a few weeks before she went missing. Every time I looked at it, I wondered if we'd both known, on some instinctive level, what was drawing near. With Noelle gripping the ground like she didn't want to be torn away, and me staring like I was trying to memorize every aspect of her that I could, it wasn't so hard for me to believe that we'd heard a whisper carried on the wind. If only the message had been a shout, if only we could have prepared, everything in my world might have remained right side up.

Lying on my bed, clutching the photograph, I glanced at the television on my dresser. I'd muted the sound when I flopped down in the middle of my bed, deciding as I waited for the interview to start that it was finally time to prepare the gift I'd held on to for years.

I slid the picture into a frame and secured the back in place, then dropped it into a slender box and sighed. Noelle had been home for over a week, and every time I gathered the nerve to call, one of her parents or Coop told me she wasn't ready to talk. So far, this interview was the best shot I had at getting any new information about her. And this gift was the best plan I'd come up with to see her face-to-face.

"An act of denial," my therapist had said when I told him about the picture and how I planned to give it to her one day. During that session, he made me choose a date when I would admit she was gone, acknowledge that she was never coming home. The date became a big deal to him, and when it arrived, I lied, telling him I had put the framed picture in a box, wrapped it, and buried it in the woods behind the park.

For effect, I added that I had played our theme song, "One Step at a Time" by Jordin Sparks, on my iPod while mounding damp dirt on top of the entombed box, pressing it deeper into the ground as the melody swept through the swaying treetops.

He steepled his fingers under his chin and nodded slowly, then said he thought I no longer needed to see him on a regular basis. When I walked out his door for the last time, I wondered if he was calling me cured and almost laughed.

I folded a piece of cream-colored card stock and opened it before pulling the cap off a purple gel pen.

Forever friends, I wrote.

And then, *Love you. Tessa.*

I stuffed a few pieces of white tissue paper into a gift bag and gently placed the box inside, then tucked the handmade card beside it and pushed everything away from me, pressing my face into my patchwork comforter. Part of me wanted to call Dr. Anderson and tell him how very wrong he had been. Noelle was home. If I had actually buried the picture, I wondered, would the box still be there, waiting for me to dig my fingers into the soft soil and pull it into the sunlight?

I looked up to see Noelle's parents seated at a table behind a line of microphones. I hit the volume button and heard the rustle of paper and the rush of hushing voices.

Mr. Pendelton looked at the scene before him, wiped his scruffy cheek with one hand, and then started speaking. "First of all, we want to express our gratitude to all the people who have helped from the very beginning."

Mrs. Pendelton nodded. "There is no way to thank you enough. All the long hours of searching, following up on leads, the prayers—they all played a part in Noelle's safe return."

"Noelle is home now," Mr. Pendelton said. "Nothing matters more."

"How is she?" asked a voice from behind the cameras.

"She's okay. Struggling a bit, as expected." The camera zoomed in on Mrs. Pendelton, highlighting the dark purple bags under her eyes. "We just want to give her some normalcy after everything she's been through."

"So . . . as I'm sure you will all understand and respect"—Mr. Pendelton cleared his throat—"we will not be doing any additional interviews. We need to allow Noelle some space. And to keep the media circus as far from her as possible."

"You mentioned normalcy. When will she be returning to school?" This was a different reporter. His voice was softer, not as close to the microphones. I turned up the volume, leaning forward as I watched the Pendeltons glance at each other.

"We're not sure. We're seeking advice on how to deal with the different situations that will arise. Right now, we're just trying to love our daughter." Mr. Pendelton's voice cracked.

"We know how lucky we are," Mrs. Pendelton said.

"Do you know anything about what happened to Noelle during the two years she was gone?"

Mr. Pendelton closed his eyes.

"We're going to let her share those things when she's ready." Mrs. Pendelton reached over and grasped her husband's hand.

"The arraignment was today, and Croft pleaded not guilty," another reporter stated. "What about the trial? Will Ms. Pendelton testify against Croft?"

The camera zoomed out as a man who was seated next to Mr. Pendelton leaned toward the microphones. His thick red beard looked scratchy and rough. "I'm Garrett Kelley, the lead prosecutor for this case. All I can say about the issue is that I have spoken with her and I am very impressed with her strength and fortitude."

Noelle's parents thanked everyone again and then stood. Cameras flashed brightly and reporters shouted as the couple walked offscreen. I took a deep breath and closed my eyes. How could Noelle's life ever return to normal?

I sat up, grabbed my cell phone, and dialed the first three numbers of the Pendeltons' house, then threw the phone down on my bed.

If I called, they would tell me the same crap about Noelle not being ready for visitors. And I couldn't let that happen.

As I drove through the familiar neighborhood, my mind wandered back in time, recalling the details of one of the last days I had spent with Noelle.

"What are you gonna do with this old thing anyway?" Noelle slid forward in her chair and picked up the camera I'd set on the patio table, turning it around in her hands. I wanted to fling its thick strap around her neck to make sure she wouldn't drop it on the concrete.

"Dunno." I shrugged. "Use it, I guess."

"It's not digital, though?" Noelle crinkled her nose.

"You have no appreciation for the finer things, Noelle," Coop said as he hopped down the kitchen steps with an orange Popsicle in his hand, plopping into one of the padded chairs around the table.

"Who asked you?" She kicked at his bare feet, which he swept off the ground and propped on the table.

"Eew." Noelle swatted at his long legs. "People *eat* here, you know?"

Coop rolled his eyes. "Like Mom has ever let anyone enjoy a meal outside without dousing this table in Clorox first?"

"But your toenails are *disgusting*." With her eyes narrowed to slits, Noelle inspected her brother's toes.

"A little length never hurt anyone," Coop said, sliding his foot toward Noelle's face with a laugh.

Noelle flung herself back into her chair before he could make contact. "If any of your foot fungus gets on me, I won't hesitate to kill you."

My eyes fluttered back to Noelle's hands. I held my breath, waiting for my grandfather's camera to crash to the ground, smashing its lens into a thousand tiny pieces.

"Is there any film in here?" With one hand, Noelle shielded her eyes from a wave of sunlight that burst from behind a passing cloud.

"I loaded a roll this morning," I said. I held out my hands, and Noelle passed the camera over. "My dad had to help me figure it out."

Noelle stood up, pulled at the waist of her tank top, and ran barefoot into the Pendeltons' grassy backyard. "Take one of me!"

"Uh-oh," Coop said. "This could be trouble."

"Come on, Noelle. My grandpa used this camera for serious stuff."

"I'm not a serious subject?" Noelle flung her arms in the air and spun in looping circles, like we used to do as kids, trying to get that drunken-dizzy feeling and seeing who could stand up the longest.

"Just this morning, my dad spent twenty minutes on a grueling version of his this-is-not-a-toy lecture." I stood and pointed the camera at a red bird perched on the branch of a tree that butted up to the back of their house. "He's waited three years to give me this camera. It's the one thing Grandpa Lou left just for me. I don't want my first roll of film to—"

"How offensive." Noelle stopped spinning and placed one hand on her chest, holding the other out into the air to steady her balance. "I'm pained beyond words that you don't feel I'm good enough to photograph."

"You're a drama queen." Coop balled up his Popsicle wrapper and launched it at Noelle. She ducked, her hair flaring out, and the paper spiraled over her head.

I secured the camera's strap around my neck and centered the bird in the frame. My finger found the shutter-release button and pressed. The shutter clicked and the bird startled, flying into the air.

"Hey!" I placed the camera against my stomach, walked back to the table, and sat. "Stupid bird."

"I won't run away," Noelle said in a singsong voice.

"No," Coop said. "We'll never be that lucky."

Noelle stuck her tongue out at her brother. "You love me, and you know it."

"Like I love gnarly foot fungus," Coop said.

"Just one, okay?" Noelle propped a hand behind her head,

her elbow sticking up toward the deep blue sky, jutting her hip into the air in a way that made her teal miniskirt sway back and forth.

I sighed, stood up from the table, and stepped into the silky grass. "Fine," I said, raising the camera to my face.

"Have I ever told you," Noelle said as she moved toward me with a huge grin on her face, "that sometimes I feel like a shooting star?"

"Stop there," I said, pressing the shutter-release button.

"But I'm a star, and I'm going to fly!" Noelle leaped toward me, her face filling the entire frame just as the camera snapped her picture.

"Noelle, you ruined the shot," I said with a slight whine. "I want this entire roll to be perfect."

She giggled and started spinning again, her long chestnut-colored hair twirling around her body.

"Leave it to her," Coop said from behind me, "to mess everything up."

"Oh, shut up, Pooper," Noelle said with a giggle.

Coop shoved the Popsicle stick into his mouth and crunched it, smiling at Noelle.

"That drives me crazy," she said.

Coop crunched again, splintering the wood into several tiny slices. When he pulled it from his mouth, it looked like a miniature broom. "I live to drive you crazy."

"I'm gonna go," I said, reaching for the camera case and tucking the Nikon into its cool dark security. "I'm gonna head to the park and get some shots of the ducks or trees or something."

"Oh my God!" Noelle clapped her hands and ran to the table. "That's perfect. Pooper, go get your shoes. You're coming, too."

I shouldn't have said anything. Once Noelle got something in her head, there was no turning her back. Still, I always tried. "I was going to go by my—"

"One more shot," Noelle said. "You and me by the fountain. Shoes off, toes slipping into that cool water. It'll be great."

"Noelle, I—"

"Not another word from you," Noelle said. "Pooper, why aren't you moving?"

Coop shook his head, his longish blond hair waving in the breeze. Looked into the sky like he hadn't heard a word Noelle had said.

"Ugh, fine." Noelle walked behind Coop's chair and leaned over her brother's shoulder. "*Cooper*, love, be a dear and slip on some shoes. I'd be forever indebted if you could take a picture of me and my BFF by the fountain."

Coop nodded. "Love to," he said, brushing Noelle's tanned arm with the slimy wood.

"Gross, Pooper." Noelle flicked him in the forehead.

"Watch it, sis," Coop said, pushing her hand away. "I just agreed to do you a favor."

"Fine," Noelle said with a huff. "I'll get you back later."

Coop ran up the steps and pulled open the screen door to the kitchen. "I'll meet you guys out front."

Noelle held her hand out to me, and I stepped forward, taking it in my own, not knowing that years would pass before the opportunity would arise again.

41

After I rang the doorbell and stood waiting, I couldn't catch my breath. *No*, I told myself. *You will not lose control again.*

The first time it had happened, I had been alone. It was sudden, my breathing coming a little too fast, shallow; I couldn't catch the deep breath my body demanded. My heart pounded to escape my chest, as if I'd just sprinted the entire way to the park, but in reality, I'd been hiding against the rough bark of a thick tree for at least an hour. When my chest exploded, I was certain I'd had a heart attack, knew I was going to die.

I cried out to the long line of people holding hands and taking mini steps away from the crashing fountain, but no one heard. They continued to stare at the ground, shuffling over each thread of grass, searching for any clue. I leaned back against the tree, clutching at my chest, pressing my hands against my eyes, waiting for the bright light that signified the end. But it never came. Gradually, my hearing cleared, my body relaxed, and I shuffled home. I told my mother everything, except where I had been, and she frantically dialed my doctor, who, after giving me a head-to-toe checkup, told me I'd had a panic attack and referred me to a therapist. I guess after all that had happened in the five days since I'd found Noelle's abandoned bike, I knew I needed someone to help me. So I went. And I talked. Eventually, though, I started to lie.

I thumbed the doorbell again, not caring if I was being a nuisance. I'd given Noelle's family enough privacy. It was time for me to do this. Besides, before the kidnapping drove a wedge between us, making our visits too difficult to bear, we had once been so close we were practically family. I heard footsteps after I pressed the doorbell for the third time. Coop answered the door.

"Tess." I saw a sliver of his face through a small crack in the door. He was pale, and his eyes looked sunken.

"Hey, Coop." I tried to take in a deep breath.

"She won't see you." He opened the door a little wider. "She's holed up in her bedroom, hardly seeing us."

I blinked, trying to keep the words from registering. "It's that bad?"

"Worse." Coop looked at the purple gift bag in my hand. "What's that?"

"Just a little something for Noelle."

I had a sudden urge to push Coop away from the door, to run up the stairs that were behind him and rush into Noelle's bedroom. Instead, I held the bag forward, willing him to take it.

"I dunno, Tess. My parents are being really cautious." Coop glanced over his shoulder.

"Please, Coop." Tears welled up in my eyes, and his image swam before me.

"It's just hard to tell what's going to upset her."

"Okay." I lowered the bag. "I don't want to upset her. I just need her to know that I never stopped thinking about her."

Coop looked back once more, quickly. "Trust me," he whispered. "It's not a good idea."

"Okay," I said, placing one hand on the door so he couldn't close it. "Maybe I could go up for just a second?"

He drummed his fingers on the door. "Uh-uh, Tess." He shook his head.

"I just want to see her. In person." I pushed against the door. He held it firmly in place. "Of all people, you have to understand that."

"Tess," he whispered. "The longer you wait, the better, okay? Things are not the same."

I looked from his eyes to the dark staircase that led to the second floor and removed my hand from the door. I wanted to ask him what he meant. To tell him that Noelle would always be Noelle and to give her a break. But he closed the door before I could say anything, and I was left standing alone, breathing in that thick floral scent, wondering what he'd meant by "not the same."

I walked slowly toward the driveway. My Jeep was parked next to a thick pine tree that had grown taller since Noelle's disappearance. I stared at the dark needles, wondering how I would ever reconcile with my friend if everyone was going to stand in my way.

Just before opening the driver's-side door of the Jeep, I took a quick look at Noelle's window. I flinched when my eyes found her staring out at me, a ghostly version of my old friend.

Noelle's pale face was framed by straight, midnight black hair. Her eyes matched that border, dark and lifeless. Her hand fluttered against the glass, a pale moth straining for something out of reach. The translucent skin of her palm pressed against the pane, and she leaned forward a bit.

I smiled.

She didn't.

And then there was a breeze, soft against my skin but solid against the bag hanging from my wrist, causing it to sway back and forth. I held the gift in the air and suddenly, after all this time, allowed myself to believe that she was home.

I leaned down and pulled the heavy bottom branches of the pine tree from the ground, then placed the bag into the cool, damp shadow underneath.

Turning back to Noelle, I saw only the flutter of a white curtain.

In the Jeep, I sat wondering what had broken our brief connection. A sound, perhaps, that reminded her of her captor. Or maybe Coop had knocked on her door to tell her I had stopped by.

Seeing her stare out of that window without a smile on her face made me wonder again if all the news reports could be true. If she'd really had the freedom to roam around the neighborhood she'd shared with Charlie Croft. If she'd actually been friends with the girl and the guy whom people had seen her hanging out with. But most important, I wondered what, exactly, Charlie Croft had done to keep her quiet. And why she hadn't made that phone call to Coop much sooner. At that thought, my hands started shaking so much it took three attempts to insert the key into the ignition.

As I drove away, I told myself that none of that mattered. Noelle was alive. Everything else would fall into place. It had to.

Like an Accident

I was never one of those girls with a body-image issue. You know, the type who, after reading somewhere that celery sticks have negative calories, eat nothing but the little green stalks. (Think Jessie Richards, the skinny-minny captain of the varsity cheerleading squad.)

I didn't think I was perfect or anything. Though I secretly loved the way my sandy-blonde hair dried in soft waves that spilled down my back, and the way my eyes matched my favorite aqua tank top, I had a little pooch in my middle that needed some attention. And when I looked down, I had this disturbing hint of a double chin. But unlike some girls, when I was hungry, I ate. Unless I was at school.

On the first day of eighth grade, I decided I wouldn't go to the cafeteria without Noelle at my side. Since then, I had discovered several methods of gobbling a quick snack in hiding, my favorite being the duck-behind-a-book-in-the-library technique. I was proud that I had remained true to my friend; since her disappearance, I had not once eaten in the lunchroom. The root of this issue was superstition; I somehow felt that if I gave in and giggled over some stupid piece of gossip, the slight chance of Noelle's return would disappear.

My second reason for avoiding the cafeteria was that I didn't have anyone to sit with. I had only one person I could call a friend, Darcy, but she was two years ahead of me, and our friendship was mostly about photography. I didn't want any other friends. I'd pushed all my old friends away after Noelle went missing, ignoring them so blatantly, they had eventually stopped calling. All the stuff friends do with one another . . . that was sacred. It belonged to Noelle. Besides, I couldn't sit around laughing with a bunch of people whose only concern was what to wear to Friday night's football game when I was pretty sure Noelle would never laugh again.

I had isolated myself as much as possible. Except in photography class, where Darcy wouldn't leave me alone, even if I tried to set her on fire.

I liked things the way they were. Comfortable. Predictable. Safe.

Until the second week of my sophomore year. Noelle was home by then, which caused the structure of my avoid-the-cafeteria argument to crumble. It was a Tuesday, the day the carefully constructed bubble that surrounded me popped.

Max, who knew nothing of my years as a loner, caught me in

the hall on the sixth day of school, hooking his arm into mine and swinging me around in the bustling crowd.

"I'm sick of eating alone," he'd said. "Care to join?"

"I don't really do the caf," I answered, trying to slip my arm out of his, my cheeks burning at the soft heat of his skin brushing against mine.

"I noticed," he said, tucking my arm tight against his body. (Dear Lord, his side was incredibly hard. Was it possible to actually feel the muscles rippling under his thin T-shirt?)

As we weaved our way through the blur of people clutching textbooks to their chests, my brain whirred with questions I could never voice. Why, with his good looks and easy personality, didn't Max have ten friends already? And why, of all people, had he chosen to eat with *me*?

"Seriously," I said as we approached the gaping entrance to the cafeteria, "this isn't my scene. All the gossiping and plan making, it goes against my nature."

"*That,*" he said with a grin, "is exactly why I like you." And then he pulled me through the double doors and into the chest-vibrating, high-impact noise of four hundred shouting students.

As he led me through a maze of round tables, my attention snagged, the same question looping through my head over and over again. *Helikesmehelikesmehelikesme?*

It must have been the way that question echoed through my mind, making me feel light-headed and slightly disoriented. Or it could have been the pressure of all that noise and energy. But when Max yanked out a chair and pushed my shoulders until I sat down, I didn't even attempt to stand up and walk away. The way I would have if he had been anyone else in that building.

Two weeks later, I had a new routine. Every day after fourth period, Max stood next to my locker, waiting for me to spin the dial and exchange my books, all the while talking me into eating with him. Each time, I found myself protesting less and less. Today, I had barely even complained as we'd made our way through the crowd, toward the table that had somehow become ours.

"Create and destroy," Max said from his seat next to me.

"Oh, that's a good one," I said, comfortable now with our game of listing opposites. It had started as a brainstorming session for our photography project, but it quickly became a way for us to talk without really talking. "But how would you photograph it?"

"I dunno." He took a bite of his shiny green apple. "But I like it enough to think about it." Max squinted. I could tell he was trying to figure a way to make his idea work, like he always did when I challenged him.

The bell rang, and a mass of people stood from the tables around us. Chairs scraped the floor, books were clutched tightly, and bodies funneled toward the exit.

Max and I stood and sidestepped into the slow-moving crowd. He threw his apple core into a nearby trash can, and when his shoulder bumped mine, I was tempted to turn my face toward him and take a deep breath. I was close enough to catch his scent without being too obvious.

During the last month, since I no longer had to wonder about the location of Noelle, two new obsessions had taken over my life. Number one, which I spent most of my time on, was figuring out how to get to see Noelle. I was anxious to know if she had found my gift and I was trying hard not to be offended that she hadn't called me yet. Number two, a secret that I would certainly die before sharing with anyone, ever, was how to get good whiffs of Max's clean scent without his noticing. The effect had started to make me a little crazy.

I gave in to temptation and was turning, ready for one sweet inhalation, when I felt a hand on my shoulder.

"Check me," a familiar voice said.

Max chuckled, his brown eyes moving past me and settling on something just beyond my shoulder. "There's something wrong with you, Darcy."

"I know," she said, flipping her straight brown hair over her shoulder. "Check me." When I looked at her, her lips were pulled back, revealing a mouthful of perfectly straight, perfectly white teeth, with nothing stuck in the crevices.

"You're fine," I said. "I'm going to get you a little mirror for your purse."

"Have one," she said. "It's not as trustworthy as a friend."

"So . . . you have a thing?" Max asked, pointing a long finger at his mouth, his parted lips, making me wonder what it would be like to kiss him. "With your teeth? A . . . preoccupation."

"Yeah." Darcy crinkled her nose at him. "And my breath. If I'm not chewing gum, I don't get too close to anyone."

"Yup." Max nodded. "That's a thing."

Darcy shrugged. "We all have *things*."

"I don't," I said, shaking my head.

"Puh-lease," Darcy said, choking a little.

Max just laughed, his head tipping back in an easy way, those soft curls spilling and dipping into new places. I wanted to reach out and touch them. Instead, I shoved my hands in the pockets of my jeans.

We made our way into the main hall and started passing a bank of senior lockers. Darcy, with one hand in her purse, was searching for an open pack of Strawberry Splash, definitely not watching where she was going.

I'm not sure what happened, if there was something on the floor that tripped her up, or if she stubbed the pointy toe of her black boot, but Darcy stumbled into me. Hard. Which was okay, because I was pitched sideways into Max, who instinctively wrapped an arm around my waist, catching me.

This, I realized, was the most beautiful opportunity to catch his scent, and I kind of collapsed into him, taking a deep breath. I felt a little dizzy with the thrill of being so near him. Until that thrill was knocked out of existence as we were jolted from behind. Harder than hard.

"Watch it, loser," a deep voice said.

Max's grip on my waist tightened, and we almost went down. For a split second, I kind of wished we had, so I could know what it might feel like to get all tangled up on the floor with him.

But instead, we caught our balance as the hulking figure of Chip Knowles barreled past us. With each step, his thick shoulders swayed, and his Abercrombie jeans hugged his tight butt. As I stared beyond the 72 on the back of his football jersey, the reason he'd barged into us became clear.

Twenty feet down the hall, Chip's girlfriend, *the* Jessie Richards, stood with a guy. Her shimmery blonde hair was styled in this perfect, made-to-look-messy bun. Wisps fell around her face, highlighting her high cheekbones and sharp nose. The cheerleading uniform she wore bared her muscular arms, sculpted shoulders, and toned legs. I wondered if she went to a tanning bed every day of the week.

I wasn't up on all the latest gossip at Centerville High School, but everyone who had spent a few weeks in the building knew that the scene about to unfold would be gossip worthy. Even if the guy standing with Jessie was totally not her type. And trust me, this kid—with his tall, awkward body stooping forward, and the over-applied product in his perfectly combed hair—was lucky to be within speaking distance of the most popular senior in the building.

"Who's this?" Chip asked, using a deep, don't-mess-with-me voice. He ran his fingers through his short golden-blond hair, tufting the front up in one swift movement.

Jessie looked at Chip and raised her eyebrows. Her thin lips curled up slightly. The kid standing next to her said something I couldn't hear and held a spiral notebook up in the air. I was impressed that he didn't cower into the locker behind him but instead straightened himself, proving to be nearly Chip's height. Chip yanked the notebook out of his hand and flipped through a few pages.

"You got yourself a math geek?" Chip asked Jessie. "How sweet."

Jessie took the notebook from her boyfriend's hand and gave it back to the kid standing next to her. She smiled and tossed her head to the side. The kid said something and then turned and hurried away.

Max started walking. I did, too, because his arm was still wrapped around my waist.

"Hey!" Max said.

"Don't." I looked up at the curls that shadowed Max's face.

"But he can't just—"

"It's not worth it," I warned him. Max's brown thermal shirt was soft against my forearm as he pulled away from me. I hated myself for wanting to melt into him. I seriously could not deal with these feelings. Not now.

He looked at me, then turned to watch the most popular couple in school walk away. The crowd parted slightly as Chip slung an arm over Jessie's shoulders and she tucked herself against his body. Her obscenely short cheerleading skirt swayed from one side of her firm little butt to the other, flouncing up enough to expose her matching bloomers with every few steps.

"Hey, *Darcy*," Max said a few minutes later as we dropped our things on our desks in photography class, "wanna see some pictures I took yesterday?"

Darcy propped herself against her desk, crossing her arms over her chest. "I don't like being used, Max."

Max's lips parted in a mischievous smile. "Tess knows she's welcome to join us."

Darcy sighed. Waved a hand in the air. "Go pull them up. I'll be right there."

Max poked me in the shoulder as he passed. "I'd love to show them to you, too."

I sat down, shuffling through my folders like I had something important to do. "No strings?"

"We've been doing this for weeks, Tess." Max shook his head. "When you're ready to show me your stuff, I'll be glad to share mine."

He turned and walked away, leaving me there to stare after him.

"Are you crazy?" Darcy stabbed me in the arm with her bony elbow. "He's *interested*."

"No way." I glanced over my shoulder and watched Max's lean body fall into the computer chair, his sinewy arm reach for the mouse, his long fingers grip its frame. "But even if you're right, I can't get all twisted up over a guy right now."

"With Max, it wouldn't be like that. You can just tell." Darcy grabbed hold of my shoulder and turned me so I was facing her. "Stop. Pushing. Him. Away."

And then she left me sitting there, so very alone, positioning herself behind Max's chair.

"Ooh, that one is great," Darcy said. I turned quickly and saw her prop one hand on her hip as she leaned over Max's shoulder. She was wearing a dark pair of skinny jeans and had one foot slung out to her side, accentuating her long legs.

"Nuh-uh," she said. "How did you get that shot?" She laughed loudly and turned, looking right at me. *These are good*, she mouthed, pointing to Max's back.

I flipped my folder open and shuffled through my pictures. One of my favorites was of two girls on a wooden swing set, flying through the air, one a little higher than the other, their thin legs pumping skyward to get more lift. A few weeks ago, I'd hurried into my neighbor's side yard when I heard their giggles, and crouched behind them in the cool grass to capture the moment.

As much as I wanted to show him my pictures so I could take a look at his, my body wouldn't move. The thought made me feel like I had to run to the nearest restroom to puke up my lunch.

A few minutes later, Darcy and Max strode back to the desks that flanked mine.

"Well, the two of you don't know what you're missing." Darcy popped a bubble of her pink gum.

"Don't tell me," Max said. "This whole hide-the-talent game is all Tess's idea."

"It's not my *idea*," I said. "You say that like it's a choice."

Max flashed me a crooked half smile. "Everything in life is a choice."

Darcy nodded. I kind of wanted to hit her. Why was she siding with him, anyway?

"I've got a question." Max ran a hand through his thick curls. I tried to ignore how hot he looked when he messed with his hair.

"No," I said. "You cannot see my pictures!"

"Whoa, there." Max reached out and placed his hand over mine. "Relax. This is a different subject entirely."

Darcy looked at our hands and chuckled as she reached into her purse. Scooting her phone several inches out of the opening, she hid it from Mr. Hollon, who was showing someone a new setting on a digital camera. Her fingernails were *tick-tick-tick*-ing against the keypad as she texted her boyfriend, something she did from photography class at least three times a day.

"I've been hearing all kinds of stuff about some kidnapped

girl," Max said, removing his warm hand from mine.

Darcy stopped texting. From the corner of my eye, I saw her turn and face me.

"What's up with that?" Max asked.

Darcy opened her mouth. Started to speak. I cut her off.

"A girl was kidnapped from a park around here a couple of years ago." I worked to keep my voice steady. "They found her, and now she's home."

Max splayed his hands in the air. "That's it?" he asked. "I've gotten more information walking through the halls."

"Ugh, I know," Darcy said. "It's obnoxious. Did you hear the whole vampire thing?"

I shook my head. "Don't think I want to."

"It borders on hilarity, really. Classic tale of vampire preying on girl, girl changing, and voilà, needing the source of her violation." Darcy pointed a finger in the air. "The story, I believe, is an infantile attempt to make sense of Noelle waiting two years to escape when she seemed to have the opportunity—"

"No one knows what really happened," I said. Which killed me, because I was supposed to be Noelle's best friend.

"Some jerk in my math class was saying that she *wanted* to be with the guy." Max's voice quieted down to a near whisper. "I saw an interview with some people from the neighborhood where she'd been staying. She was seen out in public all the time, and everyone thought he was her father."

"I don't understand any of that," I said, shaking my head, trying for the millionth time to flip the information around in my mind so it would make sense. "All I know is that no matter how free she seemed, she couldn't have gotten away until now or she would have."

"Right. I'm sure." Darcy widened her eyes at Max and nodded toward me. "Tess and Noelle, the girl who was kidnapped, they were, like, BFFs."

I could not think about Noelle now. Not here. I glanced at my desktop, at the words etched in the wood. *Run, baby, run*, it urged me.

"I didn't . . . ," Max sputtered. "I had no idea."

"It's fine," I said. "I mean, it's kind of like an accident, right? People want to know about it, see it up close. But only if it doesn't touch their lives."

"Have you talked to her yet?" Darcy asked. Suddenly, the photography classroom seemed quiet. Too quiet, like everyone was waiting for my response. "It's been three weeks, hasn't it?"

"Four. And no, I haven't talked to her yet," I said. "All I know is the same stuff you do from the news."

"I can't imagine," Max said, "how awful it must have been when she went missing."

"I'm just ready for people to stop talking about it." I stabbed my notebook with my pen.

"Um, do I need to remind you that Noelle's kidnapping practically stopped *every form of life* here in Centerville two years ago?" Darcy tapped her desk with a fingernail, punctuating her words.

"What's that mean?" Max asked. "What was so different before?"

"Oh, everything." Darcy shrugged. "This used to be your

typical little Midwestern town. People didn't feel like they had to lock their doors or watch their kids when they went out to play. The kidnapping choked our entire town with sadness. And fear."

I crossed one leg over the other, wishing Darcy would stop talking.

"Huh," Max said with a nod. "I understand that the people who knew her and her family would be affected. But the whole town?"

"Trust me. Her experience has touched everyone. People all over the country, really. My cousin from Oregon called the other day to see if I know her. And now there's going to be some trial that'll be covered by about a zillion reporters who'll tromp in from all over. I'm sorry to tell you, but people are going to be on this all freaking year, Tess." Darcy gave an exaggerated shiver. "Plus, there's the whole creep factor. No one can imagine what it was like for her."

I realized that my foot was shaking back and forth in a violent manner and tucked it behind the leg of my desk.

Max had been staring at me as Darcy spoke. "I bet you're dying to talk to her," he said softly.

"Yeah. I can't wait." I reached into my purse and pulled out my camera. I ran my fingers along the frayed strap, pressed the chipped bottom edge into the palm of my hand, pulled the forty-year-old camera to my chest. "But the thing is, I'm kinda freaked out. I don't know what I'm going to say. I mean, what if everything I think of is just wrong?"

"When you see her, you'll do fine," Darcy said confidently. "Sorry it's been so rough."

"It'll have to die down sometime, right?" I asked.

"Sure."

"Of course it will," Max said. "Eventually."

I flung the Nikon's strap over my head and stood, needing to get away from the conversation, away from my own brain, which was screaming this warning that when I had my chance, I was bound to screw it up. "I'm gonna go take some pictures."

Max reached for his camera. "Want some company?"

"Nah." I shook my head.

"You sure?" Darcy asked.

"Yeah," I said. "But thanks." I turned, walked to Mr. Hollon's desk, and grabbed a pass.

When I made my way into the hall, I took one last glance into the room before I closed the door behind me. The first thing I saw was the top of Max's head as he shuffled through pictures on his desk. Then there was Darcy's hand perched on Max's shoulder as she bent forward to stare at what he wouldn't share with me.

6

My Name Is Elle

I sat at my computer, staring at the screen. I felt like throwing up and crying and screaming all at the same time. But the only thing I could do was blink at the words in front of me and hope they would somehow disappear.

I'd been excited when I'd sat down, sliding a memory chip out of the digital camera I'd borrowed from Mr. Hollon and popping it into the little slot in the tower standing next to my desk. My parents had been trying to talk me into a digital camera for over a year, and maybe they were right. A digital camera would be fun to have so I could see my pictures immediately. Like the one I'd snapped of Max yesterday in class.

But it felt like some kind of betrayal. My grandfather's Nikon was sacred, a physical link to the man I missed so much, and I would not let my parents talk me into putting it aside for some newer, better version. This week, I hadn't had a choice. Mr. Hollon's latest assignment required a digital image.

Impatient with the length of time it was taking for the photographs to download to the folder on my desktop, I'd clicked on the Internet icon and watched as the Yahoo page popped up.

I don't really know what I thought I'd see, maybe news of the latest celebrity breakup. All I can say is that I wasn't ready for what appeared.

The first thing I noticed were the eyes. Deep and black. Lifeless. Staring right at me.

Then the matted hair, the scruffy face, the thick chin.

Charlie Croft.

My computer made a plinking sound to let me know that the download was complete, and I snapped out of it long enough to catch the headline and skim the body of the article. That's what really did it, what brought on the whole freak-out feeling that kind of fuzzed the edges of my hearing and sight. Pulling me away from reality for a few minutes and threatening to sink me into one of my panics.

I looked away. Took a deep breath. Waited until my hearing came back, which felt like swimming to the surface after plunging far into the deep end of a pool, and then I looked again.

The headline hadn't changed. ONE OR MANY? it asked.

The words that followed also remained the same:

> In a press conference held late yesterday afternoon, Cuyahoga County prosecutor Ronnie Pundt announced that Charles Croft, who has been charged with kidnapping a

minor, will face an additional twenty-seven felony counts, including rape and producing child pornography.

Sheriff Paul Shott stated that new investigations regarding Croft are under way. After searching evidence taken from Croft's home, it is suspected that he is responsible for the disappearance of at least four other minors from the tristate area in the last sixteen years.

On September 10, Croft pleaded not guilty on the charge of kidnapping. He is being held at the Montgomery County Jail on a $1 million cash-only bail.

The case is still under investigation.

I closed my eyes and rested my forehead on the arm of my chair.

Child pornography? I pictured a twelve-year-old Noelle posing in front of the mirror in her room, reciting lines from her favorite movies as she experimented with different facial expressions. Her goal in life was to make her way to a stage, to feel the heat of a spotlight shining on her face. She didn't care if that dream led her to a fashion runway, a television studio, or a movie set. She'd even talked about auditioning for a reality show when she turned eighteen. I had always hated that her kidnapping was the way she had become famous. I looked at Charlie again, right into his dead eyes.

"No," I said to him. "You will not be the last thing I see tonight."

Clutching the mouse, I maneuvered the arrow across the screen and stabbed the red X in the top right corner. Charlie was gone.

With a jerky hand, I clicked on the folder holding my pictures and flipped through them until I found the one I'd taken of Max. He'd been sitting next to me, and I'd snapped the shot quickly, hoping he'd see it as some joke instead of what it really was: my need to study his face. When I came to the picture, I just stared, wondering how he could get better-looking each time I saw him. He had these super-thick eyelashes, and a few random freckles dotting the top of his cheeks.

I was unprepared to deal with the wild feelings Max was sparking to life. I had told myself for two years that if Noelle couldn't experience that giddy, falling-in-love sensation, I wouldn't, either. Yet here I was, unable to push Max from my mind. While Noelle was struggling to experience one minute of normalcy, I was totally losing control over the new guy whom every girl was gushing over, and who was this completely . . . What? Beautiful, nice, strange new complication in my life. In addition to that—

A light tapping pulled me back to my bedroom. I listened for the noise again, wondering if it had been real or imagined. It came quickly, sounding like a small pebble bouncing off the pane. Could it be him? He'd followed me home from school the other day to borrow a photography book I'd told him about. But how had he figured out which room was mine?

I felt like I'd been plunged underwater again. As I walked toward the window, every piece of me was thick and sluggish. I pulled at the curtain, ready to see Max standing in the dark grass.

I parted the blinds.

The moment I'd dreamed about for the past two years had

finally arrived. But I couldn't jump-start my body—nothing would move.

Standing in my side yard, the moonlight silvering her skin, was Noelle.

With her head tipped toward my window, her face absolutely glowed. If I hadn't been aware of her homecoming, I'd have been sure her ghost was visiting me for a midnight chat. What got me moving was her raising her hand and waving me down. My pajama pants whispered to the dark house as I ran down the stairs, avoiding the two creaky spots in the floor, because the last thing I needed was to wake my mother, who, since Noelle's disappearance, seemed to have gained superpowered hearing abilities. I sucked in a deep breath as I tiptoed through the kitchen and turned the lock and handle to the back door.

The steps were cold against my bare feet, the grass damp and slick. The chill that enveloped me was instantaneous, but nothing bothered me as I swam through the darkness. I felt detached, like I was watching the scene from just outside my body.

When she heard my footsteps, she turned toward me. I slowed, watching as a wave of unfamiliar blue-black hair swept over her shoulder and swung to rest over the right side of her chest, hanging almost to her belly button.

"Wow," I said. "I haven't seen your hair that long since kindergarten." And then I felt stupid. *That* was the first thing I said after two years?

Awkwardly, I walked to Noelle and held out my arms to embrace her. Her body was stiff as she allowed me to hug her for a moment. When she pulled away, it was with force.

"I guess everyone's doing that, huh?" I asked, wanting to hear her voice. Needing to know if that had changed, too.

Noelle looked to the ground and then at me. I stared into her blue-gray eyes, the eyes that used to be more familiar than my own gazing back at me when I looked into a mirror. Those eyes were the same. Almost. They held a hint of something new, like sadness or fear, but they were hers.

"I'm being totally suffocated," she said, her voice as rigid as her body.

"I bet." I shifted my weight on my bare feet. "This must be the first time you've left the house."

Noelle surprised me by shaking her head from side to side. "Huh-uh. I've been out almost every night. I can hardly breathe in that house." She turned her face to the sky again, closed her eyes. "Out here, I don't feel like a caged animal."

I didn't know what to say to that. How could her house feel like a cage after the past two years?

"Look," Noelle said to the backs of her closed eyelids. "Coop tells me every time you call." She finally opened her eyes and looked at me again. "And the picture . . . it was really nice. I know what you're trying to do, and I appreciate it." She swept some hair behind her ear. "I just . . . don't care. Okay?"

"I wanted you to know—"

"You never forgot me. I was always there with you. Coop told me. It's sweet, really." Noelle sighed. "This just isn't my life anymore, Tess. I'm not that girl you knew all those years ago."

"Noelle, I'll always be—"

"That's exactly what I'm talking about." Her hand shot out at the darkness, aiming to hit something that wasn't there. "I'm not *Noelle* anymore." She breathed heavily through her nose and clenched her jaw.

"Of course you're Noelle. Who else would you be?"

The girl who was not Noelle looked directly into my eyes. Her stare was hard and cold. "Noelle is gone. And she's not coming back." She blinked. "My name is Elle."

As Noelle turned on the balls of her feet, her hair whipped around her body. I didn't move as she walked away with an even stride, her back straight and tight, her arms swinging.

In those few moments, a lifetime of friendship flashed before my eyes. Licking brownie batter from a glass bowl, sledding down Killer Hill in a foot of snow, whispering in the darkness during sleepovers, having giggle fits over prank calling the cutest boys in the high school, raiding her parents' liquor cabinet late at night.

Most of all, as she walked away from me, I pictured the excited look that sparked a person's face just from being near her. She had always pulled people in, cast some strange and immediate spell. She used to shine brighter than anything I had ever known.

But the girl who walked away from me was dark. Dull. Somehow, strangely rough. I didn't know her at all.

A Matter of Perspective

When they walked in, I was standing in a bathroom stall, buttoning my jeans and debating whether to discuss the whole Noelle problem with Max over lunch. As their heels *click-click-click*ed against the tile floor, I heard the first voice.

"I can't believe he's being so weird," someone said.

"He's not worth it, Jess," a different voice offered.

I peered through the crack in the door and saw three girls staring at the large wall mirror, talking to their reflections instead of to one another. Kirsten Holmes and Tabby Lock stood on either side, both applying shiny lip gloss. In the middle was Jessie Richards. It was hard to be sure, but her eyes looked red and puffy, and her hair was missing its usual luster.

"He's a prick," Kirsten said.

"I don't get it." Jessie's voice was soft. Her eyes started roaming, finally settling on something near her feet. "I mean, I didn't do anything."

Tabby and Kirsten stared at each other. Tabby widened her eyes. Kirsten shrugged. Tabby mouthed a few words, and Kirsten nodded. Then the two turned and faced Jessie.

"I might know something," Tabby said.

Jessie's head snapped up. She grabbed Tabby's hand.

"What?" Jessie asked. "Is it bad?"

"I saw him," Tabby said. "It was this weekend, after Tom's party, so . . . pretty late. I'd just dropped Carrie off and was stopped at a four-way in her neighborhood when he passed me coming from the opposite direction."

"So?" Jessie shook her head. "Maybe he was going to—"

"There was a girl in the car," Kirsten said.

Jessie startled at the words. Then she stood very still.

"Who?" Jessie asked.

"I didn't get a good look at—"

"Who was it?" Jessie pulled her hand from Tabby's grasp. Tabby shrugged, squinted her eyes. "It kind of looked like Shelby Stadler."

"Are you for real?" Jessie sucked in a breath. "After everything I did to help her make varsity this year, she's—" Jessie tapped her foot on the floor, fast and erratic. "Doesn't everyone know he's mine? We've been together almost four years."

"Off and on," Kirsten said.

"*Kirsten*," Tabby said.

"I have to figure out who was with him. You guys'll help, right?" Jessie's voice lifted up at the end of the sentence, this sweet and juicy sound. There was a pause as the two girls nodded at her. "One thing I guarantee, when we get this bitch, we'll destroy her."

I listened as one set of shoes, crisp and quick, exited the restroom.

"Why'd you even say Shelby's name?" Kirsten whispered. "I thought you had no idea who—"

"Jessie had to have something to go on," Tabby said. I peered through the crack in the door and watched Tabby comb through her shoulder-length hair with the fingers of one hand. "Besides, Shelby was a total snot about my haircut last week."

"But Jessie's really pissed."

"I know." Tabby giggled. "This year has been way too boring. Something needs to happen, doncha think?"

"Oh," Kirsten said. "You are such a bitch."

"Yeah." Tabby smiled. Flitted her eyelashes. "I am."

"Are you guys coming, or what?" Jessie called from the hall. "I thought you were right behind me."

"We are," Tabby said.

Both girls laughed as they *click-click-click*ed out of the restroom, leaving me with an answer to the question I'd been asking myself for days. I couldn't trust anyone enough to talk about Noelle (*Elle, Elle, Elle—get it straight: her name is Elle*), not even Max.

"So, what's up?" Max asked.

"Nothing," I said, looking at my peanut-butter-and-honey sandwich instead of at him.

"I thought you said you had something you wanted to talk to me about."

"Yeah, I just . . ." I could practically feel Max's eyes on me, and it made me want to hide under the table. Like he would have any clue as to how I could crack through the icy layers surrounding Elle? "I think I figured it out." I looked up.

Max's eyes narrowed a bit. "Okay," he said. "If you say so."

The silence that fell between us as we ate was uncomfortable, and it dragged out in these long stretches. I don't know if it was sheer boredom or a way for both of us to avoid the strange vibes passing between us, but we became focused on things happening around us, ignoring each other almost completely.

"Just to let you know," Max said halfway through the lunch period, "I'm pretty good at figuring things out."

In my peripheral vision, I could see him looking at me. I ignored him. By then, I was too intent on Jessie—who had planted herself right next to Shelby Stadler—and her friends. It was like watching one of those old silent movies; I had to pay close attention to facial expression and body language if I was going to determine what was happening in the middle of the lunchroom.

Max cocked his head to the side and turned to follow my gaze. "You're certainly into something over there."

"You can't look." I smacked his arm. "They might see."

"You're kidding, right?" Max rolled up a ball of cling wrap from his ham sandwich. "You sound like you're some secret agent."

"I'll tell you about it later, okay? I just need to see what's going to happen."

Max looked at me. "I thought you weren't a gossip girl."

I rolled my eyes. "I'm not, okay? But there's a potentially explosive situation over there. Forgive me for hoping it ignites and takes some focus off Noelle." I turned my eyes to the girls and shook my head. "I mean Elle."

"Okay, then," he said with a shrug. "Here's to hoping for a major scandal."

Not much happened while the girls were eating. It wasn't until the last ten minutes of lunch that I noticed Jessie turn her body, sliding her knees up against the side of Shelby's chair.

They were both laughing, and part of me wanted to run to Shelby and warn her that Jessie was about to bring the whole world crashing down on her head. But that wouldn't give the students of CHS anything tantalizing to gossip, text, or IM about, and I was hoping for a full-scale blowout. So I didn't move.

Jessie reached up and tapped one of the pencils that secured a twisted bun on top of Shelby's head. Shelby ducked away and shook her head back and forth. Then Jessie spoke, and the smile that had been saturating Shelby's face dried up to nothing. I watched her squint and the lines on her forehead pull tight. She shook her head once again, harder now, and her lips mouthed the word *no* several times.

"Here we go," I said.

Jessie looked at Tabby. Shelby's eyebrows shot up, and her mouth started moving quickly as she glanced at all the girls seated at the table. Next, she looked at the girl on her right, who started nodding and moving her hands as she spoke. The girl across from them nodded as well.

Then everything stopped. Jessie's chest puffed up with a few deep breaths. She looked at Tabby, who shrugged as she crunched on a carrot stick. Jessie nodded, and Shelby's body hunched forward, the tension streaming from her like the air from a too-full balloon.

"Damn," I said, stomping my foot into the ground.

"Crisis averted?" Max asked.

"Unfortunately." I planted an elbow on the table and propped my chin in my hand. "It would have been perfect. A breakdown in the highest rung of senior-class popularity."

"People will move on," Max said. "That is, once the news coverage dies down."

I tried not to think of how the media had grabbed hold of Elle's story and couldn't seem to let go.

"You heard the latest about the kidnapper?" Max asked. I looked into his eyes, the caramel color reminding me of melted brown sugar. "That he changed his plea?"

I shook my head. "He did?"

"Yeah. Saw it this morning while I was eating breakfast. He's going with guilty."

The noise around us faded away as I focused on Max's words.

"The reporters were saying tons of money will be saved because now there won't be any trial. All I could think about is how much your friend Noelle will be relieved that she doesn't have to testify."

"Elle," I said. "She wants to be called Elle now."

"Okay. Elle." Max nodded.

I didn't know how to feel. I should have been happy. But I was scared. Somehow, Elle's being so different, keeping herself from me, had made some kind of sense. I'd been telling myself that our distance was due to her need to hold everything in while she prepped herself for the trial. But now, if there was no trial, if all of that was over and she still stayed away, I would have to start facing the fact that she just might not want to have anything to do with me.

"Have you seen her yet?"

It came back in one quick flash, my need for another opinion, the utter confusion that swelled whenever I thought of Elle these last few weeks. I almost let the story of my late-night encounter with her tumble from my lips. Instead, I slowly shook my head.

"Hey." Max pointed to something over my shoulder. "Isn't that her brother?"

I turned, following his gaze.

"Four tables away. There's a kid wearing a shirt with a red skateboard. Next to him, the one in the green hoodie. Isn't that him?"

I found him right away. It was definitely Coop, sitting there with his freckled hands on the table. He was with three other guys, and they were all cracking up about something.

"You *want* to see her, right?" Max asked.

My brain fumbled over the question. I knew what I was supposed to say. But the encounter I'd had with her three nights before had been so awkward. I took a deep breath and nodded.

Max stood from the table, grabbing his trash. "Come on," he said.

"Where are you going?" I stood and grabbed my lunch.

"Do you trust me?" Max asked over his shoulder.

"I don't trust anyone."

Max stopped walking, and my foot skidded into his heel. He turned. Looked me in the eye. "Fine," he said. "Maybe this'll help you start." He walked toward the trash can near Coop's table.

I followed, the trail of his soapy scent wafting into my nose, mixing everything up even more than it already was.

"What if I don't want to?" My words were hijacked by the voices of others around me and never reached Max's ears.

Max stopped and pitched his trash. Leaning against the brick column next to Coop's table, he grabbed my arm when I reached out to dump the remains of my own lunch.

"Say something to him," he said. "Start a conversation."

I shook my head. Max gave me a little push, and I bumped into Coop's table. I looked down and pretended to see him for the first time.

"Hey, Coop." I smiled. He raised his head and nodded. "I, eh, have a question for you."

Max walked up beside me and suddenly our legs were touching. I was already having trouble with what to say next, and the warmth of Max's touch garbled my thoughts even more.

"Well, not a question exactly." I was totally blank. I couldn't think of one thing to say.

"What's up?" Coop asked.

"I, um . . ." I looked at Max.

"She wants to come over for dinner," Max said. "To see your sister."

Coop looked from Max to me and shook his head. "Elle's not ready yet," he said.

Max plucked a few jelly beans from an open bag on the table-top. "But they're best friends." He shook the little candies in his hand, the hard pieces clicking against one another.

"I don't know, Tessa." Coop sat forward. "She's different."

"Nothing will erase all the years Tess and Elle spent together. That kind of friendship is healing, man." Max sat on the tabletop and looked at Coop. His face and eyes were soft, understanding. In that moment, I wanted to kiss him more than ever. "There's got to be some way you can—"

Just then, the bell rang, and the crowd stood simultaneously. Coop, though, stayed planted in his seat.

I moved around the table until I was just a few inches from him. The noise level had almost doubled, and I wanted him to hear me. "I really need to see her."

"Tessa," Coop said, "I can't make any promises. But I'll work on it."

I mouthed the words *thank you* before turning to Max. We were pushed up against each other in the crowd, and I had to stop myself from thinking about how much I liked being so close to him, and how the sweet grape jelly-bean scent that rode Max's delicious breath was making me want to taste his tongue.

You Don't Mean That

"So she just called and said she couldn't make it?" Max was sitting next to me, looking out the side window of the Jeep. We were driving through the country a few miles from town, and the thick green grass of the farmyard we had just passed gave way to a field choked with tall cornstalks.

"Pretty much," I said, staring at the two-lane road ahead. I was lying by omission, but that couldn't be avoided. Darcy had called my cell just before I'd driven to Max's house to pick him up, and when she said she couldn't meet us, it all clicked into place. She'd masterfully plotted the outing, planning from the start to ditch us at the last second, when she knew for sure I'd be stuck. As I thought about how she'd leaned against her desk with a smirk on her face in life photography the day before, telling me that we had to take Max because the field would be too hard for him to find on his own, I was positive.

"You're such a schemer," I'd said to her. "This time, I'm not sure I'll forgive you."

"Oh, shut up, Tessa." Darcy's laughter sprang through the phone. "Have some fun for a change."

"You know my parents would freak themselves into a panic, me being alone with a mysterious guy from out of town."

"First of all, he's not mysterious, he's Max. And he lives *here* now, in warm and cheerful Centerville." Darcy sighed. "Stop using your parents as an excuse. When you get home, you can simply forget to tell them the whole *alone* part."

About a half hour later, with Max at my side, I slowed for a tight curve and immediately pulled to the side of the road, parking next to a wooden fence that was slathered with some viny vegetation.

"This is it?" Max asked, turning to me.

I nodded.

"Darcy was right. I would have passed this a hundred times."

I turned and reached into the backseat for my camera. "Wait'll you see what's around the bend." I paused and looked at my backpack, wondering what I was waiting for, wondering if I had the guts to share what was inside. *No,* I decided. *No, no, no.* Instead of grabbing for the blue bag, unzipping it, and spilling its contents, I picked up my camera, opened my car door, and stepped out, the cool air chilling me instantly.

I led the way through a shady patch of tall grass. We rounded the corner of the fence and walked under the golden-red canopy of a large maple tree before finally stepping into a wide field washed in sunlight. I stopped, and Max walked into my back.

"This is . . ."

"Unbelievable," I said. "I know."

Before us, a sea of sunflowers swayed lazily in the breeze, their dark faces surrounded by luminous orange-yellow petals, just staring like they'd been waiting for us since their seeds had been pressed into the ground.

"It looks like they're dancing," I said.

Max stepped to my side and held his camera up to his face. The shutter snapped.

"How many do you think there are?" he asked.

"Hundreds," I said, "and hundreds. We're lucky Darcy drove by earlier in the week. This field will be wilted and falling soon."

"You ready?" he asked, looking at me.

"Always," I said, holding my camera up in the air. "Why don't we split up? Make sure we don't get in each other's shots?"

Max shrugged. "Okay."

For the next half hour, I walked through the rows of sunflowers, their petals grazing my shoulders, kissing my cheeks. I took close-ups of the dark seeds swirling from their centers in a dizzying spiral, the thin white hairs sprouting from their thick stalks, the velvety green leaves spreading out like reaching arms. Some of my shots I aimed from the ground up, making a single flower look as powerful as one of the Three Sisters. Others I took from the side, so I could capture an entire row, standing proud like decorated soldiers.

I tried to keep an eye on Max without his noticing, but he

caught me staring a few times. Once, he aimed his camera my way and snapped a shot or two. Laughing, I ducked down quickly and had to dig my fingers into the damp earth to keep from falling.

When I finished my third roll of film, I found Max close to the front of the field. He was stooping over a shorter flower, aiming his camera into its center.

"They're crazy," he said when he heard my footsteps.

"I know. I love the way the light moves through them." I looked over the field, watching soft rays of the waning sun flicker through the flowers' waving bodies.

"I mean these bees," Max said.

I stepped closer and peered into the center of the flower Max was standing beside, finding that he was focused on three bees. "Yeah. They're all over the place," I said as one took flight and buzzed around my head. I swatted the air until it was gone. "Did you get some good shots of the sunflowers?" I asked.

"I did. But once I saw all the bees, I decided they should be my focus instead."

I heard the shutter of Max's camera snap a few more times. "Coop found me after school today," I said. "He talked his mother into inviting me for dinner."

"Really?" Max lowered his camera from his face and turned to look me in the eyes. "That's great."

Uncomfortable with the weight of his stare, I kicked the thick grass clawing at my feet. "I'm going tomorrow night. It's because of you, you know."

"I'm glad I could help."

I shook my head. Then I spoke without thinking, all my

worries tumbling from my mouth without any filter. "I'm not sure what to say. Or what not to say. She went through some awful stuff, Max. I mean, how do you talk to your best friend after she's spent two years with some greasy pedophile?"

Max let his camera fall to his chest. "How did you talk to her before?"

"I dunno." I paused, considering this for the first time. "I just talked. I didn't think about it."

"There's your answer."

I turned toward the Jeep and started walking. "It's not that easy," I said.

"Maybe it is." Max spoke from a few steps behind me. "Tell me about her."

"Elle?"

"No. I want to hear about Noelle. The girl she was before she was kidnapped."

I looked over my shoulder and slowed until he was walking beside me. For several seconds, the only sound was the grass whisking against our jeans.

"It's been a really long time since I've thought about Noelle," I said. "Just Noelle."

Max nodded. Like he already knew.

"She could remember every word of a song after hearing it just a few times. That used to drive me crazy. I'd spend hours in my bedroom listening to the same thing over and over, writing out the lyrics if it wasn't sticking, just so I could sing along with her."

Max stopped when we were under the maple. I looked up, noticing that the leaves above us were a flickering fire.

"She was crazy about her clothes. This one time, I borrowed a sweater and spilled barbecue sauce on it. She flipped out." I laughed, remembering how red her face had been as she'd told me she'd never loan me anything for the rest of her life. "Honestly, she could be a real bitch."

Max smiled. "What else?"

I took a few steps back and leaned against the side of the Jeep. "She was more daring than me. Noelle used to tease me, saying that it was her job to break me out of my goody-goody mold. She made me try my first sip of alcohol and my first cigarette."

Max chuckled. "I had a friend like that back in Montana."

"Noelle was always sneaking out of her house. Her bedroom window opens onto the roof of her garage. Some nights she'd just sit there and look at the stars; others she'd go tromping through the neighborhood. That's not how she . . ." I took a deep breath and ran my thumb along the cool silver button that activated the camera's shutter. "When she went missing, it was the middle of the day."

I looked at Max. His head was down, his hands clasping the body of his camera as his fingers tapped the lens cap. The sun behind him was setting, and the golden glow lapped at him like a warm, buttery liquid.

For weeks, I'd been debating, unsure if or when I would give in. I'd wondered about it often, and in this silent moment, after he'd asked me to tell him about Noelle, I knew it was time.

"You wanna see them?" I asked.

Max looked up, his eyes crinkling.

"My pictures?" I turned and walked to the driver's side of the Jeep. "It's now or never."

Max was in his seat, closing his door before I could pull my backpack from behind him. My hands felt numb as I lifted the envelope containing my pictures. I shoved it at him without looking, and then, after securing the camera, turned the key in the ignition. The Jeep rumbled to life, and soft music hummed through the speakers.

Max's hand was over mine before I could put the Jeep in drive. "Wait," he said.

"If I don't drive," I said, turning off the radio, "I might throw up."

Max laughed. "I'll take my chances."

I took a deep breath and let my hands fall into my lap, ignoring every instinct that told me to drive so I could avoid eye contact.

He dug his hands into one of the most private places in my world and slid out all of my favorite pictures. A few tumbled on his lap, and he gathered them, tapping the sides of the bundle until they were neatly stacked one on top of another.

"I get it," Max said. "You know that, right?" He looked at me, flicking a curl from his eye. The sky outside had melted into a soft orange-pink, reminding me of cotton candy.

I shook my head. "I'm not sure anyone gets it."

"It's kind of like letting someone inside your head to listen to your thoughts." Max hadn't looked at the pictures yet. He was staring into my eyes, his velvety-looking lips almost close enough to kiss.

"Just look at them already," I said.

Max bowed his head and began to shuffle slowly through my pictures. At first, I stared out the windshield, focusing on the yellow lines in the middle of the road, the way the leaves of one tree were this crazy deep orange, how the squirrel scurrying from one high branch to another looked like he might take flight. Then I studied the long shadows cast by the setting sun.

"You took this?" he asked. "Really?"

My nervous energy flashed into irritation. "I took all of them," I said.

"Easy," he said. "I didn't mean it like that." He held up a photograph. "Where's this?"

One quick glance and I knew.

"SunWatch Indian Village. They have this summer solstice celebration with a drum circle and bonfire."

On the paper between us was a Native American. He was suspended in the air, his arms spread like the wings of a bird, the beaded fringes of his long shirt tossing out all around him. His mouth was open, and his eyes were closed. His moccasined feet, several inches off the ground, had flung particles of dust into the air. Everything was so vivid—the colors of his large headdress, the paint on his face, the beadwork that adorned every piece of his clothing.

"It was sunset," I said. "They were dancing to honor the passing of spring, and to welcome the coming of summer."

"I can practically hear him chanting," Max said. "And the way you captured his movement, I expect him to just float off the page."

I looked down so Max wouldn't see my smile. A car sped past, rocking the Jeep a bit.

A few minutes later, Max laughed. "Finally," he said, holding another picture in the air. "These are as awesome as I expected they would be."

I knew before I looked. He'd seen my shots of the Three Sisters.

"You were wise to use both color and black-and-white film that day," he said. "These are much better than mine."

"That reminds me," I said. "We had a deal. When do I get to see your pictures?" I slid sideways in my seat, leaning toward him a little.

Max looked down, flipped through a few more pictures, and smiled. "How about over dinner? Next weekend?"

I moved so suddenly, I hit the car door. "What?" It was almost completely dark on the backcountry road, and I was glad for the cover of shadow blanketing my face.

"Dinner," he said. "It's usually where a date starts."

"A date." I pointed. Like an idiot, I pointed at him and then at myself. "Like, you and me?"

"Am I that far off base?" Max put the stack of photos back into the manila envelope and shut the clasp.

"No. You're not—"

"Good, because I was starting to wonder." He put the envelope on his lap and patted it with one hand. "These are really good, by the way. I can see why you got into life photography a year early."

I didn't know what to say. Had he really just asked me out on a date? I wanted to jump out of the car. Rewind the last thirty minutes. I would take back my revelations about Elle. I would never show him my pictures. And I would *not* look at his lips.

When I let my mind flitter over the reality of what had just happened, I was overcome by that floaty, detached-from-my-body feeling. But I couldn't actually go.

"So, do you do Thai?" Max asked.

"Max, no, I can't—"

"There's always Italian. You just—"

"It's not the food. I can't go out with you," I said, looking down at my hands, which were now clasped around the bottom of the steering wheel, vibrating a bit under the hum of the engine.

"I don't get it." Max turned to face me. "Look at me," he said.

I let go of the steering wheel. Turned just a little. "I want to," I said. "I just can't."

"That doesn't make any sense." Max shook his head. "I like you, Tessa."

"I like you, too, Max. There's just too much going on right now. With Elle and everything, I can't—"

"Oh. Now I get it." Max nodded, his lips tightening into a thin line.

"What does that mean?"

"You're afraid, aren't you?"

"Afraid of what?" I asked. "You?"

"I dunno," he said, the silhouette of his body leaning back against the seat. "I know this is going to come out all wrong, but I just don't buy the whole I-need-to-be-there-for-Elle line."

I wanted to open his door and shove him out. "Do you even know what it's been like?" I asked.

"I can't imagine how hard it's been. But one thing has nothing to do with the other."

I hated that he was actually calling me out. But what did I expect? My argument was pretty weak, considering the fact that Noelle . . . *Elle* and I weren't exactly speaking. "You don't know what you're talking about," I said, putting the car in drive.

"Oh, I think I do," Max said, a little chuckle in his voice.

"You're annoying, you know that?" I asked as I pulled out onto the street.

"You always so nice when a guy asks you out?" His face glowed from the passing streetlights.

I elbowed him, wishing that he would lean over and kiss me or try to kiss me or do anything that would cause his lips to make contact with my skin. And. Hating. Myself. For. That. Thought. "Just leave me alone," I said.

"You don't mean that," Max answered, with a tilt of his head.

We were silent for the rest of the ride. Max just stared out his window, watching the night grow into the deep blue-black that felt like it could swallow you whole. His fingers played with the metal tab on the manila envelope, and more than once, I wanted to tear my pictures from his grasp.

When I pulled into his driveway and he stepped out of the Jeep, the ceiling light stung my eyes, exposing me, making me feel naked.

He turned, looking back at me. "Just be yourself," he said. "With Elle, I mean."

I looked at him, but not in his eyes. He placed my pictures on the seat, grabbed his bag from the floorboard, and swung it over his shoulder.

"I hope it goes okay tomorrow." He tucked his hands in the front pockets of his jeans.

"Thanks," I said.

He closed the door slowly, as if giving me one last chance to change my mind, to tell him I'd love to go on a date. Instead of speaking, I pressed my lips together and watched him walk up his cracking driveway, then reversed into the quiet street.

When I rounded the curve of the park and passed the crystal plume of the fountain, I decided to let go. I pulled over and put the Jeep in park, then, looking at that dark patch of concrete where Noelle had disappeared, I opened my mouth and screamed as loud as I could.

God Had Nothing to Do with It

"My mom's been running every day," I said from one of the wooden stools at the island in the Pendeltons' kitchen. My feet slid off the lowest rung for the third time, so I let them hang free.

"Good for her," Mrs. Pendelton said as she adjusted the thick headband in her hair and pulled five bowls from a cabinet near the sink. "I wish I had the motivation to exercise."

"Gimme those," Coop said, taking the bowls from his mother's thin hands.

"She's trying to guilt my dad into going with her." I watched Coop place the bowls on the island.

"Tell him not to fall into that trap," Mr. Pendelton said as he filled water glasses with ice. "If he starts, she'll never let him stop."

"Mike," Mrs. Pendelton said to her husband, giving him a smack on the arm with a large silver spoon.

I pulled at the sleeves of my green sweater, trying to keep myself from worrying about how it would go when Elle finally came downstairs. *Elle, Elle, Elle. Remember to call her Elle.* And I hoped that any lingering spirits creeping through the town in celebration of Halloween would help with our reunion.

"It's true. You'd never let me—"

"What's *she* doing here?" Elle's voice rang through the air, a low pitch that resonated in my chest. I turned to find her leaning against the doorway that led into the front hall. *Crumpled,* I thought, taking in her slumped posture.

"We invited Tessa for dinner," Elle's mother said without looking up from the loaf of Italian bread she was slicing.

"She's here to see you, moron." Coop picked up the bowls and walked out of the kitchen, shaking his head.

"You guys forget to tell me, or was this supposed to be some kind of great surprise?" Elle stood there in a baggy blue sweatshirt and ripped jeans, seeming to wait for an answer. She looked thinner than I had expected, and her skin was almost translucent. Especially without makeup. I tried to remember the last time she'd walked around without a hint of makeup and couldn't come up with a memory later than fifth grade.

"Hey, Elle," I said, feeling the strange new name roll off my tongue.

"Hey, Tess, how's it goin'?" Elle batted her eyelashes. *Like she always used to when she flipped into bitch mode,* I remembered.

I looked at Elle's mother, who had taken her attention from the bread and was now staring intently at the bare feet of her daughter. "Okay, girls, I need some help. Tess, will you carry the salad? Elle, you get the dressing. We've got five kinds to choose from."

"Yippee." Elle flipped her long blue-black hair over her shoulder and grabbed the bottles of salad dressing. I followed her into the dining room, where Coop was already seated with a napkin spread across his lap.

"You could at least try to be nice," Coop whispered.

"You could at least try to keep your nose out of my business," Elle snapped.

"If you'd stop acting like an asshole, I would." Coop glared at her. Elle stared back, her lips a tight line, until he looked at the salad I'd set on the table.

I sat across from Coop, beside Elle, and counted the little rippling wrinkles in the tablecloth. Taking a few deep breaths (slowly, so neither of them would notice), I tried to clear my brain. But the questions kept poundingpoundingpounding. *What does she think of me? What should I say? What will it take to be friends again?*

"You hear the news?" Coop asked.

It wasn't until I looked up that I realized he was speaking to me. Was he talking about something to do with Charlie Croft? Right in front of Elle? I'd figured the subject of that man was totally off-limits in this house.

"Chip and Jessie . . ." Coop drew out Jessie's name and widened his eyes.

"Oh, that." I unfolded the cloth napkin on my plate and spread it over my lap. "Who hasn't?"

"What?" Elle asked. "Are they gay or something?"

Coop and I laughed. The sound was too loud and too free, and I didn't realize it until too late.

Elle sat back in her seat and rolled her eyes, her face tight, jaw clenched. "So are you going to fill me in or just make me feel like an idiot?"

"Jessie's a girl," I said. "They're seniors, and they've been dating since their freshman year. Well, off and on. He plays football; she's a cheerleader. You know, totally stereotypical of every high school's supreme order of popularity."

"Disgusting." Elle propped one elbow on the arm of her chair and started twirling a strand of that blue-black hair between two fingers. "So what about them?"

Everything about her had flipped into this nonchalant mode, but something was off. I couldn't decide if she really didn't care, or if she just wanted me to *think* she didn't care. Maybe she sensed what I already knew. That this would take the focus off her kidnapping and return like nothing else could.

"In what could be called the biggest breakup of the year, he dumped her at lunch yesterday. Right in front of everyone, which is totally rude, if you ask me." I sighed, fluttering my hand to my chest in fake empathy. "All for some other girl."

Elle raised her eyebrows. "Well, that makes it a little more interesting."

"Hell, yeah," Coop said, and then whistled. "So . . . you think I have a chance, Tess? If I move in while Jessie's feeling defeated, I could do the whole concerned-and-supportive thing for a few weeks and then, when she's crying on my shoulder, make my stealth move. She'd never know what hit her."

"Because you're such a stud, right?" Elle laughed. It was a real laugh and caught me by surprise.

"You haven't been around for a while, Elle." Coop leaned back and put his hands behind his head. "I am the most sought-after freshman in the building."

Elle threw her napkin. It soared across the table and landed in Coop's face.

"It's not nice to lie to your sister," Elle said.

As Coop threw the napkin back at Elle, Mrs. Pendelton made her way into the room with a casserole dish full of steaming mani-cotti, followed closely by Mr. Pendelton, who was carrying an open bottle of wine.

"We've been having all of Elle's favorites," Mrs. Pendelton said as she placed the dish on a metal stand in the center of the table. "Dig in, everyone."

When the doorbell rang, Coop jumped up and ran for the door. Elle's shoulders stiffened as several children's voices sang out, "Trick-or-treat," the sound echo-echo-echoing off the walls of the dining room.

"I thought you were going to keep the porch lights *off*." Mrs. Pendelton's eyes narrowed, directed at her husband. "With all the media, the last thing we need is—"

"I put the candy away." Mr. Pendelton sighed, pushed his chair back, and stood, heading for the door. "I made *sure* the switch was down."

"Dad." Elle's voice was hard, the word short and sharp. "It was Coop's idea, and I told him it was okay. Just leave them on."

The front door clicked shut, and Coop rounded the corner, bumping into his father. He looked at all of us, silent and tense. "What?" he asked. "What'd I do?"

Mr. Pendelton shook his head, the creases around his eyes making him look sad and old. "Nothing, Cooper."

"Sit." Mrs. Pendelton waved a fork in the air. "Eat."

We all served ourselves in silence and began eating. Elle's father and I made the obligatory comments about how wonderful everything tasted, while Coop and Elle kicked each other under the table.

"So," Elle's mother said into her napkin as she wiped her mouth, "how have you been, Tessa?"

"Fine," I said. "Doing the whole school thing, and that's pretty much it."

"Oh, now, don't lie," Coop said. "There's a guy in her life."

Elle stopped chewing and turned her head sideways slightly.

"Isn't that neat?" Elle's father smiled and drummed the table with his fingers.

"Neat?" Elle asked, her voice low. "You're kidding, right?"

I took a bite of manicotti, wishing Coop had kept his mouth shut.

Elle put her fork down and pushed back in her seat. "What's he like?" she asked.

"He's not my boyfriend or anything." I shrugged. "We're in the same photography class."

Elle stared at me and said, "Hmm." Then she picked up her fork and took another bite of her food. "Finally decided to give yourself up?"

I moved a bite of salad to the back of my mouth and forced myself to swallow. "What is that supposed to—"

Elle's mother cleared her throat and sat up straighter in her chair. "Elle will be going back to school in a few weeks. Isn't that good news?" Her voice was high pitched and a little shaky.

"Yeah. I'm flat-out giddy," Elle said under her breath.

"Tessa, I was thinking it might be nice if you could drive Elle to school." Elle's mother looked at me, her chest puffed out from holding her breath.

"I'm not going to school with her," Elle said. "I'll ride the bus."

I heard Coop snicker, part of a joke that none of us knew.

"You," Elle's mother said, her voice taking on the authoritative tone from years ago when she'd caught Noelle and me watching an R-rated movie, "will *not* be riding the bus."

"Didn't you know?" Coop turned a bitter smile toward Elle. "Pendeltons don't ride the bus. It's not safe."

"Give me a break, Mom." Elle flung her fork onto her plate, and it clattered noisily. "It's not like I'm going to be kidnapped again. Jesus."

"You, young lady, will not speak like that in my house." Mr. Pendelton's deep voice boomed from his mouth. "You should thank God for bringing you home safely."

"Is that what you think?" Elle stared at her father, her eyebrows pulled tightly together. "That God brought me back? God had nothing to do with it, Dad. And sometimes"—Elle stood from the table and threw her napkin on top of her manicotti—"I wish I hadn't had anything to do with it, either." She turned and ran from the room.

We all listened in silence as her feet rumbled up the steps. I watched the bright tomato sauce soak into the cloth napkin and hoped it wouldn't stain and be a permanent reminder of this disastrous meal.

"Another peaceful dinner at the Pendelton household." Coop looked at me. "Aren't you glad you came?" He raised his eyebrows and sighed.

"I think I'll go up," I said softly. "If that's okay."

"I'm guessing it can't make matters worse." Elle's father took a sip of his wine and placed his glass on the table. The thick red liquid swirled around the inside of the wineglass until it lost momentum.

I didn't knock. I just walked in. She didn't hear me at first, and I stared at her for a minute or two. She was on her bed, propped against a pile of pillows that was stacked against her headboard. The white eyelet canopy that her parents had given her for her tenth birthday was still suspended above her bed, making her seem innocent and untouched. With one hand, she was writing furiously in a spiral notebook that she balanced on her lap. With the other, she wiped tears from her cheeks.

It shouldn't have surprised me to see her crying, but it did. She'd seemed so hardened that I'd thought the only emotion flowing through her was hostility. I felt a little sick as I realized that she might be struggling with feeling anything real again after shutting down for the last two years.

She looked up. Her face was red and splotchy, her eyes slightly swollen.

"You okay?" I asked.

"Do I look okay?"

I started to turn away and then forced myself to keep facing her. *This is Noelle*, I reminded myself. *The girl who has been your best friend since before you knew what it meant to have a best friend.*

"No. You don't."

"Well, I'm not."

I looked away, finding the cold stare of her eyes too oppressive. The room seemed to be floating in the past. Except for the clothes piled on the plush carpet, which were larger and more grown-up, it hadn't changed one bit since the last time I'd been here. The butterfly border still fluttered around the top of the walls, the lavender paint still made me feel as if I were standing in the middle of a spring flower, and the music box Coop had bought Elle for Christmas one year with his allowance was still planted in the middle of her dresser. I studied the two windows in her room, their curtains drawn tight. The one above her desk, looking out over the front yard, was where Noelle had peeked out at me the day I'd brought her gift. The other window, next to her bed, faced the side of the house. Staring at it brought back a wave of memories.

The last summer we'd spent together, Noelle had pulled me out that window and across the roof of her garage several times. She was all legs as she climbed down the fence that butted up against the back of the house, me fumbling behind her, both of us trying to stifle laughter as we went. It was during one of those nights that I had my first and only kiss with a boy. I wondered if she remembered all of that. Then I looked at her, crumpled on her bed, and wondered how this girl in front of me could possibly be the same person.

"This whole thing sucks." She choked on the words, trying to contain her sobs.

"Yeah." I stood there, unsure of what to do with my hands, so I shoved them into the pockets of my jeans.

"People are walking on eggshells around me. Even my shrink." Elle wiped her nose with the back of her hand. "And me. I just want to see something break."

"Yeah, I can kind of tell." I smiled, and the corners of Elle's mouth pulled up a little, too. It made my heart stop, because she almost looked like the old her.

"I know I need to chill. It's just that . . . God." Elle slid the notebook and pen onto the comforter and sat forward, grabbing a pillow from behind her and squeezing it to her chest. "It's hard."

"Maybe if you think more about how glad we are to have you home . . ."

"For two years"—Elle pressed her palms into her eyes—"all I thought about was everyone I'd left behind."

When she lowered her hands and looked at me, I reached out to touch her, but I didn't know if I should go for her shoulder, or her arm, or her hand, so I tucked a strand of hair behind my ear instead.

"Everyone's judging me, you know?" Elle looked down at the bedspread, waving her hand at the TV on her dresser. "Reporters who've never met me are saying I should have talked. I just want to scream at them. It may have looked like I could've gotten away, but it's like I was tied to this invisible leash."

"It was weird." I rubbed my wrist, scratched at my thin, pale skin. "Hearing that you weren't actually locked away the whole time."

"The thing is . . . I was," Elle said.

Her words hit me hard and made me feel like I was sinking. Like I couldn't get enough air.

"I wish I could explain it. But I lived it, and I really don't understand." Elle looked up at me.

"Elle, I'm sorry—"

"I'm so *sick* of that!" Elle slammed her fist into the mattress. "Everyone's sorry, pitying me and trying not to say anything that might upset me. Jesus, I wish people would just act normal for once. Coop's the only one who has the balls to say what's really on his mind."

"You want to know what's really on my mind?"

Elle's head snapped up. "Yes."

"I missed you. We all missed you." Tears welled up in my eyes. "And now you're back, and we're still missing you. As long as you keep this wall around yourself and refuse to let anyone in, he wins."

Elle nodded. "Okay, maybe."

"Unless you speak up and tell us, we're not going to know what to say or do. Nobody's psychic."

"We used to be." Elle smiled, and I felt a little surge of my old friend coming through. "Psychic twins?"

So there was hope after all. This was the first time she had referred to anything from our past.

"You don't have to remind me." I smiled back, remembering all the mornings we'd arrived at school wearing almost identical outfits, in the exact same color, accessorized with shoes and purses so similar they could be interchanged. Then there were all the times we'd called each other at the same moment, only to get a busy signal. And the zillions of times we'd finished each other's sentences.

I decided to sit on the bed. When I did, the notebook between us slid toward me, and I looked down at the familiar writing, catching three words — *can't believe I've* — before Elle grabbed it and flipped it shut.

"What's that?" I asked.

"Homework." Before she threw the notebook on the floor, I saw a flash of a huge butterfly in the center of the blue cover. It was some kind of fabric patch, the raised wings stitched with varying shades of blues, greens, and purples.

"Are you totally dreading going back to school?" I traced my finger along a thread in the bedspread.

"Yeah. Everyone's going to stare and whisper like I'm some freak. Plus, I'll be in all freshman classes. I don't know which part will suck more."

"I didn't even think about your being held back."

"Me either. Not until my tutor came in and started testing me. She's cool, though, says I'll be able to catch up with my own class — your class — after summer break, if I keep working hard."

"I guess so, if you're throwing yourself into homework like that." I pointed toward the edge of the bed, where the notebook had disappeared.

"What?" Elle's nose crinkled up. She looked to the floor and waved her hand. "Oh. That's different. It's for therapy. I'm supposed to keep that notebook with me and write down anything that comes up. Like if something happens that's frustrating, or that brings up a bad memory. How the scent of coffee reminds me of his sour breath . . . stuff like that."

I listened to Elle breathe, watched the digital clock on her nightstand for two minutes, tried not to think about how close she'd had to get to smell his breath.

"And she gives me assignments, too," Elle added.

"What kind of assignments?"

"The first one was to recall everything that happened that day. When he took me."

"Will you tell me?" I asked, the soft words springing from my mouth before I could stop them. "What happened, I mean. I've spent two years envisioning different stuff. And I just want to know—"

"Everyone *just wants to know*." Elle stood. "You're exactly like everyone else, aren't you?"

I shook my head, wishing I could grasp the words that floated on the air between us and stuff them back through my lips, swallow them whole, bury them deep inside. "No, Elle. I just—"

"All you want is to know every sickening detail."

"Elle—"

"People don't have to ask. Their darting eyes, never making contact with mine, scream all their questions. How'd he get you? How'd he keep you? Why. Didn't. You. Tell?" Elle leaned down. I scooted to the end of her bed. When she stood up, the butterfly notebook lay in one hand while the fingers of her other hand tore through pages until she found what she was looking for. "You wanna know?" she screamed, every part of her shaking. "Here!"

She threw the open notebook on my lap and stormed out of the room, leaving me alone with her words. Leaving me alone with the answers I'd been waiting two years to learn.

I don't understand why it's so flipping important.

Who cares how? Or why?

It happened. End of story.

But Shrinky Dink wants details. She says the memories will heal me.

I wonder if you can really heal a person who's been ripped open and gutted.

But, whatever.

I'm riding my bike feeling the wind rush through my hair and thinking about the graham crackers and Hershey's Kisses tucked in the cabinet over the toaster oven.

I hear my name I stop I turn.

There's a man in a car he tells me my mom is in the hospital he works with her.

I fall for it.

Bam. My bike drops to the ground.

Slam. The car door closes me in.

Whoosh. I am gone.

Gonegonegonegonegonegonegonegonegonegone gonegone.

I look at him he smiles his teeth are crooked and need a good bleaching.

"You thirsty?" he asks and passes me a plastic bottle of Coke.

And. Then. There. Are. The. Flashes.

A small, dark room a dank-smelling mattress the slimy eggs he makes me eat.

The metallic-tasting drink that always brings me sleep sweetsleep.

The gun pressing against my bruised back the soft spot under my chin my throbbing temple.

My feet scraping the concrete steps my fingers trailing the cold brick wall my eyes blinded by the harsh light illuminating the door.

A cold shower his coffee breath gagging me I am shivering watching red-brown streams rush down my legs swirl around the drain.

At least part of me escapes.

Funny, the first time I saw my face on a milk carton, on the flyers posted at the mini-mart down the street, all I could think was how much I HATED that picture. I mean, really, couldn't they have picked a better one? It was bad enough it ended up in my seventh-grade yearbook, but to have it splashed all over the news made me want to die. My flat hair and half smile. That stupid photographer caught me before I was ready. I wondered if he remembered. If he had the sense to feel bad.

Funny to think how stupid I was.

Funny to think how much I didn't know.

Not so funny, though,

how he kept me quiet.

"You've been crying," Elle said from her seat on the couch.

My hand flew to my cheeks, fingers rubbing the slight swell beneath my eyes. "I rinsed my face with cold water."

"I can still tell." Elle shifted under the pale yellow blanket spread across her legs. I remembered making a fort with it years ago, stretching it from the back of the couch to the bar stools that were now pushed against the far wall, and whispering and giggling under its shelter.

I waved my hand in the air, indicating the wide space of the Pendeltons' basement. The recessed lighting was on its dimmest setting, allowing Elle the perfect hideout. "But it's so dark down here. Am I totally transparent?"

Elle shook her head. Rolled her eyes. "That little red dot you always get when you cry. It's there. Under your right eye."

I walked to the arm of the couch and leaned against it. "It's crazy. How well you know me."

Elle fluttered her lashes. "Don't kid yourself, Tessa. I don't know you any better than you know me."

"But we've been best friends since we were—"

"You do realize that I've been gone for two years, right?"

I opened my mouth, but I didn't know what to say. This huge space was cracking open between us, gaping in front of me, daring me to jump to her side to try to keep her from disappearing all over again. But all I could do was stand there and stare.

"Everything's changed." Elle jutted her chin forward. "We can't just go back to the way we were."

"But—"

"But what?" Elle leaned forward, her eyes glaring at me. "You got what you wanted, right? Now that you know what really hap-pened, you can leave. Go tell all of your loser friends what they're dying to know."

I shook my head. She didn't understand. And I didn't have a clue about how to make her.

"Close the door on your way up." Elle grabbed the remote from the coffee table and clicked on the television. The pale blue light bounced off her face as she gave me one last hard look. "I want to be alone."

In Sync

When I pulled out of the Pendeltons' driveway, I switched off my radio, deciding to make my way home in silence. The sun had set, and all that was left in its wake were creeping shadows that shaded the world with a purplish tint. It could have been all the kids in costumes running from house to house, carrying pillowcases and plastic buckets filled with sugary treats. Or the flickering luminaries and jack-o'-lanterns that lined the street. But I was pretty sure the real reason the night felt so eerie was Elle. And that journal.

I remembered the last Halloween we had spent together. Dressed as Thing One and Thing Two, Noelle and I had pranced around our neighborhood for hours. Our blue Afro wigs had been fluffed high on our heads, and we had collapsed into giggle fits each time we'd looked at each other. But the best part was the freedom. Back then, most parents were fearless and chose to stay home.

I let out a long sigh as I glanced at the packs of moms and dads, bundled and cluttering the sidewalks. Centerville was no longer safe or untouched. Not since the middle of August two years ago.

After turning onto my street, I noticed a car parked in front of my house. I didn't think much of it; our next-door neighbors had two young children, and their grandparents came over for all the photo-worthy holidays. But as I approached my driveway, I realized the car was familiar. And someone was leaning against the black hood.

He stepped away from the Mustang and walked toward my car as I pulled to a stop. But I couldn't move. My hand froze on the key ring. I didn't have time to think before Max's face peered in my driver's-side window, his hand perched on the handle of my door.

His lips moved, and I heard the muffled sound of his voice rising at the end of the sentence. A question. And I was all out of answers.

I shook my head.

He pulled my door open and spoke again. "You gonna come out of there or what?" He held out his hand, offering help.

I didn't understand how he possibly could have known, but I definitely needed steadying.

"I just wanted to check in." He pulled his cap off his head, and his curls spilled out around his face.

I watched as, behind him, a stream of kids ran through the

trampled grass of my front yard and hopped up the steps to my porch.

"You know," he added, "to see how it went with Elle."

I didn't know what to say. Unfortunately, my lips opened and let my very first thought escape without any censor.

"Why are you being so nice?"

He looked away then, facing the closed garage door. I couldn't tell anything from his profile, and I wondered if he was mad. Or maybe he was just plain done with me. In that moment, I was kind of scared he might walk away. I had to plant my feet on the hard ground to keep from swaying forward and placing my hands on his chest in the hopes that he might curl his arms around me in a deep hug.

"Trick-or-treat?" A blast of voices shrieked through the air, breaking Max's eyes away from whatever had held his attention. He turned toward my house, and we both watched in silence as my father appeared in the doorway, smiling at the kids who stood in the bright porch light. Tinker Bell sparkled, the Incredible Hulk flexed, and the pirate with the macaw on his shoulder arrghed.

My dad dropped a handful of candy bars into the outstretched bags. The kids shouted hurried thank-yous before turning away, running back to their parents, and dashing off to the next house. My father watched them go, stepping backward into the foyer. Just before he swung the door closed, he caught sight of Max and me standing in the shadow of the driveway. He stopped, unsure, I could tell, of what to do. Slowly, he raised his hand and waved. Max and I waved back. Then my father closed the door, and I heard the brassy *thunk* of the door knocker hitting its bed.

"Come sit with me," Max said. He reached out for my hand, then stopped several inches short and waited. I reached out (it felt a little like some crazy magnetism took over), and his hand enveloped mine. For a second, we just stood there, kind of breathing in the moment. And then Max started toward his car, pulling me along with him.

We sat on the edge of the curb, listening to the patter of feet scurrying behind us. From all around, little voices called out with excitement.

"I'm being nice because I like you," Max said softly. "And I'm here tonight because I thought you might need to talk."

I wrapped my arms around my legs and rested my chin on my knees. "It went okay," I said. "It's hard, though. Coop's right. She's different."

"I'm sure," Max said.

"I think she's really angry."

"She's got a lot to be angry about."

"Yeah." I started to shiver and squeezed my arms tighter around my legs.

"Cold?" Max scooted so close against my side that the gap between us disappeared.

I felt the heat of his shoulder, his side, his thigh, and wanted to melt into him. "It'll work itself out, won't it?" I asked.

Max looked at me, the light from the luminaries across the street dancing in his eyes. "What'll work out?" he asked.

"Everything with Elle." I thought for a second that he might have been hoping I meant something different. Like us, maybe.

He looked down at the pavement. Pulled his feet toward him with a long scraping sound.

"Being home after all this time." My words shook. "Fitting in. Finding her way."

Max took a deep breath. He reached around my shoulders and pulled me in tight. "Yeah." His hand rubbed along my upper arm, firm and slow. My shoulders relaxed. I allowed my body to slump into his.

"You really think?" My vision was getting swimmy, and I couldn't make it stop. I hoped Max was totally unaware, but I had to keep swiping at my cheeks, and I did that whole stutter-sigh thing a few times.

"I'm sure," he whispered, his breath warming my cheek.

I finally rested my head against his shoulder and we sat together in silence. At one point, I noticed that our breathing was perfectly in sync.

Lie to Me

"I don't understand all the reporters," I said, stretching my legs out on the backseat of my father's car. The plastic bag next to me crinkled against my thigh. "It's like their brains aren't attached to their mouths."

"Don't let them upset you, honey." The flicker from the head-lights of a passing car washed over my father's head and shoulders. The skin on the back of his neck reminded me of a smooth rock. "They're just doing their jobs."

"Gossiping. Spreading rumors. Telling blatant lies." I looked out the window at the final glow of the sunset, at the raindrops racing sideways on the outside of the car's windows, at the flat grassy pastures where horses and cows spent endless days. "Seems to me like they should've just stayed in high school."

My mother twisted in the passenger seat, her plump lips and

rounded cheeks forming a half smile. "They wouldn't get paid to be in high school."

The tires beneath us jumped a division in the pavement, the sound rumbling through the car.

"Last night I watched this panel of total morons discuss Elle and the kidnapping. They started talking about that Stockholm syndrome thing, practically saying she'd wanted to be there with him."

"I know it sounds odd," my father said. "But the Stockholm syndrome is a very real response some victims have toward their captors."

"I think it's a bunch of crap." Outside my window, three fat raindrops merged into one and dashed toward the rear of the car.

"In a way, it helps make sense of the situation." My mother turned and faced me again. Her silver earrings, the birthday gift she had chosen while we'd shopped through outlet stores earlier in the day, sparkled in the headlights of the car behind us. "Allowing herself to relate to him just might be the reason she's alive today."

"Elle might be really pissed off, Mom. Even messed up from her two years away," I said. "But she's not mental."

My dad chuckled. "No one's saying she's mental, hon."

"Just that she used the defenses she had available to her," my mother said gently.

I closed my eyes, wanting to shut out the reality of our words. That we weren't simply discussing the story of a person we didn't know made me sick to my stomach. But after stuffing myself too full of filet mignon and garlic mashed potatoes at my mom's favorite restaurant, riding in the car with my eyes closed made me feel even worse, so I opened them again.

"I looked up Stockholm syndrome, you know," I said. "And it does *not* describe Elle. She wasn't loyal. She didn't form some emotional bond with him. She's certainly not defending him." My voice cracked, and I swallowed before continuing. "She even made sure he'd be caught."

"Yet she stayed." My mother was facing forward now, but her words were strong. They lifted above the sound of rain pelting the windshield, the steady swiping of the wipers, the thrum of the tires running on the highway.

"That's not because of some dumb syndrome." I tugged at the seat belt crossing my chest and slid toward the front seat. "It's like he broke her or something.

"Here's my question," I said, sliding back again and staring out at the darkness. "If he had her so brainwashed, or Stockholm syndromed or whatever, that she stayed with him for two years"— I paused, biting at my lip—"what made her leave?"

"Something big certainly pushed her to plan her own escape." My mother looked back at me, her eyes tired and sad. "The truth is that we might never know her motivation. And we have to be okay with that."

I ducked against the window again. The tires jumped the road, and my forehead bumped the hard glass. I wished that the hum of the car's engine could ease us back into the comfortable silence that had enveloped us when we'd first left the restaurant. That the shadowed world pressing against the car would make everything so sleepy our mouths wouldn't be able to form words.

"I like the shirt you picked out today," my mother said, her voice soft.

"My favorite thing about your birthday," I said, "is that we all get stuff."

"It's not about stuff, Tessa," my mother said.

"Right." I nodded. "It's about bonding."

"You'll learn," my father said. "Family is the most important thing."

"Mm-hmm."

I reached into the bag on the leather seat, ran my hand along the small buttons strung like beads down the shirt's front, and imagined Max's fingers slipping each tiny circle through its own little opening. I closed my eyes and felt the silk of his hair brush against my cheek. And then I shoved him out of my mind. As much as I wanted him there, I couldn't allow him to stay.

My mother looked over her shoulder. "Remember that last time Elle's mom and I took you girls shopping?"

I stared at her, the memory coming back in one brilliant flash. "Back-to-school clothes? It was right before . . . she went missing."

"Yeah," she said. "That was fun. Maybe we can invite them to do something like that again. A mother-daughter day might be just what they need."

I pictured Noelle posing in front of a three-way mirror in the dressing room of J.Crew. Wearing a denim miniskirt and a black tank top that were barely within the limits of the school dress code, she twirled around so the skirt fanned out, showing off her long legs.

"Think this makes me look older?" she'd asked, fluffing her hair.

"How much older are you going for?" I stood behind her, pulling my wavy hair back with a thick headband I'd found near the register, wishing I'd opted for highlights a shade or two lighter the day before at the salon.

Noelle shrugged. "Dunno," she said. "How old do you think the hot guy is who's out there folding jeans?" She turned and fluttered her eyelashes. It was a dangerous look.

"Gross, Noelle. He's probably in college. Or maybe older." I tore the headband from my hair and let my hand fall to my side. My hair swooped into my face.

"Yeah, but he's hot." Elle turned and shook her butt at me. "It's just a test," she said. "If he asks for my number, I'll know I look at least eighteen."

"And then what?" I asked. "Older guys expect things, Noelle. You don't—"

"Oh, please," Noelle said. "Don't be such a prude. It's not like I'm going to have sex with him." She tipped toward the mirror and pressed her lips together, making sure her gloss was evenly distributed. "I just want to see if he's interested. I swear he was checking me out when I was looking through those dresses."

I laughed. "You were practically mooning him when you bent over in that skirt," I said, flipping up the back of her mini. "I couldn't keep my eyes off you. And trust me, I'm totally not interested."

Noelle turned around and shook a finger in my face. "You're wrong. And I'm going to prove it."

As she sauntered from the dressing room, I peered around the corner, watching, my heart beating quick-quick-quick as the hot guy stopped folding jeans and ran a hand through his ruffled hair. My eyes darted from Noelle and the guy to the entrance of the store. Our mothers had gone to the food court for a drink, and I could just imagine their expressions if they saw the way Noelle had leaned herself against the clothing display.

Noelle turned in a slow circle, modeling herself more than the outfit. The guy nodded, answering some question she'd asked, and she struck the Confident-Girl Pose she'd refined by practicing in front of the full-length mirror in her room. When he walked around her, grazing her side, and moved toward the register, Noelle turned and smiled wide, giving me two thumbs-up. *Score*, she'd mouthed.

"So," my father's voice boomed, bringing me back to the car, the rain, and the darkness. "What's up with the guy who came over the other night?"

"Way to be subtle," I said with a laugh.

"Give him a break, honey," my mother said.

"Hey, I did it your way, my dear." My father tilted his head toward my mother. "If we keep waiting for Tessa to tell us on her own time, we might be a hundred and ten before we learn anything besides his first name and the fact that they're in photography class together."

I leaned forward into the light created by the instrument panel. "His name is Max Kinsley, and he's a junior. His family moved here this past summer from Montana." I plopped myself against the door, hating that Max's smile had wriggled back to the forefront of my mind.

"That's it?" My father rotated in his seat, looking back at me.

"Road," my mother said, tapping the dashboard.

My father turned, facing forward again. "But that's all I get?"

"He's got brown hair, brown eyes, and an olive-toned complexion," I said, trying to use an official reporter voice. "He's approximately six feet tall and probably weighs between one hundred sixty and one hundred seventy pounds."

"Does he have any tattoos?" My father's voice was strained, his words pulled tight. "Piercings?"

"Dad." I rolled my eyes at the rearview mirror.

"I'm serious."

I started to chew on my thumbnail. "No tattoos or piercings that I'm aware of."

"Your father's just nervous because that boy had his arm around you." My mother didn't turn around, but I heard the amusement in her voice.

"Were you spying or something?" My words flung through the air, hitting my father in the back of the head.

"Tessa, it was Halloween. The doorbell rang every three minutes, and the two of you were sitting on the curb in front of the house."

"Yes," my mother said with a nod, "he was definitely spying."

"Nan!"

"Well, you were." My mother playfully smacked my father's shoulder.

"You didn't have to give me up so fast." My father tipped his head toward my mother. "I'd never tell her that you called her photography teacher to check up on this young man."

"Mom," I said. "Please tell me you didn't."

"Sorry, honey." My mother shrugged and slid down in her seat. "You can never be too careful."

"It's not like anything's going on with him." My hand found its way back into the bag that held my new shirt. My fingers counted the buttons. How long would it take Max to undo them?

"Good," my father said. "His hair was too long."

"What's wrong with his hair?" I asked.

"Is it long?" My mother looked back at me.

"It's long*ish*." My lips betrayed me and pulled back into a smile. "He's got these great curls."

"He's cute?" My mother was smiling, too. It was the first time we'd ever talked about a boy like this.

"Cute?" My father's voice was way too loud for the car. "You're not supposed to encourage her."

"Oh, Ted, stop. It's not like the kid's an ax murderer."

"And you know this for a fact?"

My mother laughed, a high-pitched sound that threatened to shatter the windows and let the rain stream in.

"Look, he doesn't have to be a murderer or a drug dealer. He's a boy. And he seems to be interested in Tessa. That scares me enough right now."

"Tessa's teacher was very impressed with him." My mother looked back at me and reached between the two front seats, patting my knee. "I can't wait to meet him."

"You're not going to meet him," I said. "There's nothing going on."

She just smiled and nodded. I could tell by the way her lips parted that she wanted to say more. But instead, she clicked on the radio, flipping it to her favorite light-rock station.

Sheryl Crow's voice purred through the car, asking someone to lie to her, and promising she'd believe. My mother hummed along with the slow strumming of the guitar.

I looked out the window and counted raindrops, wishing they could wash away everything that complicated my life.

No Fishing

"Don't think the ride means we're all BFF again," Elle said without looking at me as we walked through the crowded hall.

I'd nearly exploded with excitement when she'd called me the night before, asking if I'd pick her up for her first day back to school. And watching her now, as she faced all the stares with her shoulders pulled back, her chin jutted forward, and her hair tucked behind her ears, I felt like making up some cheesy cheer routine. *Go, Elle!*

"I know," I said, narrowing my eyes at a girl pointing Elle's way. "You didn't want to ride the bus. And you'd rather die than have your mom drop you off. I get it."

"No way," Elle said, sounding for two seconds like my old friend.

Around us, people spun the dials on their lockers, tugged at the little metal doors, and shoved backpacks into the small openings.

"Was that Lisa Albers?" Elle leaned into me, half whispering.

I looked over my shoulder and saw the profile of a girl wearing a very tight sweater, the stretched cotton clinging to her sultry curves.

"Yeah," I said.

"Those can't be real." Elle pressed the three notebooks in her arms against her chest. Pulled the strap of her purse higher on her shoulder. "What'd her parents do, give her D cups for her last birthday?"

I laughed, silently thanking Lisa for this moment of normalcy. "Actually, she had a pretty major growth spurt during eighth grade."

"I guess," Elle said, her voice softer as she studied the faces of people passing us.

It seemed like everyone was staring but in a way that showed they were trying not to. A few people smiled and nodded at Elle; others slowed a bit when they saw her, then stepped twice as fast to make up for the blunder. I was getting jostled in the traffic more than usual, too, like people wanted to brush up against Elle to make sure she was real.

"You have Mrs. Frazier for English," I said as we neared Elle's first-period classroom. "She's all about the art of answering an essay question; you'll have, like, three a week. Couple of novels, a few papers, but nothing too difficult."

"You had her last year?" Elle asked as we stopped at the open door.

I nodded.

"Score. Maybe you could hook me up with a paper or two?" She raised her eyebrows, and I looked into the classroom, where Mrs. Frazier stood behind her desk, tucking loose strands of dirt brown hair into the bun twisted on top of her head.

"Want me to introduce you?" I asked.

Elle rolled her eyes. "You really think that's necessary?"

"I just thought that maybe—"

"I can handle this," Elle said, her chest puffing up with a deep breath. "I really can."

I wasn't sure if she was trying to convince me or herself.

As she stepped through the door, I called after her, "I'll be here when the bell rings," and held the pass the counselor had given me in the air. I was Elle's official welcome committee, her tour guide through her first day of high school.

She turned and nodded once, then walked right up to Mrs. Frazier with a smile on her face. It was fake, I knew, because the deep dimple in her left cheek was missing.

Later that morning, I rushed down the hall trying to make it to my locker before the bell rang. I was permitted to be late, since I was taking Elle to all her classes, but I'd forgotten my homework for history. Besides, my teacher was kind of scary, and even if I was allowed to be late, I really didn't want to stand out in his classroom for any reason.

My brain was in overdrive, so I almost didn't see him.

But obviously that radar you get when you like someone had

already kicked in, because I caught something familiar from the corner of my eye and swung my gaze in his direction.

It might have been the comfortable posture that caused him to stoop forward like he didn't care what people thought about him. Or the deep green of his fleece jacket. I guess it even could have been pheromones, drifting toward me on a current of air kicked up by the bodies churning through the hall.

None of that really matters.

What matters is what I witnessed. And how it made me feel.

I glanced so quickly the scene was reduced to three snapshots in my brain.

First: Max leaning into a bank of lockers, smiling and reaching toward a girl with long blonde hair and a short little skirt. She was pulling something out of his reach in a very flirty way, her giggles vibrating my heart.

Second: A close-up. Her French-manicured hand batting at his chest, gripping the zippered edge of his jacket and pulling him closer.

Third: Shoes. Mine. Other people's. And the alternating black-and-white tiles of the floor.

I ducked into the nearest restroom and rushed into the corner, tucking myself against the wall and sliding down, wishing, wishing, wishing I could jump into the large trash can beside me and ride down into some rabbit's hole that would take me far away from my life.

"How's your day been, Elle?" Max asked.

I stuffed a french fry in my mouth, glad to have Elle at our lunch table for more than the obvious reason. After seeing Max and that girl flirting in the hallway, I needed Elle for a distraction.

"Okay, I guess," Elle said, glancing around at the people sitting nearby. "Except all my teachers are totally annoying. Acting like I'm some move-in and not the kidnapped girl with a nationally known background."

Max asked, "What do you want them to do? Ask about it?"

"You sound like my shrinkette." Elle lowered her gaze and narrowed her eyes. "But you make a good point."

After three more french fries, I realized my stomach was too agitated to deal with food. Thinking about that girl's hand on Max's chest made me feel like I was going to throw up. So I sat there without eating and avoided his eyes.

Coop stopped by our table a few minutes before the bell and punched Elle on her arm. She punched him back—hard, I think, because he winced.

"Give us the scoop, Poop," Elle said as she pulled her hair back into a barrette. "When was Teddy Brown hit with the ugly stick? He used to be so cute."

"You're awful, Elle." Coop crossed his arms over his chest. "He's on some meds for the acne. It's actually getting better."

"Wow." Elle looked toward the table where Coop had eaten lunch, glancing again at the topic of their discussion, and waved. A red-faced boy whose chin was tucked against his chest waved back, a thin smile parting his lips. "If that's better, I'd hate to have seen him before."

As they spoke, Max caught me looking at him. *What's wrong?* he mouthed, reaching for my hand. I yanked my arm from the table, slapping it down in my lap, and shook my head.

Coop propped a foot on the seat next to Elle as she pulled a compact mirror out of her purse and started glossing her lips with a tube of pink-tinted stuff that smelled like cotton candy.

Coop grinned and patted Elle on the head. "Who're you trying to impress?"

"Get offa me, Pooper!" Elle swatted at his arm, then checked to make sure her barrette was still in place and that the perfect number of wisps framed her face.

"Seriously," Coop said, "you look different. It's nice."

Elle threw the compact and lip gloss into her purse and turned her face up to her brother. "Thanks," she said.

When the bell rang, we made our way through the tight crowd, past the rows of senior lockers, and stopped under the circular glass ceiling of the atrium.

"I'll be a few minutes late to photography," I said to Max, kind of waving him away. He didn't get the hint, though, and kept standing there. I felt like shoving him. But I just took a deep breath and glanced at Elle, who was looking over my shoulder. She was seeing many old faces, reacting differently to each one, so I didn't even wonder who was behind me.

Until I saw that dimple.

And the way she ran her fingers through her thick blue-black hair, tilting her head down slightly so she was looking up through her eyelashes.

She was giving someone her Flirty-Girl Look, which she had

perfected during the spring of seventh grade, posing for hours in front of the mirror to make sure she had it just right. This was back when she was obsessed with Jack Dorsey. It took one week of using the Flirty-Girl Look during science class, and finally Jack started to get all tripped up when he spoke to her. Soon after, over a starfish they were dissecting, he asked her if she wanted to hang out. Later that day, when I asked if it had worked, she tossed her head back and laughed. *Of course it worked*, she'd said. *And he's bringing Trevor Ryan, so you're coming, too. Our park. Midnight Saturday.*

"Tess, did you hear me?" Max asked, placing a hand on my arm.

I shook him off. "No, I—"

"Hey, *you*," Elle said in a voice I hadn't heard since before she'd gone missing. She was still looking over my shoulder. Part of me was dying to turn, but the rest of me hardened to stone to keep my body in place. Especially when I saw the look of shock that washed over Max's face.

"S'up?" a deep voice asked.

Max nodded and then stepped forward to give the owner of the deep voice space to walk around us until he was standing beside Elle.

I almost laughed. But there really wasn't anything funny about watching Chip Knowles fling an arm around Elle's shoulders. Or about how Elle looked up at him and batted her lashes (not in the bitchy way, but in the I'm-so-into-you way).

"You guys know Chip?" Elle asked, reaching up to brush something off his lips. "Crumb," she said to him.

What. The. Hell?

"Um, yeah," Max said, pinching my arm. "You guys had a great season."

Chip shrugged and tipped his head forward, as if he were even a slight bit modest.

"Thanks, man." His skin was puffy below his brown eyes, like he hadn't had enough sleep. There were little pricks of stubble on his chin and lower cheeks, and his golden hair was mussed all over. I wondered if he'd showered that morning and carefully constructed the look, or if he had just rolled out of bed and swiped some product along the top of his head. My eyes moved from his face (devoid of expression) to Elle's (dangerously excited) and back again.

"How do you two . . ." I didn't even know how to form the question that was screaming inside my brain.

"It was kinda funny," Elle said with a giggle. "We ran into each other one night at the park in our neighborhood. You know the fountain?"

I nodded. I knew the fountain all right.

"He was fishing at like three in the morning. Fishing!" Elle tipped her head back and laughed.

"And this one came up and scared me half to death." Chip goosed Elle from behind, and she jumped forward a step, swatting at his arm while a squeal erupted from her mouth.

As all of this played out, I realized that the girl standing before me was much more like my old friend than I'd realized. She'd always craved the attention of guys and was used to getting exactly what she wanted. The thing was, I'd expected her to be different.

More guarded and aware. But the only change I noticed was that her actions seemed to be fueled by a deeper level of recklessness. And that freaked me out.

"I didn't even know there were fish in that dirty old pond," Elle said. "Did you?" She looked at me, her eyes wide.

I nodded. "Aren't there NO FISHING signs all around the edge of the water?"

"Puh-lease tell me you're not still a total goody-goody." Elle's eyes pulled into narrow slits as she looked at me, daring me to say more. Then she held two hands up and spread them wide. "I swear he caught one this big! Don't go all PETA on him, though. He threw the slimy thing back in the water."

About this time, I noticed Chip's eyes roaming off to my left. His lips curled up slightly in this wicked smirk. It didn't last more than a second or two, but I was certain of what I'd seen. I also knew exactly what I would find when I turned. I didn't want to, but this time, my body just took over.

Jessie Richards sauntered past us without even looking, her long legs swinging in a perfectly even stride. Her face and body showed no sign of emotion. She was good, I had to give her that much, because everyone else in the atrium and the four attached halls that spread out like spider legs was staring openly, their mouths agape, their fingers pointing. Not even Jessie's entourage, Kirsten Holmes and Tabby Lock, could hide their wide-eyed shock.

"You ready to go?" Chip asked as soon as Jessie was out of sight.

"Sure." Elle giggled, and I remembered how much her flirting had always annoyed me. "You don't mind, do you, Tess?

Chip's gonna walk me to class." Elle wrapped an arm around Chip's waist and squeezed his hard body to hers.

"Yeah," I said. "I'll just meet up with you after this period."

But she and Chip had already started walking down the hall, the crowd parting for them in the same way they always had for Chip and Jessie.

"She should think about going into acting," Max said. "I mean, what'd she do to her voice? That didn't even sound like her."

"Did that really just happen?" I asked. "Please tell me it didn't."

Elle and Chip were gone by then, swallowed by the mass of people in the hallway.

"It happened, all right," Max said. "And I have one question." He stepped forward. "If she can date," he whispered, a smile creeping to his lips. "Why. Can't. You?"

I took a step back. And then another. "Stop invading my space," I said.

"Is that supposed to be some kind of answer?" Max's lips tightened, like he was trying really hard not to smile.

I was feeling so much, all of this stuff was just swirling around in my head, and I didn't know how to sort through it. Or even where to start. Elle had broken up the most popular couple in school? She was dating Chip Knowles? And for weeks I had been pushing Max away. I stood there, completely lost, wondering why I had been fighting this thing with him. Hoping I hadn't blown it.

"What about that girl I saw you with today? Are you dating her too?" I asked, my voice high pitched, the words running together. "Little Miss Miniskirt."

As soon as the questions were hanging in the air between us, I regretted speaking. Max's mouth split into a wide grin.

"So that's what has you so bothered?" It was like someone told him the answer to a tricky math problem, the way his voice lit up. "Renee is my lab partner. She's got a boyfriend. A *serious* boyfriend."

Max tucked his arm into mine and, with a little squeeze, started to tug me through the hall. "You've got nothing to worry about." He moved in close, his breath warming my cheek. "I'm all yours."

"What if I don't want you?" I asked as we walked past a group of giggling freshman girls.

"Renee's my proof. You want me, all right." Max looked at me, this spark of humor lighting his eyes. "Almost as much as I want you."

I couldn't help it. That made me smile. "Fine," I said. "I'll let you take me out."

"Well, don't sound so excited," Max said with a laugh. "It's okay, though, I'll take your yes any way I can get it at this point. I'll even let you name the time and place."

It took only three steps for me to figure it out. And my idea was utterly perfect.

"Christmas in Centerville. First weekend in December," I said. "You'll want to bring your camera."

"So you know her?" I asked Darcy as she slid into the seat beside me.

"Renee? Yeah." Darcy plopped her purse on her desk. "We

were on the same soccer team until I quit last year."

"Is she dating anyone?"

"She's practically married to some Steven guy," Darcy said. "He drives that beat-up yellow thing. You know, the car that looks like a banana."

Walking up from behind, Max knocked his knuckles on my desk. "See?"

"Didn't your mother teach you not to eavesdrop?" I asked.

"I was finished with the computer. You're just mad because you don't have any reason to be mad."

"Oh, whatever." I kicked his feet, which were crossed at the ankles.

Max bent at the waist and leaned down until his face was inches from mine. He smiled. I tried as hard as I could not to. It didn't work. "You *have* to go out with me now," he said.

"I know." I nodded. "You win."

"As gushy as I feel about this moment"—Darcy smacked my desk, and her silver ring made a pinging sound—"I need info. Is it true?"

"I told you it wouldn't take more than five minutes," I said to Max.

"For what?" Darcy asked.

"For everyone in the building to hear."

"That's totally true," Darcy said. "But is the rumor true?"

"I don't know anything more than the rest of you." I put my hands up to my face and squeezed my eyes shut for a second. "But they were all touchy-feely in the atrium just now."

Darcy widened her eyes. "You have to tell her to back off,"

she said. "Trust me, Jessie's revenge will be off the charts. This has been going on for weeks now, longer than any other time those two have broken up. Jessie won't take pity on Elle just because she's the girl who got kidnapped. She's going to *crush* her."

"I don't get it," I said. "What does Chip want with Elle?"

"What's not to get?" Darcy lowered her head, her bangs falling forward, and looked up at me. "Chip loves attention. Being with Elle will put him in the spotlight even more than being the star quarterback and dating the hottest hottie in school. Plus, Elle's probably pretty experienced. If you know what I mean."

"Darcy, that's disgusting," I said.

She shrugged. "Disgusting or not, I guarantee it's what he's thinking."

"Oh, God," Max said. "That's pretty sick."

"Right." Darcy lowered her voice and started talking really fast. "I'll never forget these identity papers we had to write when we were in the fifth grade. We were supposed to describe what we wanted to accomplish in life. Most people listed cheesy stuff like finding a cure for cancer, feeding the world's hungry, or creating world peace."

"But Chip?" Max asked.

"His goal in life was to become famous. He didn't care how it happened, just that it did. Maybe he'd join a rock band, he said, or become a professional football player. As long as people knew his name."

"And now he'll be seen with the most well-known person in town," Max said.

"Okay." I waved my hands in the air and stood, then reached

into my bag for my camera. "I feel sick. I can't take any more of this." I walked toward Mr. Hollon's desk, snatched the pass, and rushed through the door into the quiet stillness of the hall. I pressed my back against the nearest locker and closed my eyes, concentrating on a solution to the colossal mess Elle had somehow created for herself.

After wandering for half the period, I stood in a different hall on the opposite side of the school. I was hunched down a bit with my fingers wrapped around the body of the camera hanging from my neck, prepared to duck away from the window in the classroom door if anyone looked my way. I'd angled myself so the teacher, who was standing in front of the classroom writing algebraic equations on the board, couldn't see me. Only the back two rows had a chance, but no one was paying attention.

Several people stared blankly toward the front of the room. One guy wrapped a string around his pointer finger and pressed on the tip, which turned a deep shade of purple.

And then there was Elle, right between a sleeping lump wearing a hoodie and an empty seat. I had a feeling that I was more aware of her surroundings than she was. I didn't think she noticed anything, not the void next to her, not the line of drool that had to be oozing from the mouth of the guy taking his midday nap.

She was completely focused on whatever was streaming from her mind, down her arm, and through her pen to stain the pages of a spiral notebook. *The* spiral notebook, I assumed, because of the way she was writing, one hand moving at a cramping pace, the other clenched into a fist. I ached to read every last page of that notebook. To know the details so I would have a better idea of what to say, what not to say, and how to help make her feel like she was really, truly, all the way safe.

I raised the camera to my eye and zoomed in on Elle's face. Her lips moved a little, like they were testing the words as she wrote them, making sure they were true. I focused, depressed the button, and snapped. I knew the picture would be a little grainy because of the glass that separated us, but I didn't care. I had her now. Elle. Home.

Not a Big Deal

I had just turned off my light and crawled into bed, hadn't even had time for the covers to get all toasty from my body heat, when my cell phone rang. Startled, I slammed against the headboard of my bed as I grabbed the phone off my nightstand. I noticed the time before the caller.

Twelve twenty-three.

Elle.

I snapped my phone open. "You okay?" I asked.

"Mmm," Elle answered. "Juss peachy."

"Are you . . . Have you been drinking?"

"A little."

"Where are you?" I kicked my covers off and stood, reaching for the jeans I'd slung over the chair by my computer.

"Park," Elle said. "Our tree."

I zipped my jeans and grabbed for a notebook, flipping to a blank page. I scribbled an I'm-okay-Elle-needed-me note for my mom, just in case she woke up and found me missing.

"Don't move," I said into the phone. The vision of Elle sitting on the bench flashed through my head. It sent a shock through my system, the thought of her alone in the dark. I didn't understand what could possibly drive her to go to that park. And I wasn't sure I wanted to find out.

"Elle, what are you doing out here?" The words streamed cloudily from my mouth as I sat on the bench, the cold from the hard wood seeping through the seat of my jeans in an instant. "It's freezing!"

Elle slumped back and stretched out her legs. "Waitin'."

"For what?" I rubbed my hands together. "The first snow?"

I looked at the fountain, which had an internal light to fully illuminate the spray of water. Soaring up and then crashing down to the surface of the pond, the water continued uninterrupted.

Just like always, I thought.

"Nope." Elle chuckled and shook her head, a thick section of dark hair falling between us. "'Member that last winter, all those times we sledded down Killer Hill thinkin' we were so cool to be hanging out with people who were in high school?"

"Mm-hmm." I smiled. "As if anyone in the crowd knew we even existed."

"I missed that. Every time it snowed, I thought about those

days. How we'd spend hours out in the cold and then run in for hot chocolate with all those melty, goopy marshmallows."

"Or the s'mores that your mom made in the toaster oven."

"Yum," Elle said. She scratched her cheek, flipped her hair back over her shoulder, and looked at me. Tears glistened in the faint light that reached us from the fountain's base. "You wanna know what I missed the most?"

I nodded. Squeezed my hands together.

"My bed. And being there all-all-all alone . . ." Elle's voice trailed off. She tipped her head back and looked up at the sweet gum branches, spreading like a canopy above us. When I looked at her, her eyes were closed. Then her head snapped toward me, and she was staring right into my eyes. "And your nail polish! All those crazy colors you used to wear. I thought about that a lot, wondering if in that very moment you were wearing Rockin' Raspberry or Tizzy Teal. How's come you don't wear nail polish anymore?"

I shrugged. "Dunno," I said, not sure what else to add. How could I tell her that absolutely everything was because of her?

Elle reached into her purse and pulled out her phone, flipping it open.

"I think I'm being ditched." She kicked the grass with the toe of her shoe.

"Chip?" I asked.

"Yup." Elle nodded in an exaggerated way. "I've texted him and left him a buncha voice mails. I'm getting nothing."

"Maybe it's for the best." I looked up at the bare branches clicking in a sudden gust of wind. "His ex—Jessie—she's kind of scary. I really don't think you want to be in the middle of all that."

Elle pulled a pack of cigarettes out of her purse and lit one. She cocked her head to the side and blew out a stream of smoke. "Don't you think I've faced worse than some stupid little cheerleader?"

"Listen," I said, taking a deep breath. "I just want to say what I'm thinking. Once. And then I'll leave it alone, okay?"

Elle shoved her free hand in her purse and pulled out a little bottle, reminding me of the summer after fifth grade. My parents and I went to Florida that year, and Elle came with us, making the usually boring family vacation much more exciting. We were in hysterics the night she pretended to raid the hotel room mini-bar, walking around the room with lurching steps, speaking with a slur.

The liquid inside the bottle Elle now held was clear, like water, but I was pretty sure it was something much stronger. She took a swig and then offered the bottle to me. I held my hand up, planning to decline, but then something else took over. There we were, the two of us together after all this time, in the same quiet park, under the same old tree, next to the same roaring fountain. I grabbed the bottle and took a stinging sip. Then opened my lips and swallowed a mouthful. The fire melted me.

"Go on and finish it," Elle said, reaching into her bag and pulling out another miniature bottle. I heard a snap as she twisted off the cap. "And by the way, I know what you're thinking."

"Really?" I asked. "I doubt—"

"You think he's using me." Elle tilted her head, her long hair swaying to her side. She took another drag off her cigarette and slowly blew smoke into the night. "Getting back at Little Miss JR for some indiscretion, maybe? Needing attention now that football's over? Looking like a hero for dating the dirty, broken girl? Am I right?"

"I wouldn't call you dirty or broken," I said.

Elle rolled her eyes my way. "Am I right about the part where you think he's using me?"

"Well, yeah." I nodded. "This is Chip Knowles we're talking about."

"Let me tell you something, Tessa." Elle pressed the tiny bottle to her lips and turned her face to the dark sky. I watched her throat, counting one, two, three large sips. When she looked back to me, her face was pinched tight. "I'm not stupid. And just so you know, I'm using him, too."

I shook my head, not understanding.

"For the last two years I have been *dying* to have a totally normal, tortured-adolescent experience. Fighting over the most popular boy in school, pissing off the head cheerleader: it's absolutely perfect," she said, her slow and calculated words causing a flash of panic to shiver through me.

"Okay, I get that." I took in a deep, icy breath, wishing that the invisible crystals of water surfing the air around the pond could infuse me with strength. "But seriously, Elle, you don't know what you're getting into with Jessie."

"I can handle that girl, Tessa." Elle took another puff of her cigarette, then threw it to the ground and stubbed it out with the toe of her shoe.

Both of us stared at the glowing water shooting up toward the sky. Our backs were turned to the rear edge of the park, where the field of grass ended and miles of wooded trails began. The darkness felt heavy, pressing against my back, and I wanted to turn and face it. To make sure nothing was behind us.

"Maybe you'll get it if I share my list. Don't laugh, but I actually wrote one," she said, tugging her butterfly notebook a few inches out of her purse so I would understand. Elle looked at me, her eyes wide, and cleared her throat. "'All the Things I'm Getting Out of Chip.' Ready?"

"I guess," I said. But I wasn't. I really, really wasn't.

"One: I'm having that totally normal teenage experience I've been dreaming about, in the form of a battle over some stupid boy." Elle held one finger in the air. "Two: my first morning back to school, I was just the girl who'd been kidnapped. After lunch, when people saw me with Chip, I became the girl who broke up the most popular couple in school. One second of standing there next to Chip changed everything." Elle popped another finger into the cold air.

"Elle, people didn't just think of you as the girl who'd been kidnapped."

"You're totally right." Elle gave me a crooked half smile. "Thanks to the news reports, they thought of me as the girl who'd been raped and the girl who'd been the star of child pornography. I could see it in everyone's eyes, Tessa. Not just pity, but curiosity. People wondered how many times I'd been pinned under his naked, bloated body. How many times I'd given him head. Or if he bit me or burned me or tied me up. Yes, yes, yes, by the way."

I didn't know what to say. I was shaking all over, and my lungs felt like they would explode with one more frigid breath. I couldn't show her, though, so I kept staring into her eyes, tensing my body so my sudden shivers wouldn't give me away.

"So number two on my list is real. Between lunch and fifth period, Chip turned me into someone else, gave people something new to think of when they looked at me. Three is simple, Chip is the only person who isn't trying to fix me. He's not waiting for me to magically flip back to the person I used to be. Plus, he didn't know that girl from before, so he can't remind me of her."

I ran my fingernails along my legs and felt the mouth of that little bottle peeking up from between my knees. I grabbed it and downed the rest of the fiery liquid in one last gulp, relieved to be sharing this moment with Elle, but nervous that she was getting into something very messy.

"And then there's number four. Chip didn't know, but tonight he was supposed to help me accomplish something very important. Again, I'm not stupid. I know I'm a mere distraction and that Mr. and Mrs. Popularity will be back together in a matter of time. So tonight, before I lost my chance, I was going to make sure Chip became my first."

"Your first what?" I asked.

"That's good," Elle said, looking at me. Something about my expression made her laugh. "Please tell me you're not still a virgin, Tessa."

"Well," I said. "I am. Still a virgin." I wouldn't dare tell her that the only boy I'd kissed was Trevor Ryan that night in middle school, right here under this very tree.

"Oh, that's . . . really sweet." Elle slapped my leg. "I mean, good for you, right?"

I felt totally out of place, uncomfortable in my body, uneasy on the bench that had once been a daily part of my life, cringing in the familiar space of our neighborhood park. I wanted to run fast and hard, until I was far away from this person my best friend had become.

Elle flattened her hand against her chest. "We all know I'm not a virgin anymore, but I never gave myself to anyone, see? Char—" Elle pressed her fingertips into her eyes and pulled them away, clasping her hands together. "*That man* took everything he wanted. Tonight, I decided I would give myself away for the first time."

"But, Elle . . . Chip?"

"It doesn't matter *who* it is. Just that it happens." Elle shivered. "I can't stand to think that *he* was the last man to touch me. I have to do something to change that. Chip's as good as anyone. Actually, better." Elle laughed. "He's pretty freaking hot."

Suddenly, Elle's phone tinkled a string of notes into the air, reminding me of wind chimes. When she looked at the screen, a huge smile spread across her face.

"We're on," Elle said. "He's almost here."

"Whoa," I said, sitting forward. "Almost here?"

"Yeah." Elle dug through her purse.

My body started to speed up—my pulse, my breathing—and I was suddenly hot.

"You can't go with him," I said.

"Of course I can," Elle said, popping a stick of gum into her mouth. "It's exactly what I want."

"Elle, there's got to be another way." I grabbed her hand and squeezed. "Just come home with me. We have stuff for s'mores, and we'll take them up to my room and listen to—"

"Thanks, Tess"—Elle shook her head—"but I have to do this."

I saw the headlights before she did, the white of the Range Rover sparkling in the streetlights' glow. Chip crept to a stop next to the square of sidewalk where I'd found Elle's bike that terrible summer day. To get in the passenger seat, Elle would have to walk right across that slab of concrete. I worried that she might fall through, get sucked into some vortex, and be lost to us all over again.

It's a sign, I wanted to say. But instead I bit my bottom lip until I tasted the tang of my own blood.

"I'm glad you came out tonight," Elle said. She squeezed my hand and then pulled away, standing and slinging the strap of her large purse over her shoulder. "See ya later."

I sat there and watched as she jogged toward Chip's car. The driver's-side door opened, and Chip stepped out, unfolding himself to his full height. He reminded me of one of those transformers Coop used to play with. Rounding the front of the car, his legs sliced through the headlights. I was surprised when he stopped at the passenger door and opened it; the demonstration of chivalry fit nothing that I knew of him.

Not wanting to watch Elle disappear, not wanting to think about what she would be doing in the next hour, I looked down, and when I did, I saw it. The blue was darker in the shadow of the bench, but the fabric of the butterfly glinted in the fountain's light. Elle's notebook lay at my feet, looking as alone and forgotten as I felt.

My mind rushed through all my options.

The one that screamed the loudest was: *Keep it. Read it. Give it back later.*

After all this time, the answers to my questions were lying at my feet.

But I couldn't . . . could I?

I reached down and grabbed the notebook. Before I could think another thought, I did what I knew was the right thing. The only thing.

"Elle!" I screamed into the night. Competing with the rush of the fountain, my word faded quickly. Chip slammed the passenger door and started around the back side of the Range Rover.

I stood and ran toward them. I couldn't hold on to it. If I did, I wouldn't have the strength to keep myself from betraying her.

"Chip!" I shouted.

He was walking past the back window when I saw his thick body stop and turn.

Chip moved slowly toward me.

"Elle dropped this," I said. I held the notebook in the air. Chip's large hand reached out and took it from me, his solid fingers running across the wings of the butterfly.

"Fascinating read," he said with a quick nod. His baseball cap was on backward, and strands of golden hair poked from the little hole in front.

"What?" I asked.

"I found it one night after Elle passed out." Chip ducked his head, playing it off in this casual way. "I've seen her write in it, and I thought it was some paper for English or something."

"It's not," I said.

"Yeah. I figured that out." Chip laughed. He actually laughed! The sound made me feel this intense need to claw at his face, but I controlled myself by digging my fingernails into my palms. "You've read it, too, then?"

"No," I said, my jaw tight.

"Don't tell her I did." Chip took a few steps back. "She'd be embarrassed."

"I won't tell her." I shook my head. "She'd be a whole lot more than embarrassed."

"It's not a big deal," he said. Then he turned and made his way to the opposite side of the car, tromping right over that sacred square.

"Yeah," I said. "It really is."

Chip folded himself back into the SUV, and I watched as he passed the notebook into Elle's hands. It wasn't until that point that she turned and saw me.

She nodded.

Smiled.

And then she was gone.

Get a Grip

I knelt on the cold, hard ground, staring through the viewfinder of the Nikon. The miniature house before me was made up of nothing but sugar. I could hardly see any gingerbread under the colorful gumdrops, M&M's, Red Hots, and licorice. White icing glued the candy in place, piped around each piece in looping circles, cementing the chocolate-covered pretzels that stood side by side to form the little picket fence that wrapped around the entire green rock-candied yard.

"I can't believe I won," Darcy said as she shifted her position for a picture.

"I can," I said. "Look at that thing. How many hours did it take?" I snapped a shot just as three moms wearing fuzzy scarves stepped into the background, blocking the CHRISTMAS IN CENTERVILLE'S 10TH ANNUAL GINGERBREAD HOUSE COMPETITION poster that I'd intended as Darcy's backdrop.

"I lost count after twenty-three." Darcy adjusted the silver star on top of a large coconut-covered evergreen in the front yard. She had decorated it with crushed pieces of peppermint candy. "After I lost to Eden Pertly last year, I knew I had to step up my game. But let's get to what's really important—are you guys having fun?"

I nodded. Tried not to smile.

"I knew it!" Darcy clapped a couple of times, the sound muffled by her thick mittens, before I reached out and dug my fingers into her arm.

"Calm down," I said. "It's really nothing. We're just hanging out, okay?"

"No." Darcy breathed her strawberry breath into my face. "It's not nothing. It's totally a date. Your very first ever, if I'm not mistaken."

"Yeah, but if I think like that I might freak out," I whispered. "So, for tonight, it's nothing."

"Oh, whatever." Darcy patted my cheeks with her mittened hands. Her brown hair fell forward over her shoulder, and she flung it out of her face. "I feel like your big sister, you know? And you're spoiling my moment, Tessa."

"Kind of like my dad spoiled mine." I grunted, remembering the uncomfortable moments of introductions when Max had picked me up.

"Oh, no." Darcy laughed. "Did he give Max a lie-detector test? Force him to submit fingerprints?"

"Practically." I ducked my head. "Let's just say that my parents have all of the Kinsleys' phone numbers."

"How embarrassing."

"Tell me about it." I nodded toward the gingerbread house. "Enough about my humiliation. I need another shot of you and the masterpiece. Some admirers got in the way earlier."

Darcy leaned down again, her hand perched beside the tray holding her first-place masterpiece, and blew a huge pink bubble with her gum. I snapped just before she sucked the wad of Strawberry Splash into her mouth with a big pop.

"Come on," I said. "You ruined the picture."

"I thought I was adding some panache."

"One piping hot cup for you," Max said, stepping to my side and handing me a Styrofoam cup, "and one for the Master of Gingerbread."

"Mmm," I said as the hot chocolate warmed my throat and chest. I licked my top lip, tasting sweet, melted marshmallows, and thought of Noelle. "That's just about right."

"It's almost warm in here with the heaters," Max said.

We stood in one of seven large tents lining Main Street, much warmer than we had been earlier, when we'd shivered on the side of the street as we'd watched the holiday parade.

Darcy pulled her phone from the back pocket of her jeans and smiled, then typed something before looking up.

"I gotta go," she said, peering around a group of people and waving toward the tent's entrance. "T just got here."

"Congrats again," I said. Taking another sip, I looked at Max and found him staring at me. "What?"

"Nothing." As he adjusted his tight-fitting wool cap, several black curls fought for freedom. He gave me a mischievous little smile, and I ducked my head. "Let's get outta here."

I wondered if he'd noticed any difference in my hair, which I'd straightened and clipped up in several sparkling barrettes. Or my extra layer of raspberry-flavored lip gloss. I'd felt silly as I chose my outfit, giggling a little as I pulled my favorite wool sweater over my thermal shirt, turning to check my butt in the stretchy jeans I'd bought special for the evening.

"I got something for us," Max said, placing his hand on my back as we passed a large group of skinny middle-school boys on skateboards.

"Oh, yeah?" I said, trying hard not to smile.

"Yeah."

Several large snowmen walked past on the street. One waved at me and tipped his hat.

Max pulled his hand from the pocket of his black coat. "Ever ridden in a horse-drawn carriage?"

I stared at two red tickets fanned out in his hand. Looked into his eyes. He tilted his head, and for a second I got the urge to brush my lips against his pink cheeks to see if they were as cold as I imagined.

"No," I said. "I haven't."

"I figured." Max grabbed my hand and squeezed. "You said you usually skip the whole Christmas in Centerville event."

"Well, yeah. Since . . ."

"Elle, right? And I heard this is the first year they've had the carriages." Max pulled my arm and started toward the line. "So I thought maybe you'd like to go with me." I couldn't say anything, so I just nodded.

Minutes later, Max and I stood in the roped-off line for the carriage ride. In front of us an elderly couple dressed in long brown coats stooped slightly, as if time were pressing them forward and they could hardly resist the pressure. Between their frail bodies, their bare hands were clasped, their fingers intertwined. That was what made me grab my camera . . . those two gnarled hands.

"That oughta be good." Max lowered his face and looked up at me, half smiling.

"What?" I asked.

"The hands. You thinking of the assignment? Tension of Opposites?"

"Strength and weakness in the same shot," I said. "How'd you know?"

"I know you better than you think." Max met my eyes, held them for a little longer than usual.

Suddenly, I had no idea what to do with my hands, so I clasped them around the body of the camera, then let go and tried to shove them in the pockets of my jeans, but my mittens were too bulky. When our carriage arrived, I breathed out this huge sigh, then immediately wished I could suck the cloud of frozen breath back into my mouth.

I didn't dare to look at Max's face until we were stepping up into the carriage. I knew it would be there, that annoying half smile of his, and I was right. But somehow, when I saw it, I felt a little better. Until we sat on the velvety seats and I lost my balance, almost pitching into his lap. Grabbing my waist, he caught me and eased me down next to him. That was how his arm ended up around me, his fingers playing with the flowy white belt looped through the rings in my jeans. As I listened to the horses' hooves *clip-clop* along the pavement of Main Street, I couldn't believe I was actually sitting in a horse-drawn carriage with *Max Kinsley's* arm wrapped around me.

"Cold?" he asked.

"No. I'm not—" I turned toward Max as our carriage went over an uneven patch of pavement. The tilt was just enough to ease me into him, our noses grazing.

Oh. My. God. I thought. *We're totally close enough to kiss.*

And I started to freak. If it happened, would it be glaringly obvious that I had never been kissed? Like, *really* kissed.

Max looked at my lips, brushed a strand of hair off my cheek, and finally met my eyes. The winter wonderland surrounding us ceased to exist. Jingle bells quieted and twinkling lights faded, leaving only the whinny of the horses, the gentle motion of the carriage, and us.

He smiled. I giggled. His arm moved to tighten around my shoulders, and he pulled me a little closer. I moved toward him, wondering about the scent of my breath. Then his lips grazed mine, and I finally knew the answer. That mouth I'd been staring at for months was as soft as I'd imagined.

It was brief, our first kiss. My first kiss. But I couldn't have asked for more.

When we separated, he leaned his forehead against mine.

"Not bad," he said.

I squinted.

"I'm just saying," he said, with a tilt of his head.

"Oh, shut up." I laughed and leaned into his shoulder, letting my body sway with the carriage as the two horses pulled us through town. Max swayed, too, his warmth pressed against me, making me tingle all over.

After our first kiss, I felt all twisted and loopy inside. I wondered if people around me noticed, but no one flashed me a knowing look or a too-wide grin. Max held my hand, leading me through throngs of people littering the sidewalk, past tents stuffed with Christmas crafts, and around carolers dressed in clothes that looked like they had been worn on the set of *Little House on the Prairie*.

We were on our way to Max's car, my mind sifting through all the possible ways I could ensure another kiss, when we passed the line for pictures with Santa, and a little girl sucking on a large candy cane hopped right in front of us. We nearly knocked her down, but Max tore his hand from mine and grabbed her shoulders to keep her upright. The girl's mother, wearing a large puffy coat, gripped the girl's upper arm and thanked Max while trying to keep her squirming daughter under control.

"It was my fault," Max said.

"No." The mother pried the gooey candy cane from the fingers of her child. "She's had way too much sugar tonight."

I couldn't believe so many people were standing in the roped-off line, which zigged and zagged through one of the side streets near the center of town, finally ending at a large display, where Santa was seated in front of a shimmery green wall. I was thinking that the man they'd found to play Santa was perfect—his beard looked real, and his eyes held that sparkle mentioned in every Christmas story out there—when I saw Elle step toward him from the front of the line. Behind her, Chip strutted to the platform, his hand running through his golden hair.

"Tessa?" Max grabbed my hand and squeezed. "You ready?"

I shook my head and pointed toward the front of the line. Elle sat on one of Santa's knees, and Chip planted himself on the other as Santa let out a merry "Ho, ho, ho!" I watched Elle throw her head back and laugh at something Chip said.

"I want to wait for her," I said. "How do we get over there?"

Max stood on his tiptoes and looked over the heads of all the people separating Elle and me. "C'mon," he said. "I think I see a way."

I followed him, taking in whiffs of hot cider and sugary pastries, until we made it to the opening in the rope wall that signified the exit. Elle and Chip had just walked out and were ten feet ahead of us, his arm wrapped around her shoulders, hers around his waist. They stopped at a picnic table planted in the middle of someone's front lawn. Elle sat as Chip pulled some money out of his pocket and flipped through the bills.

"Can we?" I asked.

"You really want to?"

"No." I touched my forehead to Max's shoulder. "But I should."

"Okay." Max rubbed his thumb against the back of my hand. "I understand," he said as we started walking toward them.

When I tapped Elle on the shoulder, she jumped and let out this abrupt sound that was a cross between a growl and a scream.

"Sorry," I said, feeling awful, especially as I watched Chip's face screw up in a look of disgust at the noise. "I didn't mean to scare you."

"It's okay." Elle pressed her elbows into the wooden table as Max sat across from her. "Want some hot chocolate? Chip was about to go brave the line."

"No, thanks," I said, not moving from my place at the side of the table. "We already had some."

Chip didn't say anything, just folded the money in his hand and shrugged before turning and walking away. Elle, her face illuminated by the white twinkling lights that outlined the house behind Max, didn't see when one of Chip's friends stopped him in the street. The guy stepped close and said something, then shrugged and pointed over his shoulder with his thumb. When Chip turned our way, I rotated my body quickly, not wanting him to know I'd been watching.

As Elle and Max talked about how the center of town smelled like horse poop, I watched Chip duck between two houses and disappear.

"Elephant ears!" I said suddenly, my voice way too loud.

"Please tell me that's not some cuss word you've made up, Tessa." Elle laughed. "It was kind of cute in the fifth grade. Not so much anymore."

"Funny." I shot Elle a sarcastic smile. "I meant exactly what I said. Elephant ears. I'm going to get some."

Max started to extricate his legs from underneath the picnic table. "I can go."

"No," I said, already walking away. "I got it."

When my feet hit the street, I started jogging, counting the houses as I passed them. I looked over my shoulder when I reached the final yard, thankful that Elle and Max were engrossed in a conversation and weren't paying any attention to me.

I walked past the last house at a quick pace and turned when I reached the driveway that Chip had taken. I crouched against the bricks of the front porch, peering around the corner to see what, exactly, was going on.

Ten feet away, Jessie Richards stood against the side of the house. Her hands framed her face, and her shoulders slumped forward. One of her legs was bent, and her foot was propped against the brick wall for support. Chip stood right in front of her, shaking his head.

"Seriously, Chip, when's it going to be enough?" Jessie asked.

"Why are you going all psycho on me?"

"Oh, God, Chip." Jessie sobbed and bowed her face into her shaking hands. "I feel like I don't know you anymore."

"Jesus." Chip stepped forward and placed a hand on her shoulder. "Get a grip, would you?"

"No, Chip!" Jessie's foot flung from the wall and stomped the concrete ground as her fisted hands struck his chest. "You get a grip. What the hell are you doing with that girl, anyway? And don't try to tell me you're falling for her."

Chip smoothed his palms along the front of his jacket. "We're just hanging out, Jess."

As Chip's hand swung down to his side, Jessie reached out and grabbed for it. He pulled away quickly, and she stepped back.

"You had sex with her, didn't you?" Jessie's voice was quiet, icy cold. "Chip, do you know how repulsive that is?"

"Oh, shut up, Jess. You're just jealous because you know she's better than you'll ever be."

Jessie sucked in a deep breath and held it while Chip's words registered in her brain. I could almost see her processing center spinning like a CD in a disc player, faster and faster, trying to come up with some kind of response.

But she didn't have one. She just turned and rushed away, her long legs gliding past me so fast she didn't even notice my presence.

Chip straightened himself, pulled his shoulders back, and cleared his throat a few times. He kept staring at the brick wall where Jessie had been standing.

He was still. Really, really still.

Until he turned and walked toward a large trash can that was parked in the darkest shadow of the driveway. In one swift movement, he kicked out his leg, slamming his foot into top half of the plastic container. I heard a pop as the trash can split, and then, not daring to wait any longer, I turned and ran back to Max and Elle, deciding to explain my empty hands with details about long lines and irritated crowds.

There's No Emotion Involved

"Just one," Elle said, reaching into my snack-size bag of potato chips.

"You've never in your life," I said, slapping her hand, "had just one."

"Well, if you're gonna be like that"—Elle slumped back in her seat—"I'll just watch the fat slide onto your ass."

I sighed and turned the bag her way. "Fine," I said. "Have at 'em."

"No." Elle tilted her head toward me. "I was trying to have one of those best-friend moments my shrinkedelic keeps telling me I need. You ruined it, Tessa. I'm disappointed in you."

I wanted to jump up and wrap my arms around her, to squeeze with every ounce of strength in my body. Elle had called me her best friend! Could we really have found our way back to normal, after everything?

As I tried to keep myself from screaming out to the lunchroom that I had a best friend again, Max reached a hand into the crinkly bag and grabbed three salty chips. "I'll take a few," he said.

"Just so you know," I said, "I have issues with sharing."

"Well, now that you have someone worth sharing with," Max said, "that should change."

"Oh my God," Elle said, leaning forward against the edge of the table, staring across the lunchroom, her blue-black hair falling over her shoulders and grazing the tabletop, reminding me of the soft tip of a paintbrush. "How hot is he? I mean, *look* at him."

I followed her gaze, knowing in advance who I'd see walking through the cafeteria line. "Elle, you're scaring me," I said as I watched Chip's hulking figure pause over a basket of muffins. "I thought you were going to keep your distance. Emotionally, I mean."

"There's no emotion involved, Tessa." Elle licked her lips. "I'm just saying he's hot as hell, okay?" Elle pushed her chair from the table, stood, and took a few steps away.

"Elle, come on. You'll see him in the atrium in a few minutes." My eyes darted to Jessie's table and found what I expected. Jessie was staring at Chip with wide eyes that seemed to be brimming with anguish, or longing, or just plain old desire. Whatever it was, I knew it wasn't good.

"Just stop worrying, will you?" Elle asked over her shoulder. She raised her eyebrows, waiting for my response.

"Yeah." I took a chip from the bag and crunched. "I'll try."

And then she was gone, weaving her way through the mass of tables, chairs, and bodies.

"I'm thinking that's not going to end very well," Max said, taking a swig of water from his bottle.

"Me, too," I answered. Elle stepped through the tall archway separating the food line from the dining area. She was reaching for Chip's shoulder when Max grabbed my hand.

"You gotta let it go." He tapped my arm with his bottle.

"Right." I nodded, focusing on how Jessie's eyes had narrowed, taking on the glazed look of hatred, her lips pinched tightly together.

Quickly, I turned back to Elle and Chip. Elle's hands were clasped around his biceps as she stood up on her tiptoes to kiss him on the cheek. He kind of knocked into her, and her mouth opened wide with laughter that I couldn't hear.

Jessie, by this time, was trying to stand up but couldn't because Kirsten and Tabby were holding her arms, grabbing her shoulders, pulling her down.

"Tessa," Max said. "Stop staring."

"I can't."

"I *challenge* you to stop staring."

"You're not allowed to do that."

"I just did."

Chip and Elle stepped into the line, waiting to pay. Chip started juggling three individually wrapped muffins. Elle just cracked up, sticking her hand in his way every few seconds. As the muffins somersaulted to the ground, they both bent down to pick them up, and I lost sight of them.

By then, Jessie was standing, yanking her arm from Kirsten's grasp, her lips moving quickly. When she freed herself, she smoothed her hair and nodded silently at the table of girls staring her way, who, like me, were all waiting to see what would happen next.

"The challenge is on." Max leaned in and whispered in my ear. "At the moment, you're losing."

Chip and Elle were almost at the front of the line. I willed the cashier to hurry as Jessie sauntered away from her table of friends.

"Look at me," Max said, his breath swishing against my cheek.

I did. Looked right into his chocolate brown eyes. "I didn't take you for the romantic stare-into-my-eyes type."

"I'm full of surprises." The corners of Max's mouth turned up. "Whoever looks away first loses. Go."

"Loses what?"

"The stare-off."

"How do you win?"

"You can't look away. Geesh, have you been paying attention?"

"You blinked."

"The rules say nothing about blinking."

"I wonder what's happening with Elle."

"I think if any eye clawing or hair ripping were taking place, we'd know."

"It could be seconds away. She might need me."

"Who cares? This is fun."

"It's torture."

Max laughed. "You have nice eyes."

"So do you. Can we stop yet?"

"No. I have an important question."

"Oh, really?"

"Yes. What are you doing for New Year's Eve?"

I almost looked down at the floor but caught myself just in time. "I don't know yet."

"Wanna hang out with me?" Max lifted his eyebrows.

I started to get a little hot. Squirmed in my seat. But didn't look away. "Elle and I have this tradition. We usually—"

"Oh, right. I wasn't thinking." His words were flat and clipped, cutting our playful exchange short.

"But maybe we could all—" I glanced toward Elle, catching sight of Jessie as her progress was halted by someone pushing away from a table, his blue chair almost knocking her to the tiled floor. I couldn't see her face, but I watched as her hand reared up and smacked him on the back.

Chip and Elle moved away from the cash register, turning to face each other. Chip nodded at something Elle said; then he stepped into her and bent down, whispering into her ear.

I looked back to Max's eyes, which were still trained on my face. "Maybe we could all hang out."

"Yeah. Sure." He nodded. I could tell from the way his lips were scrunched and wrinkled that I'd upset him. It was the last thing I wanted to do, screw this thing up, whatever was going on between us. But I couldn't help it. Then he half smiled, and I started to breathe again. "You're aware you just lost, right?"

"Oh, no," I said with a laugh. "I did, didn't I?"

"Just let me know," he said, turning toward the table. "About New Year's, I mean." His voice was soft and distant, like he didn't really care. But I believed his eyes, instead, which creased with something like irritation or disappointment.

"Yeah. Okay," I said. Elle finally walked away from Chip, the smile on her lips indicating that everything she'd told me about not being emotionally involved was a lie.

"I'll cash in later." Max's voice was still soft, but it held a hint of humor. "I'll have to think about what prize my overwhelming victory deserves."

"Dream on." I nudged my elbow into his side.

"I'll add it to your tab," he said. "You still owe me for getting you an invite to dinner at the Pendeltons'."

Elle walked back to the table and sat in her seat. "On. Fire," she said.

I rolled my eyes. "He's not that hot."

"You know, Elle," Max said, "you could give a guy a complex."

"You're much better than Chip Knowles." I patted Max's knee.

"Oh, God," Elle said.

"What?" Max sat up straight. "You think I'm that bad?"

Elle shook her head and pointed. I'd already seen. Jessie and Chip stood by a table where a man was taking orders for class rings. The ex-couple stood close together, their mouths moving tight and fast, their eyes bright and glaring. The few people who were standing in line for rings slowly stepped away from the table to avoid getting caught in the crossfire.

"Can't she just leave him alone?" Elle asked.

I didn't want to say what I was thinking. But as her best friend, I had to.

"Didn't you say you expect them to get back together?" I asked quietly.

"Yeah. But not right now." Elle shrugged. "I was just starting to have a little fun."

The bell rang, and people stood, gathering their things. Elle jumped up and perched on her tiptoes to maintain her view of Chip and Jessie.

"She's got her finger pointed in his face like he's some stupid little kid," Elle said as she reached for her stack of books. I threw my leftovers onto Elle's tray and grabbed it, turning to head for the nearest trash can.

"Got it," Max said, taking the tray from my hands and walking away.

"I mean, who does she think she is?" Elle asked.

"She's the girl who dated him for four years, Elle."

Elle all of a sudden flipped into bitch mode. "She's not dating him anymore, Tessa."

"C'mon," I said, wondering how I could possibly put an end to the situation. "Let's go."

Elle ran her fingers along the spine of each book tucked against her chest. "Maybe I should wait for him."

I shook my head as Max came back to the table and grabbed his things.

"What's up?" he asked when he noticed my foot *tap-tap-tap*-ing the floor.

"Elle here was just wondering if she should wait for Chip." I propped a hand on my hip. "What do you think?"

Max looked from me to Elle. Elle attempted to focus on Max but couldn't keep from gazing back toward the argument near the man and his rings. "Um . . . I'm gonna go with *no*?"

I nodded once and put a hand on Elle's shoulder. "See?"

Elle pulled away. "Yeah, I see that he said exactly what you wanted."

"Hey, Elle." Max stepped forward to keep from being bumped by the people moving toward the exit. "A lot of people might be like that. But I'm not. I really think you should walk away."

"Oh, yeah?" I felt like smacking her for giving Max attitude. "Why?"

"For one, you'll look like an idiot standing here by yourself staring over at them. You'll either seem weak or demanding, neither of which is too desirable."

"People are already going to talk." I stepped in closer, looking around the room, which had lost half of its population. "Do you want them to feel sorry for you or admire you?"

Elle's eyes hardened. "You talk to her, don't you? The shrinke-delic? She must give you tips on how to worm into my brain and make me do the right thing." Elle's lips tightened as she glanced over at Chip and Jessie. I tried to ignore them, but their narrowed eyes and waving hands made it difficult.

"She's right. You have a choice." Max put a hand on Elle's back and steered her toward the exit. "If you stand here and wait, you'll be the victim. People will be all, 'Poor Elle, she doesn't have a clue.' But, if you walk away with a smile and show everyone you're confident enough to leave them alone, people will envy your strength."

Elle's feet started moving a little faster. I saw a gap between Max's hand and her shoulder blade. "You think?" she asked.

"Absolutely." Max nodded and a few curls bounced forward. I

was dying to reach out and tuck them behind his ear, but that was too much. Too close. So I doubled my pace until I was at Elle's side.

"Hold your head up," I told her. "And look everyone in the eye."

"So," Darcy said as she scanned the dresses hanging on the rack in front of her, "I saw Jessie and her death rays in the lunchroom last period."

"Close call," I said from my seat on the arm of an old couch.

"I noticed." Darcy pulled a blue dress from between two others, yellow and red. She held it up against her chest, wrapping one arm around the front, cinching the fabric to her waist. "What do you think?"

The dress was so long it scraped the wooden floor of the stage. The high, lacy neck was strung with pearly buttons. A large poofing shoulder stood at the top of each arm, tapering off around the elbow, where it pulled tight.

"I think that neck looks like a doily my grandma would have used under an ice-cream bowl."

Darcy looked at me and laughed. Then she swooped to the front of the stage and danced in a large circle, her hair swinging across her back. When she finished, she faced the darkened rows of the auditorium, curtsying to the empty seats. "I think it'll match your eyes."

"Whatever," I said. "Can we just do this?"

Darcy fluttered my way and spread the dress beside me on the couch. "You gotta take off your shirt."

"Darcy, I did not agree to—"

"Oh, just do it, Tessa. I can tell you're wearing a tank top under there." She unzipped the back of the dress. "This'll look great next to the dress I saw at the mall the other day. Total opposites."

"I can't believe you already know you're using fashion as the theme of your project." I pulled my long-sleeved shirt over my head and tucked my wavy hair behind my ears.

"Be patient. It'll come to you," Darcy said as she pulled the hanger from the dress and moved toward me. I held my arms up and bent at the waist so she could wiggle the dress over my head. "So, how would she have handled it? Elle, I mean, in the lunchroom, if Jessie had attacked them both?"

"You really think Jessie would do that?" I pulled the dress down and lifted my hair to the top of my head, turning so Darcy could slide up the zipper.

"Totally. It'll happen one of these days. And Elle had better be ready. Jessie is heartless when it comes to stuff she wants." Darcy spun me around and put a finger to her chin. "Take off your jeans," she said with a nod.

"No way!" I laughed and twisted sideways.

"You have this unnatural lumpy thing going on right here." Darcy poked the top of my jeans, hitting the button with her finger.

I shook my head and crossed my arms over my chest, that doily lace scratching at my neck. "Where do you want me?"

Darcy looked at the scenery propped along the back of the stage, walking toward a tall piece of white lattice. "That's perfect," she said.

"Why's all this stuff out here, anyway?" I asked as I walked toward her.

"Mrs. Irvin said they had to clean out the storage rooms after the last play. Something about mouse poop. Back up a little, will you?"

I did as she asked, placing one hand on my waist to hide my unnatural bulge. Darcy focused her camera and took several shots, then shook her head and walked toward me, snapping a hair elastic off her wrist.

"Put your hair up in a bun. It'll pull the look together." Darcy circled her hand over her head and waited. "Back in ninth grade, when Jessie was trying out for the cheerleading squad, she terror-ized Nikki Rader. Like, daily. Nikki, who was a year older than Jessie, was a sure thing for the JV squad. Until she quit. Jessie got her spot instead."

"Yeah, but that was back when she was a freshman." I twisted my hair up on top of my head and wrapped the elastic around the bun. "She's older now—"

"And more spiteful than ever. She's gotten everything she's wanted since that JV position; she expects life to go her way. But Elle came home and turned Jessie's world upside down."

I pulled a few strands of hair down so they fell on either side of my face.

"That's better," Darcy said. She turned and took several steps away before pointing the camera at me again. "All I'm saying is that Elle had better figure out how she's going to handle it when Jessie makes her move."

"Have you seen pictures of that Charlie guy?" I asked.

"The kidnapper?"

I nodded.

"Yeah. His eyes creep me out."

"Elle dealt with him for two years. Got away. *And* made sure he was arrested." I took a deep breath. "I'm pretty sure she can handle Jessie Richards."

"I dunno." Darcy shrugged. "I hope you're right."

I posed for several more pictures, twirling around a few times so Darcy could get a motion shot with the dress flying around my legs. It was after we'd finished and Darcy was back at the rack of dresses, hanging the blue one in place between the red and the yellow, that she mentioned Max.

"I heard about Max's ex," she said, all matter-of-fact.

"Ex?" I asked. Max had an ex? As in, girlfriend? "How?"

"I asked. Duh." Darcy spun around and sat on the arm of the couch, patting the seat next to her. I collapsed into the dingy cushion.

"Do you know much?" she asked.

I couldn't speak, didn't want to tell her that I knew absolutely nothing, so I just shook my head.

"Okay, here's the deal. They dated for, like, two years. Sounds like they were really different. She was a soccer player, really into the game, and he, well, you know, is the shy, quiet type who likes to take pictures. I guess she was really into him, and when he tried to break it off she freaked out."

"Freaked out how?" I leaned back. Maybe this wasn't so bad.

"He didn't go into details, but it didn't sound pretty. He said he felt stuck. Especially when her parents decided to get divorced. That's why he didn't break it off until his family moved here over the summer."

I sat up, my eyes wide, and stared at Darcy. She gave me this oops-I-thought-you-knew look and popped another strawberry bubble. "It's totally not a big deal," she said.

"He just got out of a two-year relationship?" I stood and started pacing.

"One in which he felt stuck. His word. *Stuck*."

My brain went into overdrive. Two years meant anniversaries and middle-of-the-night phone conversations. Inside jokes and nicknames. Birthdays wishes. New Year's Eve kisses. And sex.

Oh. My. God. *Sex*.

"Talk to me, Tessa. You look like you're losing it." Darcy was by my side, her hands reaching for my shoulders.

"I didn't know about any ex. And two years is a long time."

"He likes you." Darcy smiled. "A lot."

I shook my head. "This is such a bad idea, Darcy. Getting all caught up in him. I'm just going to get burned."

"Why do you do that?" Darcy batted at the side of my head with both hands. "Tell your brain to stop already. Have a little fun. Stop being so flipping guarded all the time. *Live* for a minute. You might actually like it."

"It's scary," I said, my voice a whisper.

"Yeah." Darcy shrugged. "But it's also pretty fun."

Darcy's butt chimed, and she pulled her phone out of her back pocket. She read the text her boyfriend had just sent her and smiled.

"See?" she said, turning her phone my way. *Have a surprise 4 u later. Bring a blanket 2nite. Love.*

Make Yourself Like It

"I can't believe your mom finally got you one of those things," I said, pointing to the lava lamp on Elle's nightstand. Blue globules oozed up and down its center, lazily somersaulting around and into one another. The color of the lava matched the wings of the butterfly on Elle's notebook, which was sitting next to the lamp's base, making me sweat with desire to grab it and run. I should have kept the journal that night in the park. Then I would know everything.

"I should write in to *Seventeen* magazine." Elle tucked her legs under the covers of her bed and leaned back against her pillows. "Tips on how to get everything you've ever wanted from your parents. One: Have an epic battle that ends in stomping, screaming, and sobbing. Two: Get yourself kidnapped. Three: Come home, but only after enough time has passed for maximum guilt to set in."

"Too bad you only asked for a lava lamp. You might have a new car right now." I knelt down beside Elle's bed. "It's still here, right?"

Elle nodded. "They didn't change anything."

I reached under the white eyelet dust ruffle and found the handles to Elle's trundle bed. With one solid tug, my old bed was free. "I wonder how many nights I've slept in this bed." I walked over to the door and flipped off the overhead light before hopping onto the mattress, stuffing my legs under the covers, and pulling my hair back in a low ponytail.

"No less than a year's worth," Elle said as she dropped a pillow down to me. I lay back and glanced up to her bed. She was staring down at me, her chin propped on the edge of the bed. She blinked, the shadows from the lava lamp floating across her skin. "Remember the night your grandpa Lou died?" she asked.

I nodded and turned to my side, curling into a ball. "My parents rushed out of town, thinking he'd survive the stroke."

"They should have taken you."

"I had this feeling it was almost over," I said. "I begged them to let me see him, but they brought me here instead. I just wanted to say good-bye."

Above me, Elle's covers rustled as she situated herself. "You said the same thing after your parents called to tell you he didn't make it. I thought about that all the time while I was gone. That all you wanted was to say good-bye. But it was too late."

Shadows oozed up the wall, slithering over the framed picture I'd given Elle, which was propped on top of the tall chest of drawers next to her closet. Elle's breathing evened out, slowed.

Her legs twitched, a sign she was almost asleep. The clock on her dresser read 12:27.

"You don't know how many times I wanted to call you," she said, her voice thick with sleep, her words rough as sand. "To say good-bye."

I squeezed my eyes shut. "I knew," I said. "Just like I knew about Grandpa Lou."

"Good. I'm glad." Her words fell at the end, a whisper I could hardly detect. Then she was asleep. And I was alone.

The numbers on the clock flipped and fluttered me toward 1:00 a.m. I didn't feel tired. Not even a little heavy. It was that journal—it was calling me, daring me to read it.

The heat kicked on, and the steady whir of air tethered me to the moment. I wanted to turn off the lava lamp. The creeping shadows made it impossible for me to fall asleep. But earlier, Elle had told me that it was her night-light and that it kept away the nightmares. Helped her know where she was when she opened her eyes in the darkness.

I turned to my stomach and stretched out my legs, willing myself to ignore the temptation. Elle shifted on the bed above me. When I looked up, I saw the edge of the spiral notebook. It snickered and taunted. I propped myself on my elbows, checking to see if Elle's legs had stopped twitching, which always indicated she had entered a deep sleep. Nothing. Except for the blue wings, shimmering in the soft light of the lava lamp, urging me to open the front cover. I reached up and ran a fingernail along the spiral. Elle didn't move.

I snatched the notebook from the dresser. My chest tightened, explosive with tension and excitement. I never thought I'd hold it again.

All the questions collided in my brain. The blast sent shock waves down my arms, to the tips of my fingers, and flattened me on the bed. I swiveled so the pages would lie in the faint glow of light that hit the right side of the trundle, telling myself that if I could just understand, I might be able to help.

SHH! QUIET NOW.

It was like some stupid game. Really.

Shrinkenstein says I shouldn't trivialize my experience, but I can't come up with another analogy. Simple directions. Easy to play. It went just like this . . .

His objective: To stalk, pounce, use, kill. And to make sure I didn't talk. Game Piece = The Hunter.

My objective: To survive. Game Piece = a Speckled-backed fawn.

During the day, I'd watch TV. Talk shows and game shows. Or the Lifetime Movie Network. Those people became like family (gag me, I know, but I didn't have many options). Except for the times my real family made the news. I inhaled every detail, starving for more. My mom's fingers clasping a picture of me, a delicate suture stitching her broken heart. My dad standing beside her, his thick hands gripping her shoulders, holding the rest of her together. His voice cracking as he said that it had been six months, one year, more. As I sat there breathing in the smoky air of Charlie's world, I could hardly believe.

Those days I flipped off the TV and tried to scrub the sour smell from the refrigerator, sank down into a bathtub filled with scalding water, or walked around the block, hoping someone somewhere would recognize me, every minute fearful that Charlie would get away and make his biggest move of all.

Cooper.

Charlie whispered Cooper's name in my ear when I wasn't a good listener. If I wasn't as fast/hard/slow/gentle as he wanted. The Cooper card was his power play. By using it, he could get me to do anything.

Anything. At. All.

Crazy to think it took only one word. Just two little syllables stitched my mouth shut for all that time. Until I found the stuff in his room. And I had to take a chance.

Then I actually won. The little fawn beat the big bad—

Elle's phone tinkled its little song into the dim light of her room. I slammed the notebook shut and plopped it back in place on her nightstand. Turned my head so it faced the closet door. Closed my eyes. And tried to steady the pounding of my heart.

The phone rang again. Elle stirred. "Are you kidding me?" Elle flipped her phone open and slid it to her ear.

"Hey." Her voice was groggy. "What's up?"

Pause.

My breathing came out in huffs. I hoped she didn't recognize the sound of my betrayal.

"No way!" I flipped over as Elle sat up, looking at me, her eyes puffy but alert. "Are you crazy? It's like twenty degrees out there."

Pause. Big smile.

"Yeah. I guess so."

I shrugged. Elle mouthed, *Oh my God*, fisting her hands into tight balls.

"I still have it. You want me to— Sure. We'll be there in fifteen."

Elle snapped her phone shut. Her entire face scrunched up in this excited smile.

"Lemme guess," I said. "That was Chip."

"Mm-hmm. They're at the park. Sledding! Can you believe it?"

"It did snow a lot today," I said, trying to prolong what I dreaded was coming next.

Elle flipped the covers off her legs and shot out of bed like she'd taken a bunch of caffeine pills.

"He wants us to meet him out there."

"Us?"

"Well, me, but you're coming, too."

"Elle, sneaking out onto the roof and trying to climb down the side of that fence in this weather is just crazy."

"I'm not stupid." Elle opened her closet door and stepped inside. Within seconds, hooded sweatshirts, long johns, and slick pants were flying onto the foot of the trundle. "We'll skip the window and go out the back door."

"Oh, so you don't even bother to sneak out anymore? You just take off." I almost slapped my hand over my mouth to keep more words from coming out. The whole night with Elle, I'd felt like I had my old best friend back, and the last thing I wanted was to screw it up by putting her on the defensive.

"Pretty much." Elle twisted her hair into a loose bun, dark

frays of blue-black spilling out in a few places. "The worst thing that'd happen is being caught and getting some lecture on sin and forgiveness."

"What happened? They didn't used to be—"

"Bible freaks? I guess after I went missing they resorted to prayer, and now they believe that God the Great is responsible for bringing me home." Elle slid her legs into a pair of long johns, then pulled on a pair of slick pants.

"Well, you could totally freak them out."

Elle rolled her eyes. She walked to the music box on her dresser and flipped open its top. The pixie wearing a pink tutu started twirling as "Dance of the Sugar Plum Fairy" rang through the air. "Are you coming or not?" she asked, tugging the velvet fabric from the side of the box and sticking her fingers into the lining. She pulled out something small, and I caught a flash of white before she plunged the item into the side pocket of her pants, yanking the zipper up to ensure its safety.

"You need some socks?" she asked, walking to her dresser. "It's gonna be freezing out there."

I shook my head. "I don't like this."

"Well, do something to make yourself like it." Elle threw a balled-up pair of wool socks onto my blanket. "Why don't you call Max?"

"I can't call Max. It's after one."

"What are you afraid of?" Elle pulled her socks on and walked to my purse, which was sitting lopsided on her dresser. She yanked out my cell and flipped it open, pressing button after button. "You don't have much of a phone book in here, Tessa." She pressed the phone to her ear and smiled.

I bolted out of bed as her hand floated to the air near her chest. One finger popped up, then another, indicating how many rings she had heard. I grabbed for the phone but missed as she ducked into the corner, giggling.

"Max?" she said. "Hey there, it's Elle."

"Give me the phone, Elle." I swatted at her arm, but she circled around and went the other way.

"No, Tess is fine. Nothing to worry about. We were just heading to the park for a little moonlight sledding. Thought you might want to join us."

Elle grabbed a fleece jacket from the back of her computer chair and stuffed an arm into the sleeve.

"Cool!" Elle smiled and nodded, giving me a thumbs-up with the hand that erupted from the jacket. "We'll see you in ten."

I crossed my arms over my chest as she snapped my phone closed. "What did you just do?"

"Get over it," Elle said, stepping to the door. "You have about two minutes to bundle yourself up, or I'm leaving you behind."

I looked at myself in the mirror hanging on the back of Elle's closet door. Standing there with my arms tucked against my body, with my foot thrust forward and tapping the floor, I reminded myself of my mother. Why did I always have to be the one to think about consequences? How was it that Elle, after everything, still didn't see any reason to be cautious? I sighed and pulled off the bottoms of my flannel pajamas.

As I reached for a pair of pink flowered long johns heaped on the trundle, Elle clapped her hands and said, "That's right, Tessa. Let's go have some fun!"

"What the hell are you guys doing?" A deep voice whisper-shouted from behind us. Elle's fingers froze midtwist on the handle of the back door. I closed my eyes. Mr. Pendelton would *not* forgive this. I didn't want to see the look of disappointment on his face.

Elle turned and stepped around me. I heard a loud smack. "Ouch!"

"That's what you get," Elle said, "for scaring the crap out of me."

I turned to find Coop behind us, his hair mussed in the soft light glowing from under the microwave.

"Do you know what time it is?" he asked, pointing to the clock on the wall, which read 1:14. "Or how freaked out Mom and Dad would be if they found your room empty?"

"Oh my God," Elle said, holding her hand in the air. "You two are killing me. Enough with Operation Maturity, okay? I just want to let loose for a few freaking hours."

"Where are you going?" Coop grabbed a Tupperware container from the countertop and popped off its lid off with a quick snap.

"The park."

"Are you kidding?" Coop asked, taking a bite of a Christmas cookie left over from the batches Mrs. Pendelton had made for Elle's and Coop's teachers. A last-day-before-break tradition that she'd started when we were in grade school.

"We're going sledding." The arms of Elle's winter coat swished as she moved toward the Tupperware container full of sprinkled cookies.

"Sledding?" Coop stuffed the last bite of cookie through his lips and started on another.

Elle nodded. "You're not gonna tell, are you?"

Coop shook his head and licked red and green sprinkles off his lips. "On one condition," he said with a sly smile.

Elle propped a hand on the counter and chewed her cookie. "What?"

"I get to go, too."

"No way, Pooper." Elle dusted the crumbs and sprinkles off her hands and turned to open the door.

Coop stopped her by bracing his foot against the floor, pressing his toes into the bottom of the door. "I'm serious."

Elle didn't turn around. She sighed and shrugged. "Fine," she said. "We'll get the sleds out of the garage. Meet us out front in five minutes."

"Who're you meeting?" Coop asked, his breath coming out in a cloud. "Please tell me it's a bunch of hot chicks."

"Gross, Pooper."

Our feet crunched on the thick padding of snow, sinking inches deep with each step. Coop dragged three sleds behind him, the trail smoothing the sidewalk as we made our way past dark houses on the silent street. Up ahead, steam rose from the pond in thick, undulating layers. The usually powerful fountain was more of a slight trickle now that a thick crust of ice had grown around its base. The light, still glowing from under the cumbersome crystals, cast a mystical glow over the shimmering snow.

"It's not Chip, is it?" Coop groaned. "You know I can't stand that guy."

"It doesn't matter how you feel about him," Elle said.

"It should." Coop shook his head, the tassel of his wool hat flopping from side to side, and hitched the rope attached to the sleds higher over his shoulder. "I'm very perceptive when it comes to people."

"Coop, I know you're trying to be all brotherly and take care of me, but I don't need it."

"He's an ass," Coop said.

"Shut up, will you?" Elle sped up and left Coop and me several steps behind.

"There's a rumor going around," Coop said, his voice carrying through the quiet, "about you and Chip and a pool table. I'm assuming you didn't start it. That means he did."

I'd heard the rumor at the end of the day and had been trying not to think about it. The last thing I would have done, though, was bring it up to Elle. I had hoped that she wasn't aware of what people were saying, and that two weeks of vacation would give people something new to talk about by the time we were back in school.

"Who says it's a rumor?" Elle asked, her words trailing cloudily over her shoulder.

Coop stopped. "Why do you have to be such a bitch?"

Elle spun around, her boots sliding a few inches before she caught her balance. "Why do you have to take everything so personally?"

"You're my sister," Coop said, pounding the front of his coat with a mittened hand. "How am I supposed to react when I hear something like that? If I was even close to his size, I'd have kicked his ass by now."

"Ooh, brilliant way to solve a problem."

Coop dropped two of the ropes and bent down, picking up a single sled. "I don't even know why I waste my time trying to look out for you," he said.

"Me neither." Elle shrugged.

"I'm done," Coop said.

"Good." Elle's eyes narrowed into slits. She jerked her woolen-capped head toward their house. "You better not say anything to Mom and Dad."

"Whatever." Coop turned and trudged back toward their house, his footsteps squeaking in the snow.

When I looked at Elle, her hands were dripping with snow, balling a wad into one large snowball. She swung her hand back and lobbed the missile at Coop. It connected with his right shoulder and splattered down his coat. He didn't turn around, just kept walking, his head down, arms pulled tight against his body.

We heard them before we saw them. Loud whoops echoed through the darkness, between the trees in the depths of the wooded reserve at the back of the park. The three bulky shadows standing on top of the hill couldn't see us as we approached from behind. One of them tipped his head back, emptying what looked like a flask into his mouth. They put their hands together in a sloppy three-way high five before diving headfirst onto three waiting sleds and racing to the bottom of the hill.

A crescent moon peeked out from behind an icy crust of clouds. We watched as the three guys collided into one another at the base of six or seven large trees. Their laughter boomed up toward us.

"So you're not mad at him?" I asked, watching Chip roll off his sled into a tuft of powdery snow.

"He's annoying, but he's trying to protect me, so I can't be too pissed."

I watched Elle's words float away as the moon went back into hiding.

"I meant Chip," I said, my voice flat.

"Why would I be— Oh, because of that stupid rumor?" Elle kicked her sled around until it was in front of her. "That has Jessie Richards written all over it. Besides, I got used to ignoring all the nasty stuff people say about me. Months ago."

"Yeah?" I asked, wondering if she really hadn't been affected by Jessie's attempt to mash her into pieces. "Still. It must be hard."

Elle shrugged and took a few steps back. "It's been way too long since I've done this," she said, running forward and hopping onto her sled. She let out a long squeal of laughter as she swept down the hill.

"So she was serious?" a familiar, velvety voice asked from behind me.

I turned with a smile.

"You guys are really sledding?" Max was thick with padding. His puffy winter coat made him look like a snowman wearing a pair of snow pants and boots.

"Totally not my idea," I said.

"I know you well enough to guess you had nothing to do with this."

"Are you implying that I have no sense of adventure?"

Max squeezed my shoulder with a thick-gloved hand. "No offense."

I stepped forward, pressing myself into him, and reached around the back of his head to pull his face into mine. His lips were fiery hot, soft at first, then hard as he kissed me in return. Our tongues touched, and his arms wrapped around my waist. I tried not to think about his kissing the girl Darcy had told me about. The one he had dated for two years and hadn't gotten around to mentioning. But trying to ignore her made me think about her even more. He might have sensed the shift in my thoughts, because he pulled away slowly.

"I'll have to insult your ability to let loose more often," he said with a lazy smile.

I pulled Max down to the ground, sitting forward on the sled so he had space to fit. "C'mon," I said.

Max sat behind me, tucking his legs against mine. We pedaled with our hands and flew down the hill, crisp air rushing the exposed skin of our faces. When we reached the bottom, we were both laughing. Max leaned in for a brief kiss.

"What are they doing?" I pointed to four bodies huddled against a tree at the edge of the reserve.

"Who cares?" he asked, standing and helping me up.

"I do." I grabbed the sled's rope and pulled it to the side of the hill, heading straight for the group.

"Tess, just leave them alone," Max called from behind me.

I turned around and looked at him standing there with his arms spread in the air. "Come with me," I said.

"Can't we just hang out alone? Without worrying about Elle?"

I almost walked to him, could practically feel the heat of his breath on my face. But then I envisioned Elle, her hand reaching into that music box of hers, and had to know what she'd pulled out of the lining.

"It's not that I don't want to," I said. "Give me a minute, okay?"

I heard him sigh, saw the way his whole body moved with the deep breath, watched the air puff out of his lungs. And then I turned and walked toward Elle. I felt better when I heard Max's footsteps crunching behind me, but not much.

He'd reached my side by the time I closed in on the small circle standing next to the tree. The two guys with Chip were his teammates, both very large, towering over me. Elle leaned into Chip's side, her eyes closed, a cloud of smoke streaming from her mouth. I thought it was just her breath mixing with the air. Until I saw the thick hand-rolled cigarette she passed to Chip.

"Heeey," Elle said when she saw me. "Sorry we started without you." The sweet smoke filled my nose, and I realized more than the simple fact that she was smoking pot. I wondered if it was as clear to Elle as it was to me that Chip hadn't called because he'd wanted to spend a fun-filled night sledding with his girl. All he wanted was her drugs.

"It's okay," I said to Elle, shaking my head as Chip offered me the joint. When I stepped back, Max's body stopped me. Grounded me.

"Wanna go again?" he asked, grabbing my hand. I turned and looked into his eyes, noticing the familiar pinch of sadness (or was it irritation?) that Elle seemed to cause.

"Sure." I tried to sound more excited than I felt, but it didn't work very well.

"We're right behind you," Chip called as Max pulled me toward the sled.

New Year's Eve

For the first time, I stood in the dim light of Max's bedroom. His walls were covered with posters of snowboarders, Led Zeppelin, Bob Dylan, and black-and-white nature scenes photographed by Ansel Adams. I turned in a slow circle taking in everything. The empty bottle of water on his nightstand, his jacket slung over the back of his chair, the stacks of books piled against his wall. I wasn't sure what I had expected, but this scene fit what I knew of him. It made me feel warm from the inside out, like I'd just taken a big sip of hot chocolate.

"Here you go," Max said as he stepped through the door. "Hope this is okay. It's all we had." He handed me a cold mini bottle of Coke, and I sat on the edge of his bed.

"Thanks."

"No problem." Max walked toward his computer and sat on

the swivel chair, leaning against his jacket. "I've been working on this slide show for a while. You're about to see all my favorites."

"It's not fair you made me wait so long." I scooted farther back on his down comforter. "I mean, we only have thirty-six minutes left in this year."

Max turned and faced the glowing screen, and I heard the familiar *click-click-click*ing of the mouse as he navigated his way to the pictures he was finally going to share with me.

"It'll just take a minute to pull up. Then we can go downstairs to watch the ball drop."

The flash of a young Noelle popped into my head. She wore a fancy silver hat with the words *Happy New Year* scripted along the top in glitter. I pictured us dancing in feather boas and high heels, bleating colorful noisemakers and showering each other with handfuls of confetti at the stroke of midnight. I wondered if she was having fun at the party Chip had taken her to. Hoped Jessie wouldn't be there to cause trouble. Tried not to feel offended that Elle had decided to spend her first New Year's Eve back home with Chip instead of with me.

"So what'd you do last year?" I asked, scratching hard at my cheek to punish myself for asking the question when I knew I didn't want to hear the answer. But it was time for one of us to tackle the subject of his ex-girlfriend.

Max swiveled to face me.

"Last New Year's Eve, I mean." I looked at a pile of T-shirts stacked on Max's dresser as I waited to hear his response.

"Darcy told you, didn't she?" Max's eyes looked sad in this soft and melty way, and I hated that they were directed at me.

I took a sip of the fizzy Coke and felt a little sick to my stomach.

"It's not like I was trying to keep it a secret." Max stood and walked to me. The bed sank under his weight, tilting me toward him, but I leaned away. "It just never came up."

"You dated someone for two years and didn't think it was important enough to mention?" I sighed.

"I know it sounds awful, but it just wasn't that important." Max pulled on a strand of my hair and then tucked it behind my ear. "The whole thing was more about me figuring myself out than me being devoted to some girl."

I covered my face with my hands and groaned. "Does this 'some girl' have a name?"

"Nicole." Max pried my hands away from my face. "It's not what you think. She fell for the idea of me. And I was too much of a coward to end things when I should have."

I jumped up from the bed and put my Coke on the dresser next to an ashtray full of quarters. "Did you have sex with her?"

Max's mouth dropped open. His eyes fluttered to my chin, my hands, my feet.

"No." I shook my head. Held one hand in the air. "Don't answer that. It'll make me feel worse."

"I didn't just use her, if that's what you're implying."

"I'm not implying anything." I shook my head. Leaned back against the dresser. "I've never had a boyfriend, okay? I'm just going with this whole thing, and when Darcy told me about a two-year relationship that you'd just ended, it really threw me off balance."

"I'm sorry." Max tapped his fingers on his knee. "I was afraid of scaring you and screwing things up."

"You might have," I admitted, "if I'd known from the start." I pointed my finger at Max and he grabbed it, pulling me toward him. "But now it's too late. I've kind of fallen for you. So it'll take more than 'some girl' to scare me away."

"Good." Max spread his knees apart and I stepped into his body, running my fingers through his thick hair. He fell back on his bed and pulled me with him, rolling me over to my side. "You freaked me out for a minute there."

"I was hoping you'd say something like that." His soapy scent invaded me, making me feel that weak kind of happy.

"That you scared me?"

"Just that you care enough to be afraid you might lose me."

Draped in shadow, Max's face had this dreamlike quality as he moved in to kiss me. It was one of those moments when I wished I could stop time to snap a picture.

His lips were a little wet when they brushed against mine; then I felt the smooth heat of his tongue as his hand grazed my side, moving up and down, soft at first, then more heavy and insistent.

A wave of heat surged through me and I pressed myself into the mattress. Hot pricks, like static, danced across my body. Max's fingers grazed the skin under my belly button, skated along the top of my jeans, and slid over the button.

I opened my eyes and saw the familiar curls of his hair hanging forward. He nuzzled his face into the side of my neck, running his lips along my collarbone. He felt so good. Too good.

I pressed my hands against his chest, and he raised onto his elbows.

"What now?" He arched one eyebrow, a smile playing on his lips.

"I don't get it," I said.

"It's called kissing. I can look up the history later, but for now . . ." Max leaned in, his lips parted in the exact smile he wore that hot summer night at the Three Sisters.

"I mean, why me?"

He chuckled and flipped over onto his back, looking up at the ceiling. "Why not you?"

"In the beginning, I was standoffish and even bitchy. I was determined to keep you at a distance, but you didn't let up, you kept pushing to get to know me. You could have had about any other girl in the school, but you chose me."

Max tapped his fingers against his chest, and I wondered what song was going through his head. I stared at the bumps on the ceiling above us, trying to find a pattern where I was pretty sure there was none.

"You intrigued me. From the first moment I saw you lying under that tree, I had to know you. You were so . . . guarded and afraid, I couldn't get you out of my head. And then I ran into you in class. It was like fate."

I turned and faced him, wiping strands of hair out of my eyes, resting my hand on his shoulder, watching his chest rise and fall with several silent breaths.

"I thought everyone in this town was boring." Max shrugged. "Until I met you."

"You couldn't get me out of your head?"

Max turned his face to me, and I bumped my nose against his.

"Not for a second. You drove me crazy."

I laughed. Leaned over and kissed him on the mouth, my tongue flicking his playfully. Then with more force. His fingers pulled through my hair, tugging me closer, tighter. I pressed my body against his, inching from his side to his chest. With one solid arm, he hoisted me up and I found myself on top of him. I pulled my mouth away from his and realized that my breath was coming in fast, shallow huffs.

"You okay?" he asked. His eyelashes were so close they swiped my nose when he blinked.

"I think so," I said.

He smiled. Brushed a wave of hair off my face. "Do you trust me?"

"You really want to know the answer to that?" I tried to chuckle, but it came out sounding a little strangled.

"I'll take my chances." He raised up a few inches to kiss my lips.

I kissed him back slowly before pulling away. "I think I do trust you."

"Really?" he asked.

I nodded.

"Will you take off your shirt?" His voice was whispery soft, and cautious.

"Max," I said, trying to roll off him. "I—"

"Wait." He trapped me with his arms. "I just want to feel your skin. Against mine."

I looked into his eyes and could tell he meant it. I hadn't spent a lot of time with guys, but it was pretty obvious he wasn't trying to play me into a bad situation. At least, I didn't think so. I sat up and felt a little unsteady when I realized I was straddling him. I pulled my shirt over my head and looked down, glad I'd decided to wear a bra. I wanted to suck in my stomach but thought it would look way too obvious. Besides, he wasn't gawking or anything. I actually felt pretty comfortable.

"Wow," he said. "You're even more beautiful than I'd imagined."

"You imagined this?" I pressed my palms into his chest.

"Just a few hundred times," Max said. "You trying to tell me you never have?"

I shook my head, my hair fanning forward over my bare shoulders. "My private thoughts are none of your business."

"Ha!" Max propped himself up on his elbows. "Thought so."

He grabbed his shirt at the waist and tugged it off, tossing it over the side of his bed. I ran my fingertips along his chest, down his side, and across his stomach, feeling the terrain of his body. He tried not to laugh, but he couldn't hold it in any longer as my fingers drew up his other side.

"See," he said, "this isn't so bad."

"That's what I'm afraid of." I dropped my hands to the mattress on either side of his head.

"Afraid you'll like this a little too much?"

I laughed, nodded, and moved to kiss him again. I kept myself elevated for a few minutes, just feeling his lips and tongue move against mine. It was when my arms started shaking (I'm not sure if it was fatigue or excitement) that I lowered myself. And the heat of his skin against mine was one of the best feelings I'd had in my life. Kind of like a tall glass of ice water on the hottest summer day. Refreshing and painfully good at the same time. It didn't take long for me to wish that I'd left my bra hanging on the door handle of my closet. About a minute later, I unsnapped the thing and flung it to the floor.

Max started to say something, but I pressed a finger to his lips. "That's all I'm taking off," I said. "No more."

And I kissed him again. And again. And again.

That was how we rang in the new year, totally unaware that millions of people were celebrating across the country, oblivious to the fact that the ginormous ball in Times Square had made its descent, and deaf to the voices that sang along with the tune of "Auld Lang Syne."

You Don't Want to Know

"No freaking way," Elle said, nudging the open pizza box away from Coop's outstretched hands.

Coop flopped onto the couch so hard my soda can wobbled. "You two are never going to finish a large pepperoni and sausage by yourselves."

"Never know." I shrugged and popped half of a greasy square into my mouth. "This is Girls' Night. Anything goes."

Coop leaned forward and grabbed a handful of squares before Elle could stop him, so she smacked him on the arm. "Ouch! That was not necessary," Coop said. "And to think I was just about to offer to buy you an extra pizza if you want more once this is gone."

Elle looked at me. I shrugged. "We do have all those brownies up there," I said.

"Chocolate icing?" Coop ducked against the side of the couch and raised his arm in defense.

"You ate them?" Elle smacked him again.

"Just one. Then I smelled the Marion's pizza drifting up the steps and decided to hit the basement for some of Centerville's finest instead."

"You're the most obnoxious brother in the history of the world." Elle grabbed the remote from under Coop's thigh.

"How was your movie?" he asked, kicking the *Cruel Intentions* DVD box with the toe of his gym shoe.

"Totally heart-wrenching," Elle said. "I can't believe he died."

"Tragic," Coop said sarcastically.

"For real." Elle nodded as she flipped through the channels trying to find something worth watching.

I took a bite of my pizza, and as I pulled it away from my mouth, half of the cheesy topping slid forward, slapping against my chin. It was that exact moment when Elle shot up from her seat between Coop and me, her plate and several small squares of pizza flying into the air.

"What the hell are they doing?" Elle's voice was icy cold. The pizza squares landed with a plop, facedown on the tan carpet.

Coop sat forward, his eyes darting from the TV to Elle. "You know them?"

"Shh!" Elle reached back and Coop grabbed her hand, pulling her to the couch, but she resisted.

I looked to the TV, where, on one half of the screen, a blonde woman sat at a news desk, her mouth tight and her eyes crinkled, nodding. The other half of the screen framed two teenagers, a guy and a girl who were both so pale it seemed like they hadn't seen the sun in years. They sat on a brown couch with a picture of a country scene hanging on the wall behind them. It was obvious that they weren't on the news set but were somewhere off location.

"Tell us about the first time you saw her," the reporter prompted.

"We saw her around a buncha times." The girl propped her hands on her lap, clutching them tightly together.

"But we met her one day when I almost ran into her with my skateboard," the guy said.

"She almost jumped out of her skin." The girl's large eyes avoided the camera trained on her face, which seemed unnaturally round due to her fluffy brown hair. "I felt awful he scared her so much."

"She was always kind of skittish, though," the guy asserted.

"What else can you tell us about her?" the reporter asked, leaning forward with the hope of some juicy details.

"She was different." The girl scrunched her lips together.

"Yeah. Like, really different." The guy snorted and ran a hand through his short hair. "Always serious. It was really hard to make her laugh."

"Wonder why, asshole," I said.

"He looks dirty." Coop made a face like he'd just smelled something rotten.

"Hmm." Elle clasped her hands together as she stood in front of the television. "You summed up Kevin Staples with the most appropriate word in the English language," she said over her shoulder. "Maybe you actually are perceptive, like you were talking about a while ago."

"You want to hear more of my thoughts about the Chipster?" Coop asked.

Elle hit the volume on the remote, and Kevin's raspy voice filled the room.

"There was this one time we were all hanging out, you know, not doing much, and we saw this . . . whaddya call it?" Kevin looked at the girl sitting next to him.

"A press conference," she said.

"Yeah. One of those. The mom and dad of this kidnapped girl were being interviewed, saying all kinds of sappy stuff about their daughter. They even flashed some pictures of her."

"And the crazy thing is," the girl interrupted, "we said how much Elle looked like that kidnapped girl. Asked if there was anything she needed to tell us. We were being sarcastic, right? But she had a chance to tell us everything. We could have helped her."

"No." Elle stepped forward, shaking her head at the screen. "You couldn't have."

"But she didn't say anything." Kevin rubbed two fingers over a large zit at the base of his nose. "Just shook her head and laughed."

"Why do you think that is?" the reporter asked with a serious tone.

"She musta not wanted to go home," Kevin said, putting his hands on his knees. "She had this thing for my mother's—"

"Kevin." The girl reached up and put her hand over his. When he looked at her, she shook her head.

"You were saying, Kevin?" The reporter was staring so hard it looked like her eyes might blast out of her head.

"My mom has this anxiety thing, so she takes some pills to help her sleep. And Elle, she . . . well, let's just say some of those pills went missing every time Elle was at my house."

With his twitchy nose and thin lips, Kevin reminded me of a rat. In that moment, I felt like I could dive through the screen and grab hold of the greasy kid's neck. Squeeze. And shake and shake and shake.

Elle took a few steps back and buried her face in her hands. "Thanks a lot, Kev."

Coop looked from the screen to Elle and back again. "Why's he saying that?"

"Because it's true," Elle said, propped against the arm of the couch.

"I don't under—"

"Shh!"

"Are you telling me she's a drug addict?" The reporter's eyes were actually twinkling with excitement. It was either that or the lighting crew had figured out some way for the overheads to enhance her thrill at uncovering an unsavory detail about Elle.

"I don't know why else she'da taken 'em." Kevin shrugged.

"That's not what I think," the girl said softly.

"Thank you, Julie," Elle whispered, her body slumping.

"Why, then, do you think she would need those pills?" The reporter's voice took on an interrogative tone. Her eyes no longer twinkled but looked like small onyx stones.

Julie shook her head. "I don't know, ma'am. But I never once saw her act like she was messed up."

The screen did this kaleidoscope thing, and Kevin and Julie

were sucked into TV land, leaving a single, live shot of the reporter. She was now wearing a few additional layers of makeup and had several more inches of poof teased into her hair.

"There you have it, folks," she said with a fluid smile. "The first interview with two friends Noelle Pendelton made while she was in captivity. We've had panel discussions with various psychologists on Stockholm syndrome and other psychological side effects of surviving such a traumatic event. But these two kids have given us a vital snapshot, detailing this young girl's actions during her two years away from her family."

Elle punched the remote, and the television screen went black. "Bitch."

"Elle." I reached out to her, but she stood up and circled the coffee table.

I did the only thing I could think of to help in the moment. I knelt on the floor, peeling five squares of pizza from the carpet and blotting the stains with a paper napkin.

"Screw them!" Elle pointed at the screen, tears pouring down her face. "People think they could have helped me. What a joke. Charlie would have gone after every last one of them. And he could have, because if it hadn't happened exactly like I planned, he would have gotten away. He'd be free right now, and everyone I ever cared about would be at risk."

"You're right, Elle," I said, pressing the napkin into the carpet, thinking of the journal entry I'd read a few weeks earlier.

"And Kevin had to bring up those pills! Now people are going to think I'm some junkie when I was just trying to get some relief. A few freaking hours to myself."

"No one will blame you for trying to escape mentally when you were stuck there physically." Coop looked at me and widened his eyes in a what-the-hell-are-we-supposed-to-say look.

I got up, tossing the greasy napkin onto the table.

"See?" Elle clapped her hand against her thigh. "You're my brother, and you even think I took them!"

I squinted, totally confused. "So you didn't take them?"

"Just tell us, Elle," Coop said, leaning back into the couch and putting his hands behind his head.

"I took them, sure." Elle put a hand to her mouth and shook her head. "I mean, I stole them. But I never swallowed any."

"Then why'd you steal them?" I asked, trying to make sense of the crazy direction the conversation had taken.

"For Charlie. I'd crush them up and put them in his dinner or his beer. Once a week. I swear, on Thursday nights he'd sleep so sound, I probably could've had him arrested."

So why didn't you? I thought. *Why? Why? Why didn't you try?*

"You should call in to that show," Coop said. "To explain yourself."

Elle shook her head. "It wouldn't help. People are going to think whatever they want. Nothing I say is going to change that."

I shrugged. "It might."

"Huh-uh. I'm not going to subject myself to some totally fake reporter who'll ask a bunch of private questions."

"But if people heard the real reason you stole those pills—"

"Coop, I could go to the trouble of explaining about the pills, but it would trip all these other subjects. Why didn't I use those times to escape? Or call the police? Did I actually like being with him?"

"She's got a point," I said.

"The thing is, I could go public and answer every last question, hoping people will finally understand. But that'll *never* happen. Not like I want it to. So I just have to sit back and wait until it's over. Until the media has something else to cling to and exploit."

"You're sure?" Coop asked. "You have so much support from people. You could find a different reporter. One who'd—"

Elle shook her head. Chewed on her thumbnail. "I can't open myself up, Coop. They'd ask me the one question I can't answer."

Coop looked at me. I shook my head. But he asked anyway.

"Well," he said, "why *didn't* you try to get away any sooner?"

Elle just stared at him, tears dripping from her chin. For a second, I thought she might answer him. But what could she say? If she told him the truth, that keeping *him* safe was a link in the chain that had bound her to Charlie for two years, the guilt would break him.

"You don't really want to know that, Pooper," she said. "Trust me."

Outta Me, Onto You

"I'm feeling a little overwhelmed here," I said, tapping my fingernails on my desk.

"It'll be fine." Darcy reached over and covered my hand with hers. "Stop before you drive me insane."

"Did they do this last year? Because I don't remember—"

"Is there a problem, Tessa?" Mr. Hollon stood by his desk, his arms crossed over his chest.

Max laughed. "You know very well what the problem is, Mr. H."

"I know it'll be a challenge for you." Mr. Hollon walked to my desk, his hands falling on the folder holding my most recent pictures. "From challenge comes growth."

I snorted. "Or death."

"Don't be so melodramatic." Darcy made a little *pfft* sound.

"Tessa, you'll be fine, and you know it," Max said.

"You people, with all your confidence," I said. "You don't get it."

"It's just an art show," Mr. Hollon said. "You don't have to stand next to your work and wait for a flogging if someone dislikes one of your pictures. You simply have to figure out which shots to include and how best to showcase them."

"What if I decide not to enter?" I looked up at my teacher and saw that his left eyebrow was raised. Never a good sign.

"That is not an option, Tessa. It's for a grade." With that, he turned his back on me and walked away.

"I'll just take a zero," I said under my breath as I slid the envelope full of photographs off my desk, letting it drop to the floor.

"Not. An. Option." Mr. Hollon threw his words over his shoulder without looking back.

I tried not to freak out. But it was all getting to be too much. I didn't need some stupid art show to worry about on top of everything else. And the sound of Darcy's fingernails clicking away at her phone while she popped little bubbles of gum against her teeth was about to send me over the edge.

I reached over and was about to tear her phone from her hands, but she twisted in her seat so I couldn't reach her.

"You don't want to do that," she said.

"Yes." I nodded. "I do."

"Hang on." She looked more closely at the screen, reading the words that her boyfriend had just sent.

"Like I want to hear some stupid love—"

"C hallway," Darcy said, whipping her hair over her shoulder as she turned to look at me with wide eyes. "Hurry up! It's Elle."

I stood and stumbled over the manila envelope holding all of my pictures. Max reached out and steadied me with both hands.

"Is she—"

"She's with Jessie. T wrote their names, C hallway, and one other word."

"What?" I asked, grabbing my camera from my purse so Mr. Hollon wouldn't ask where I was headed.

"Catfight."

I used my hands and arms, even my knees, pushing hard a few times to split through people in the crowd. The circle surrounding Elle and Jessie was three rings deep by the time I made it to C hallway. They were gathered in front of the entrance to the boys' bathroom, practically pulsing with excitement over the conflict brewing.

"I'm sure you heard that I've been gone for a couple of years."

That was Elle's voice. Someone behind me said, "Ouch," and I didn't know if it had to do with my elbow in her stomach or Elle's words.

"Like I'm supposed to care?" No doubt, that was Jessie. All around me, people sucked air into their lungs in this dramatic show of disbelief. "You want my pity?"

I shoved my way into the center of the ring just in time to see Elle prop one hand on her hip. "Seems more like *I* have something *you* want."

Jessie rolled her eyes and looked to her left. Through the gap between Elle and Jessie, I found the reason she had diverted her attention from Elle. Supportive as always, Kirsten and Tabby stood a few feet away, their lips peeled back in these wicked grins. "I can have anything I want."

Elle chuckled. "Really? From my perspective, it looks like the one thing you want to call yours is just out of reach."

"You must be a little slow, since you had to take a few years off school and everything. Plus all those drugs you took . . . So let me help you out." It was really hard for me not to step up and punch Jessie in the face. I sucked in a deep breath and looked away. From the other side of the circle, Tabby leaned forward. I swear, I expected to see drool streaming from her lips.

Jessie propped both hands on her hips and stuck her neck out as she spoke: "Chip Knowles is, and always will be, mine."

Elle pushed some hair off her face, her glare never leaving Jessie. "That's really sweet and all. But I'm pretty sure he's tired of being your most important accessory."

Jessie smiled thinly and shook her head. "You should have been smart enough to figure out the way things work around here before you stole someone's boyfriend."

"How many of you"—Elle acknowledged the group of people surrounding her—"think I would steal a person?" After a few seconds, Elle found me in the crowd. She rolled her eyes and pulled her shoulders back before facing Jessie again. I was proud, watching her stand strong, facing one of the most relentless adversaries in the building. "It must kill you that he doesn't want you anymore. If it's easier for you to think that I stole him, fine."

Jessie snorted. Tabby and Kirsten reared back like they had just been slapped.

"Enjoy yourself while you can." Jessie leaned forward. "Because your ride is almost over."

I studied Kirsten's and Tabby's faces, the glimmer in each of their eyes giving away how much they were relishing every second of this showdown.

"You're terrified, aren't you?" Elle took a step forward and looked right at Jessie.

Jessie just stared at Elle, her eyes narrowing so that all I could see were thick lashes.

"You're not so sure he'll make his way back to you," Elle said.

Tabby clasped Kirsten's hand and tucked it under her arm.

"That's ridiculous." Jessie tilted her head.

Kirsten nudged Tabby's side with her elbow.

"Puh-lease," Elle said. "I may not have been back that long, but everybody, and I mean *everybody*, knows you're freaking out."

Jessie shrugged. "All I can tell you is you're wasting your time with him."

Elle chuckled. "Funny. That's exactly what Chip said about all the years he was with you."

Gasps flew through the air, varying in length and intensity. Jessie looked to the ground.

"And by the way," Elle added, "I didn't have to steal anything. Chip was very willing."

When Jessie looked up, I saw tears in her eyes. Her lips trembled, and her cheeks grew mottled with patches of deep red.

"I'll bet you made it worth his while," Jessie said, her words all quivery with anger. "You learned a lot about making a man happy while you were *away*, didn't you?"

Elle pulled back her arm and fisted her hand. I lunged at her, grabbing her elbow with about a millisecond to spare.

"I see you learned a lot about class, too." Jessie shook her head.

"Enough, people, let's move along," I heard from outside the perimeter of the circle. "Get back to lunch, or class, or wherever you belong."

Jessie turned and stepped toward Tabby and Kirsten, who still hadn't moved and still had those depraved smiles plastered to their faces. It was like plastic surgery gone wrong.

"You must feel really dejected if you have to stoop that low," Elle said as Jessie walked through the dispersing crowd.

Jessie just waggled her fingers over her shoulder. And then she was gone.

"Move along, everyone." The voice was clearer now, and I thought it might be the assistant principal.

Elle's eyes scrunched tight, and she took a deep, shaky breath, trying not to cry. A look of fear crossed over her face before she pulled herself together enough to remember she had the upper hand. Chip, for the moment at least, was hers.

"I gotta go," she said. "I'm way late for math."

"Just try to forget about this," I said.

"Yeah, yeah." Elle twisted her hair into a long rope and flung it over her shoulder as she started to walk away. "She's not going to win."

As the last stragglers fanned out, I turned and saw Max propped against a locker. He opened his arms, and I walked toward him. Stepping into his warm body, pressing myself against his comfort, I took in a deep breath of his soapy scent and wished it had the power to cleanse me of everything.

"Elle," I said, trying not to shout. I could see her up ahead, rushing through rows of cars glinting in the sun's rays. The blue-black of her hair, which had begun to fade into a drab brown, swished across her back as she looked from side to side.

"Elle!" People all around me slung backpacks into their cars, slammed doors, and revved engines, hoping to rush through the end-of-the-day traffic. "Wait up!"

She heard me. I knew she did. I pushed myself to move faster and finally caught up with her. All I got was her profile as she searched across the sea of cars surrounding us.

"I don't know why you're ignoring me," I said, "but it's not going to work."

That was when she stopped. Turned. Tilted her head. "I'm busy. What do you want?"

"To see if you're okay." The words hung in the cold air between us. I could see the anger rise to the surface of Elle's face. She hated to be considered weak. She was *always* okay.

"Can't we just forget about it?" Elle adjusted the strap of her backpack, letting the load drop lower on her back.

"I don't think so," I said. "You looked pretty freaked out when Jessie said all that stuff about Chip being hers."

"It showed?" Elle's shoulders slumped.

"Just because I know you so well." I scraped the toe of my shoe on the pavement of the parking lot. "You fell for him, didn't you?"

"I tried not to." Elle's eyes scrunched closed, and lines formed on her forehead. "Like, really tried."

My eyes stuttered from Elle's face to her feet and then back again.

Elle laughed, her head tipping back. "Looks like I'm screwed."

"You never know," I said. "Maybe they won't—"

"Little Miss Perky, always finding the bright side. Do you have some master plan to guarantee I won't lose him?" Elle raised her eyebrows. "Because Jessie has officially amped up her game."

"Maybe it'll blow up in her face."

"Nothing blows up in the faces of girls as pretty as Jessie Richards." Elle sighed.

I wanted to say something more, something brilliant that would make all of this go away. But I had nothing. So I just bit my bottom lip.

Elle looked past me, turned in a static circle, her hand shielding her eyes.

"You looking for Chip?" I asked.

"His car's gone." Elle pointed at an empty space in one of the front rows of the lot.

"Maybe he just drove over to the stadium." I nodded toward the football field.

Elle stood on her tiptoes and looked toward the tall brick building. A few guys moved around the back entrance to the locker rooms.

"C'mon," I said. "It's really cold. I'll drive you over there."

A few minutes later, I crept the Jeep around the corner near the locker rooms, watching Elle study the pink faces of everyone we passed, counting five bundled bodies before we made our way into the back parking lot.

"His car isn't here." Elle tapped her foot on the floorboard. "So he just *left?*"

Her eyes were focused on gray sky, so I didn't answer. I turned the Jeep around and headed through the main parking lot, reaching for my iPod before I turned onto Main Street.

"Here," I said, holding the iPod out. "You pick. Turn it up as loud as you want."

She looked into my eyes. "I'm not giving up."

"Of course not," I said, shoving the iPod into her hand.

I listened to her click her tongue as she ran her thumb along the face of the slim device. And then she said, "Oh, yeah," and reached forward, twisting the volume on my radio until the clanging guitar strings of Ani DiFranco's "Outta Me, Onto You" vibrated every cell of my body.

Forgettable

"Lie down." Max's feet broke through a thick layer of ice that blanketed the snow-covered ground.

I pulled at the sides of my wool hat, adjusting it so my ears were covered. "How'd you ever get so smooth?"

"C'mon," Max said, pointing his camera at me and clicking a picture. "Just do it so we can get back to the car."

"This was your idea," I said. "I mean, I could have thought of at least ten other ways to spend our snow day."

"Ten?"

"Okay, maybe eight."

"Do any of those ideas include us snuggled under a blanket on the couch in my basement?"

"If I don't freeze in this ice storm, you might find out."

A stiff breeze whipped through the treetops above us. The

Three Sisters groaned under the weight of a half inch of ice cling-ing to their thick bodies.

"The storm passed hours ago, Tessa. It's probably in Penn-sylvania by now." Max pointed at the ground. "I just need to get three or four shots. Lie down."

"You know, some girls would be offended by all these demands." I knelt on the cold ground.

"Have you even taken out your camera?"

I fumbled with the zipper on the black case and pulled my camera into the light.

"Okay, okay," I said, lying on the ground, pointing my lens skyward and adjusting the focus. Covered by the ice, everything sparkled and shimmered in the sunlight, giving the woods this glow that was more fairy tale than reality.

"That's not right." Max's feet crunched toward me. "Look at the picture again."

His mittened hand shoved a photograph that he'd taken the previous summer into my face: me lying at the base of the Three Sisters, wearing shorts and a tank top, sweating in the oppressive heat, taking shots from the ground up.

"I still can't believe you took pictures of me," I said. "It's so stalkeresque."

"Stop being so dramatic and pose, will you?"

"What am I doing wrong?"

A navy blue finger pointed at my straightened legs, which were half frozen by that point. "In the picture your left leg is bent."

"You're kidding, right?" I looked at his face, took in the way his eyes were all crinkled, how his mouth didn't even hold a hint of a smile. "Okay, fine." I pulled my left foot toward my body and stuck my tongue out at Max as he turned to walk away.

"Perfect." I heard the shutter snap as he took several shots. "Talk about an opposing image."

"You're actually excited about this art show, aren't you?"

"I think it sounds kind of cool. I'm interested to see whose projects get tagged with ribbons."

"I know mine won't." Instinct took over, and I popped off my lens cap. Looking through the little square, I watched the arms of the Three Sisters sway above me. Though I hadn't planned to, I snapped several shots while Max walked around, trying to find the exact spot he'd been standing when we'd met all those months ago.

"You never know." The shutter of Max's camera snapped three or four more times. "You just might get first place."

"Not if I don't enter."

Max walked toward me and helped me up. Pulling me against his body, he wrapped his arms around my waist. "You can say you're not entering all you want. I don't believe you."

Max kissed me on the lips, stifling my reply. I kissed him back, wishing he could understand. When our lips parted, I noticed snowflakes swirling in the air.

"It's not just that I'm terrified—which I am, by the way," I said. "It's all this stuff with Elle. Something needs to happen."

"Like what?"

"Jessie being flattened by a meteor."

"If she's gone, Chip might stay with Elle. I thought you hated them together."

"I can't stand it. But I hate the thought of him breaking her heart even more."

Max shook his head. "Tessa, Tessa, Tessa."

"What?" I grabbed his hand, pulling him up the slope and toward the trail that led us to the parking lot.

"You're getting too caught up in everything with Elle. It's kind of freaking me out."

"What's that supposed to mean?" I trudged up a small hill, watching my breath crystallize in the air.

"Pretty much exactly what I said." Max stopped a step ahead of me and shrugged. I looked at the branches behind him. They clicked against one another, all rushed and frenzied in the bitter gusts of air. It was like they were trying to tell us something important.

"Elle is my best friend. If you can't handle—"

"Tessa! All I've been doing is handling it!" Max threw his hands up in the air. His eyes were so wide and held so much frustration that I had to look to the glistening ground. "I've been understanding and patient when I didn't think I could be either of those things for one more second. I've tried to give you space, to let you do what you need to do for her."

"Max, I know. And I appreciate it. I do. It's just—"

"That's the thing. It's always *just* something." Max rubbed the top of his head with his mittened hand. He sighed and a stream of white breath flew from his mouth. "You mean a lot to me, Tessa. I want to be supportive. But you're too wrapped up in all her drama. And you're starting to make me feel a little crazy."

I looked at Max, hot tears springing to my eyes. "I have to be there for her."

"Of course you do. But you're trying too hard to be her safety net." Max's lips pinched tight. "It's great to support someone after she falls. But you're gonna break *yourself* if you keep trying to hold her up. Don't you get that?"

"No," I said, my foot stomping into the snow. "I don't get it. This girl has been my best friend all of my life. I would do anything for her. Least of all, by the way, would be breaking myself to help her. Because she didn't *fall*, Max. She was shoved down and ground into the cement, pulverized by the heel of someone's shoe."

"Listen," Max said, his tone as crisp as the air, "I'm not trying to trivialize what happened to Elle. For one freaking conversation, though, I'd like to take the focus off her and put it on us."

"Don't you mean on *you*?"

Max's shoulders stiffened. "This," Max said, looking at me with frozen eyes, "is about the part of me that wants to be with you, Tessa. If you can't . . ." Max bent at the waist, propping his hands on his knees, staring down at the ground like it was just too much to look at me. Seeing him like that made me want to run.

I looked past Max, to the clickety-clackety branches, whose message suddenly became clear. If I kept it up, I was going to lose him. The problem was, I didn't know how to stop myself. Not when it came to Elle.

I balled my numb hands into fists and squeezed as tight as I could. I wanted to scream and scream and scream. I was screwing everything up. And I didn't have the strength to pull myself off the path I had chosen. I had to play it out. To see where everything would fall in the end. I just hoped I wouldn't find myself standing alone.

"Max, I'm sorry." My words shivered in the air between us. "This whole thing with Elle, I can't explain it. It's just so huge. I know I'm doing things wrong every time I turn around. But I'm doing the best I can."

"Some days"—Max straightened up and stared at the tree-tops—"your best makes me feel like you couldn't care less."

"Do you need me to tell you that you're important to me? That being with you is the only thing that really feels *safe* and *right* in this crazy mess?"

Max's lips parted in the hint of a smile. "It would be nice." He looked at me, his chocolaty eyes melting.

"Well . . ." I glanced down at the ground, kicked at the snow with the toe of my boot. "It's true."

I looked at him just as the shutter opened and captured me.

"What was that?" I asked.

"Your cheeks are all pink, and a few snowflakes just landed on your lashes. Had to take it." Max shivered and grabbed my hand. "All I'm asking is that you stop making me feel like I'm so . . . forgettable."

"You're hardly forgettable," I said with a smile, rubbing a mittened finger across his lips.

"That's certainly nice to hear." Max wrapped his arm around my waist, and we resumed walking toward the car.

"I'm thinking hot chocolate," I said, tucking my hand into the curve of his waist.

"Under the blanket on my couch?"

"Sure." I laughed, trying to force the leftover tension from the air. "Let's go!"

We raced to his car and flung open the doors, scrambling into the front seat. I'm pretty sure we both had the same idea, because we both tugged off our mittens at the same moment. After Max turned the key in the Mustang's ignition and the car rumbled to life, he looked at me and said, "We'd better let it warm up."

Loving that every other space in the parking lot was empty, I leaned toward him, my lips parted, ready to commence with my newfound favorite pastime.

"But I'm so cold," I said, pouting my lips. I'd read in *Glamour* that guys like pouty lips, and yes, I'd even practiced the look in the mirror.

Max tugged at the zipper of my coat and grinned. "I think I can help you with that," he whispered as his lips brushed against mine.

Do You Believe in Ghosts?

"Tess, don't you think it's time we get to know him?" My mother was standing at the kitchen counter, a few dozen naked cupcakes spread out in front of her. A glass mixing bowl filled with home-made strawberry icing was shoved to her left.

"I thought you were going to frost some with chocolate," I said, plucking a cupcake from the end of one row. I plunged a knife into the icing and plopped some on top before peeling off the paper wrapper.

"I didn't have all the ingredients. And with the storm coming, I had no desire to deal with the crowd that's bound to be at the store." My mother swept her wrist along her forehead, pushing from her face bangs that had fallen from the clip holding back her hair. "Did you hear what I asked you?"

I nodded, pinching off a bit of cupcake and putting it into my mouth. "I was ignoring you."

My mother looked at me and tilted her head. "You've been spending a lot of time with this boy, Tessa."

I rolled my eyes. "Mom, if you think I'm gonna have him over for some family dinner, you're crazy."

"Why?" My mother dipped a plastic spatula in the bowl and started her well-perfected process of applying icing. When she finished, it would look like tiny waves were rolling across the top of each cupcake. "Your father and I aren't so bad, are we?"

"It has nothing to do with you." I licked some pink goo off my fingers. "It's just too formal. I'm not even sure what to call us right now."

My mother turned to face me. The apron she was wearing had a Hershey's Kiss on the front and read CHOCOLATE MAKES EVERYTHING BETTER. I'd picked it out for her about a million Mother's Days ago. "It might be formal, but this quick meet-and-greet when he picks you up will not suffice much longer. I'm not comfortable—"

I put a sticky hand in the air and munched the last of my cupcake. "Ma, let it happen naturally, okay?"

"That's gross, Tessa," she said, pointing the spatula at my full mouth. "And though you would like for it to be, this discussion is far from over."

"Fine," I said. "Just no more tonight. *Please.*" I grabbed the spatula from her and turned toward the cupcakes, reaching for another.

"No way!" My mother yanked the spatula from my hand and shoved it deep into the bowl of goopy icing. "I need the rest of these for the meeting tomorrow."

"I was going to help you decorate them." I took a step back and shrugged. "But if you don't need my help—"

"I would love your help," she said, pulling several containers of sugar sprinkles from the cabinet above the counter. "You can sprinkle like you used to when you were little. But first"— she turned to face me—"will you check the weather? I need to be in Cincinnati by ten tomorrow, and if it's going to be as bad as they're saying, I need to get up super early."

"You should just stay home." I turned and walked toward the living room, my thick socks sliding along the wood floor. I watched the wavy shadow of my reflection cross the black depth of three large windows that looked over our backyard. The bitter winter night had set in early.

"I can't afford to, and you know it," my mother called over her shoulder. "The doctors have to learn about this new asthma drug if I expect them to start prescribing it."

I sank down onto the couch and propped my feet on the coffee table, clicking on the television. The Local on the 8s wouldn't hit the Weather Channel for three more minutes, so I flipped up toward MTV. Commercial. I kept flipping. Up toward the news channels. Flip. Flip. Flip. Stop.

I flipped back, wondering if I'd really seen what I thought I had.

From my spot in the middle of the couch, I leaned forward, my elbows digging into my knees, and tried not to blink at the television. The sour-looking face of Charlie Croft occupied the entire screen. His dark eyes stared out at me. I wanted to scream, claw them out of his face.

I read the Breaking News banner once. Twice.

My teeth ground together.

The third time the words scrawled across the screen, I listened to the reporters' voices, and it started to come together in my mind, forming an entire picture.

When the doorbell rang, I didn't move. I couldn't. It wouldn't have mattered if it had been John Mayer standing out there singing my favorite song, that one about melody being his destiny. I was wholly incapable of doing anything but sitting and staring.

My mother said something sarcastic about not bothering me and swept through the walkway behind the couch. When the front door opened, the door knocker swung against its bed in a reverberating *thunk*, and I let the air I'd captured escape my chest.

"Mom!" I called, lowering the television's volume until the remote control slipped from my hand and bounced under the couch. "You gotta see—"

"Tessa, you have company." My mother's voice was higher than usual. A familiar cheer that meant only that she was trying too hard. Was the whole Max thing going to happen right now? Because it was *so* not the right time. "You must be freezing! Come in here and warm up."

The muffled sound of a soft voice flowed my way, but I couldn't discern whether it was male or female with the rustling of a winter coat and the clomping of heavy boots.

"I love your hair," my mother said, her voice moving closer now. I stood quickly and stepped around the couch.

"Really?" a familiar voice asked.

"Really. You look wonderful, Elle."

"Eh," Elle answered as they stepped into the room. "My mom

made me do it. Said it would make me feel better."

"Moms sometimes do know what's best."

My chest tightened. My body wouldn't move. It was like time had stopped, and I couldn't figure out what to do. *Block the TV*, my mind screamed. *Block her view!*

"You didn't walk here in all this snow, did you?" my mother asked with a concerned tone.

"No," Elle said. "A friend dropped me off."

"We'll make sure you get home before the storm gets too strong." My mother ran her hands down the front of her apron. A few dried slivers of icing fell to the floor. "I've got to get back to work. If you girls want to help, you can each have a cupcake."

"Mmm." Elle licked her lips. "I'm stuffed from dinner, but I haven't had one of those in forever."

Get her out of here, I told myself. But then I wondered. Did she already know? Was that why she was here? To tell me?

I sucked in a deep breath, hoping my voice would come out normal instead of shaky, because if anyone knew what I sounded like when I was freaking out, it was the two people standing in the room with me.

"Elle," I said, "your hair!" Elle swiveled her head, her now-shoulder-length hair swooshing across the back of her neck. She reached up and ran her fingers through her newly layered bangs that hung down the left side of her face. Rays streaming from the recessed light above accented the soft shade of auburn, and the new streaks of highlights and lowlights.

"You like it?" Elle's nose crinkled up, and I could tell she was uncomfortable with the change.

"I love it," I said. "I mean, that interesting shade of blue-black was okay. But this . . . is so much more you." I took a step forward, wondering if she could see any of the screen, or if I was still successfully blocking it.

"Tessa," Elle said, her voice soft. "Is everything okay? You look really pale and—"

When she stopped talking, I knew it was over. And I could tell she hadn't had any idea what had happened. She tilted her whole body to the side and looked around me. Her face froze. She wrapped her arms around her front, holding herself tight, like she was expecting to be hit from behind.

"So you haven't heard?" I asked, gripping her upper arms and steering her to the couch.

Elle shook her head.

"I wasn't sure."

"The phone's been ringing a lot today." Elle pressed her fingers into her eyes. "And my parents, they were whispering about something in the basement when I left with Chip, but I didn't know it was . . . about Charlie."

"What's going on?" my mother asked, her eyes wide.

I shook my head. Looked at my mom and mouthed, *Call her parents.*

But she didn't. She sat down on the couch, her apron fanning around her like an old-fashioned dress, and wrapped her arm around Elle's shoulders.

Elle finally opened her eyes and watched silently, clenching and unclenching her hands until her fingers were white. The sound was way down, and I could hear only the whisper of the reporters' voices, could catch only a few random and unconnected words.

Tony Stoker.

Assailed.

No. Vital. Signs.

"Oh, dear," my mother said.

"Can you turn it up?" Elle stared at the screen. An aerial view of the prison offered us a rooftop scene where a high razor-sharp fence surrounded a frozen-over basketball court. I assumed that beneath it the entire prison was on lockdown.

I knelt in front of the couch and swept my hand along the plush carpet until I found the remote. When I sat up and raised the volume, a cherry-cheeked reporter named Chase Nettles broke the silence between us. I reached for Elle's hands.

"Prison officials have yet to make a statement." Chase had a deep voice that didn't fit his baby face. "But one officer reported that Croft was attacked by another inmate as he arrived for clean-up duty in the kitchen. The assailant, Tony Stoker, used a shiv, or a knifelike weapon, stabbing Croft numerous times."

Elle's hands shook under mine.

"Okay, I'm hearing that it is confirmed," a female voice announced as the screen flipped to a shot of a blonde reporter with helmet hair. She pressed her earpiece farther into her ear as she looked just left of the camera. "Croft was pronounced dead at five fifty-three this afternoon. There will be an autopsy to confirm the exact cause of death, but it is suspected that the knife punctured his trachea, in effect drowning him in his own blood."

"Oh, God," I said.

Elle turned. Looked into my eyes. "He's dead?"

I nodded. Hugged her tight.

My mother stared at us with watery eyes.

"He's dead," Elle whispered into my ear.

My mother stood and stepped backward around the couch, bumping into the corner. She steadied herself with one hand. "I'm going to call your parents, Elle."

"He can't hurt anyone ever again," I said.

"He's-dead-he's-dead-he's-dead."

"Yes," I said, smoothing Elle's soft auburn hair. "He's dead."

"He's-dead-he's-dead-he's-dead," Elle chanted, pulling away from me and looking back to the television. She pressed a hand to her mouth and lurched forward, standing quickly. "I think I need to be sick," she whispered, rushing around the couch and into the half bath in the hallway.

I followed closely behind, unsure if she'd want me there. And then I remembered her tenth birthday. That day, I'd been so excited for her party I'd ignored the unnatural grumbling in my stomach. When the sight of hot dogs sent me rushing for the bathroom, I was mortified by the sound of laughter that followed me. But then Elle was there, right by my side, where she stayed, missing most of her party to hold my hand and tell me that it didn't matter what those jerks thought anyway.

I knew as I reached for the handle and closed the door behind me that it wouldn't be as easy to make her feel better tonight. But I had to try. So I knelt down and held back her hair as she heaved everything from her stomach into the toilet.

When she finished, she crumpled to the floor. "Ick," she said, wiping her mouth with the back of her hand. "I ate too much of my mom's chicken tetrazzini."

There was a soft knock at the door, and when I opened it, my mom handed me a glass of ice water.

"They're coming right over," she said, her worried eyes almost sending me over the edge. I was barely holding on, and her quivery chin nearly pulled me apart.

I closed the door and leaned against the wall, spreading out my legs as I passed the water to Elle. She took a large sip and swished, then spit it into the toilet. I closed the lid and flushed, surprised when Elle lay next to me and placed her head in my lap. I ran my fingers through her soft hair, watching the silky strands tumble across my jeans.

"Will you braid it?" she asked. "Like you used to?"

I smiled and grasped a small section, separating it into three equal parts. I was just finishing the fifth small braid when she turned her face to me. She was pale and looked so young. And afraid.

"I wish we could stay in here forever," she said.

I shook my head. "You're too strong for that."

"I don't feel like it."

My fingers twisted and twisted and twisted her hair. "But you will."

Her eyes fluttered closed, and she took several deep breaths. "Do you believe in ghosts?" she asked.

I ran my thumb along the braid I'd just finished, feeling its dips and curves. "I never really thought about it."

"It's just that"—Elle pinched her lips together—"I did all this stuff to get away. What if he can find me now? Punish me for escaping and turning him in?"

"Oh, Elle." I brushed my fingertips across her forehead. "He's gone. For keeps. You're safe now."

Not Ready Yet

"Elle, we've been driving around for an hour and a half." I tried to keep the irritation out of my voice, but I was getting tired. And then there was Max, who was waiting for me and whom I was trying not to think about.

"I know. I'm sorry." Elle checked her phone for the hundredth time since I'd picked her up at nine thirty.

"Have you even thought about what you'll do if we find him?" I turned right at the intersection in the center of town, picking up the faint scent of City Barbecue's wood-burning barbecue pit.

"I don't know." Elle looked out the side window of the Jeep, her breath clouding her view of the snow-covered sidewalks and the icy wrought-iron clock towering above Panera Bread. "I guess that depends on where he is."

"Well, he's not at Chris's or Josh's or Paul's." I flicked my blinker and turned onto a side street that would take us past another football player's house. "We've tried Denny's, and Bill's Donuts, and the bowling alley. Twice."

"It's just weird that he hasn't called me yet. I've texted him, like, three times."

I looked at Elle, lifting my eyebrows. "Oh, is that all?"

Elle let out a laugh and shook her head. "I know I'm pathetic, okay? But you're my best friend, so you have to deal."

"I'm driving you all over town, aren't I?" I turned onto a dark street and cruised up a hill. When my phone rang, I gave a loud sigh.

Elle pulled the phone from my purse and looked at me with tired eyes. "It's Max."

I pulled over to the side of the road and took the phone from her hand. "Max," I said into the mouthpiece. "I'm really sorry."

"Really?" Max's voice was low. Hard. "Because it doesn't seem like it."

"I know it's late, but—"

"Late?" Something on Max's end crinkled roughly. "It was late when you called me at ten, saying you'd only be another half hour."

I glanced at the blue light of the digital clock on the console: 11:03. "Please don't be mad."

Max sighed. "That's kind of a difficult request."

"So I'm guessing you don't want me to tell you I can be there by eleven thirty?"

Elle batted at my hand, reaching for the phone. *Give it*, she mouthed. I ducked against the door.

"Tessa," Max drew my name out, like he was trying to think of what to say next.

"I thought I'd be done by now," I said.

"You're still with her?"

"I swear, I'll make this up to you."

"Good. Because being put on hold over and over isn't the most fun I've had in life."

"I'll think of something." I listened to Max's soft breathing, envisioned his long lashes blinking away the seconds, and hoped I really could think of a way to make this right. "Just give me a chance." *Please, please, please.*

Max sighed. "Will it involve lots of groveling?" His voice had dropped down to a level of mild irritation.

"Maybe."

"What about kissing?"

"Of course."

"Okay," Max said. "You have one more chance."

"You're a pretty great guy," I said. "Have I ever told you that?"

"Oh, God! The kiss of death." Max sounded like he'd just been elbowed in the stomach. "Are you going to give me the let's-just-be-friends-speech, too?"

"I don't think I could just be friends with you. Your kiss is too yummy."

"Yummy, huh?"

I giggled as Elle grabbed the phone from my hand. "Maximus, you have halted all progression. I thought we had an understanding."

As she listened to Max's response, Elle nodded and chewed on a fingernail.

"Yes, next weekend she's all yours. Tonight, though, we

require complete concentration. Which specifically means no further interruptions from you."

Elle shook her head. "Literally no progress. We've been sitting at the side of the road since you called."

Elle looked at me and rolled her eyes. "Yes, I know most people can multitask by driving and speaking on the phone simultaneously. But it's against the law these days. And we're talking about Tessa McMullen."

Whatever Max said caused Elle's whole face to smile.

"Right. She'll call you first thing in the morning. Nighty-night."

Elle snapped the phone shut.

"What'd he say?" I asked.

"Will you *drive*, for crying out loud?"

"Fine!" I punched the gas and the tires spun beneath us on the slick pavement.

"I like him, Tessa."

"Me, too," I said, trying to hide my smile.

"He's good for you."

I paused, wondering if I should say what was on my mind. And then I decided that even if it pissed her off, she needed to hear it from someone. "You deserve a guy who'll be good to you, too."

"Something's up," Elle said, ignoring my last comment as she popped her thumb in her mouth and started chewing on the nail. "I can't go home until I find him. You're sure you don't know where she lives?"

I sighed and looked at Elle. "You really wanna go there?"

Elle smacked my leg. "I've only been asking for the last two hours. No wonder you wouldn't call that Darcy chick to find out where her house is. You knew all along!"

"Sorry." I shrugged.

"You should be. You're supposed to be my best friend, and best friends don't hold out on each other."

"I thought it might not be so great if you find him there."

"I have to figure out what's going on."

Five minutes later, we snaked our way through the back streets of Jessie's development. As I steered the Jeep around a deep curve, the sound of Elle's nervous breathing made me feel like I was suffocating.

When we cruised to the stop sign at the end of Jessie's street, Elle's hand shot out and squeezed my arm.

"Oh my God." Elle pointed straight ahead. "There's his car."

My throat was suddenly crackle dry. Why had I been so stupid? I should have just kept on lying. But part of me doubted that he'd actually be holed up at Jessie's. And now I was stuck.

"That monstrosity is her house?" Elle took in the double columns holding up the spacious front porch, the light pouring from super-high windows that accented every room in the front of the house, and the three-car garage protecting Jessie's prized convertible BMW.

I pulled to the side of the street a few houses before Jessie's, put the Jeep in park, and flipped off the lights. "Elle, I—"

"Please." Elle held her hand up in the air. "Don't, okay? Just take me home."

"You don't want to wait for him?"

Staring out the window, Elle chewed on her lower lip. She

shook her head and looked down at her lap, that new wave of bangs blocking my view of her face.

"You're not going to do anything?" I asked.

Elle shrugged. "What's the point?"

"Satisfaction when you bust him. Seeing the look of shock on his face. Hearing him say that's he's sorry for lying."

"That would only work if he cared, Tessa." Elle turned to me, her eyes closed tight. "He doesn't."

"Don't be so sure, Elle." I couldn't believe myself. I hated Chip, yet here I was trying to talk Elle into believing he might care for her, all because I didn't want her to feel even the smallest twinge of pain.

"It's totally obvious. And I've known it all along." Elle tapped the gearshift. "Let's go."

"Okay," I said, turning on the lights as I put the Jeep in drive and pulled away from the curb. "Maybe you're right. Sleep on it. In the morning, you'll know what to say."

"I already know."

I took a deep breath and exhaled slowly, letting all the tension I'd stored over this Elle-Chip relationship flow from my body. Finally, it would be over. Elle, who didn't take crap from anyone, would dump him on his ass.

"I'm not going to say anything," she said. "He doesn't have to know that I know. That way, things will stay the same."

I felt like I'd been punched in the stomach. My whole body slumped forward.

"I'm just not ready yet," she said, turning to stare out the window as we crept past Jessie's house. The thoughts floating through her head were so clear to me it was as if she were shouting them.

She wondered what Chip and Jessie were doing.

If they were alone.

If they were getting along. Or fighting.

Questions shot through her brain like a meteor shower.

Were they talking? Or doing something that required no words?

Did they have on all of their clothes? Or none?

Was this the way it was finally going to end?

If Today Was Your Last Day

I walked toward the origin of the Black Eyed Peas' "I Gotta Feeling," the drumbeat and lyrics pumping the air around me, the bass vibrating my chest, wondering what the hell I was doing at a stupid party.

"I can't believe I let you drag us here, Elle." The stairwell was dark, so I propped one hand on Max's shoulder as he led me into the basement of the enormous house belonging to some junior named Pete Levenfeld.

"You need to live a little," Elle said from behind me.

"This was supposed to be *my* weekend," Max said over his shoulder. His eyes told me he was only half joking. "Or did you forget the promise you made me while Tessa was driving you all over town last weekend?"

"Shh!" Elle reached over my shoulder and smacked Max on the back. "Keep it down, would you?"

"Does he even know you're coming tonight?" I asked. Chip was definitely somewhere in the large house. We'd seen his car parked in the street.

"Not exactly," Elle said from behind me.

"Actually, this might be the perfect place for our date." Max looked at me as a girl wearing an off-the-shoulder sweater pushed past him. "We can get wasted and then go bash some mailboxes with a baseball bat or something."

I laughed. "Promise?"

Max held a can over his head. "No," he said. "How about one beer and then we'll go?"

"Sounds good." I grabbed the Bud Light, clutching it in one hand as we took the final steps.

"Who invited you?" I asked Elle as my feet sank into the plush carpet of an oversize basement.

"I heard about it in math and thought a mindless evening making fun of people might be just what you two—"

We saw her at the same time: she was leaning over the pool table with a cue stick tucked against her side, aiming for a green 6 ball that was close to a corner pocket. Her golden hair hung down, whispering across the felt table. She cracked the cue ball, which smacked the 6, which dunked into the mesh pocket. In a flowing tank top and slim-fit jeans, she hopped up and down a few times with a perky cheerleader vibe. And then Chip stepped up behind her as she swiveled for a high five.

"Oh, God." Elle pressed herself into my side.

"They haven't seen you," I said. "Let's just go upstairs and—"

But then Jessie turned, her icy blue eyes resting on Elle. Her lips curled into a sneer, and she leaned into Chip and wrapped an arm around his waist.

"I'm thinking we should go now," Max said.

I slid my fingers around Elle's wrist and tried pulling her up the first step. "C'mon," I said.

"No." Elle tugged free of my grasp and straightened her body to stand as tall as she could. "I'm not going to slink away like some dog."

I glanced at the twenty or so people gathered around the room. Some sat on the couches, watching a basketball game on a flat-screen television. One guy played pinball while two of his friends shouted about his technique. But most stood in groups of four or five, just talking and swaying to the music.

"A beer would be good right about now," Elle said. "And maybe a game of pool when the table's free." She walked past Jessie and Chip, toward the stools at the bar, and sat so that she could watch them play. That was when Chip looked up and saw Max and me standing at the foot of the steps. He gave us a little nod. Even with his face shadowed by the brim of his baseball cap, his eyes looked dark and a little glossed over, like he'd smoked a hit or two of the bong going around a circle in the back corner of the basement.

Jessie watched with scowling eyes as Chip found Elle sitting at the bar. Her legs were crossed, and her arms were pulled back so that both elbows rested on the back of the stool. She tilted her head to the side and flitted her lashes at him. *Bitch mode*, I thought. *Not a good sign.*

"Heeey," Elle said to Chip. His mouth dropped open as he

looked from Elle to Jessie and back again. Then he waved this pathetic wave.

"How ya doin', Chip?" I asked as I hopped onto the stool next to Elle, hoping my smile didn't indicate how nervous I felt. This night was charged with an energy that could easily turn explosive.

Chip shrugged. He rubbed his palms on the back of his jeans, causing his T-shirt to pull tight across the muscles of his chest.

Jessie reached up, her eyes questioning, and ran her French-manicured fingers over the large bump of his shoulder. She whispered something in Chip's ear, and he shook his head. Jessie gritted her teeth, turning slitted eyes in Elle's direction.

When Chip noticed Jessie's glare, he tapped her butt with his cue stick. "Your turn," he said, as if everything about the moment was completely normal.

Max snapped his beer open and tapped his can against mine. "Here's to the stellar start of a fun-filled night!"

I opened my beer and took a deep swig. It tasted bitter, and the fizz burned all the way in my nose. Two girls walked past the pool table, heading toward the restroom, giggling and holding hands. Max rolled his eyes at them.

As I took my third swallow, Chip backed away from the table, met Elle's stare, and tipped his head toward the staircase. Elle nodded.

"I need another drink," he said.

"Already?" Jessie's voice shook a little as she bumped her hip into his side. "You should slow down, or you're going to regret it tomorrow."

"You know where another bathroom is?" Elle whispered. "I really gotta go."

"Yo, Rebar!" Chip yelled to a large guy leaning against the stones of a two-sided fireplace. The guy turned, and Chip held his cue stick in the air. "Take my place for a minute, will you?" Rebar nodded and stumbled over to play Chip's game. Chip patted Jessie on the butt before he walked past the bar and headed toward the stairs.

"I saw one in the hall leading to the kitchen," Max said to Elle.

"Keep her down here as long as you can," Elle whispered in my ear as she jumped off the bar stool and walked past me.

I swiveled in my seat, smiling at Max. He stepped in between my knees and rested his beer can on my leg.

"You're smiling?" Max leaned in, kissing me on the cheek. "At a time like this?"

"I don't know what else to do."

"We could go up to the roof and jump off."

"That's a little drastic, don't you think?"

"It might be better than watching what's about to unfold."

"I dunno," I said.

"I'm pretty sure."

I looked into Max's eyes as he glanced over my shoulder. Behind me, balls cracked, slamming into one another.

"I just want it on record that I think this is a bad idea." Max crossed his arms over his chest, tucking his beer against his side. "Tonight was supposed to be our night. And now you're getting all caught up in Elle again."

"It's not going to be like this forever," I said, hating that his voice was suddenly so hard. "It's just really intense with the whole Chip thing right now."

"My concern," Max whispered, "is that there'll be another Chip to take his place as soon as this Chip is gone."

"No way," I said. "She just needs a little help getting through this, and then she'll be fine."

"And if she isn't?" I noticed a few flecks of amber nestled in the deep chocolate brown of his eyes.

I could have stared into them forever, Max's eyes, if I hadn't seen Jessie hurrying upstairs. But I did see her. So I grabbed Max's hand, pulling him behind me, and did what any best friend would do.

When I made it to the top of the steps, I found Chip leaning against the granite countertop in the kitchen, one foot crossed over the other. Elle stood to his left, also leaning against the counter. Jessie was right in front of them, her arms crossed over her chest. As I stepped onto the tile floor, Max grabbed my hand. And then two guys and a girl stumbled through the garage door.

"Hey, Chip!" the girl said with a dramatic flip of her hair.

"Hey, man," said one of the guys. As he stepped toward the door leading to the basement, his eyes took in the entire scene and his face puckered. "Ooh, sucks to be you."

Chip nodded his response, wearing a stifled grin. It made my skin crawl, the way this guy could seemingly find amusement in the pain he'd caused the two girls standing near him.

"You were about to tell me what's going on," Elle said as the trio knocked their way through the door and down the steps. Her voice was solid and icy. I felt a wave of pride for her strength.

"I'm interested in hearing that very same thing," Jessie said, *tap-tap-tap*-ing her foot on the floor. "You told me you'd ended it with her."

"Did he now?" Elle asked, tilting her head Jessie's way, meeting her eyes. I loved the moment between the two girls, and I figured Chip didn't have a chance.

Chip looked at Elle and shook his head. "Look," he said. "I'm sorry."

"So that's it? End of story? You're back with her?" Elle pointed a finger at Jessie but kept her glare focused on Chip.

I narrowed my eyes, and Max squeezed my hand, tried to tug me back toward the staircase.

"When did this happen, anyway?" Elle asked.

I didn't move. I didn't speak. I didn't swallow or blink or breathe. I'm pretty sure my heart stopped pumping blood through my veins.

"You gonna man up and tell her?" Jessie asked. "Or should I?"

"Tess," Max whispered in my ear. "Um . . . don't you think we should"—he jiggled my hand, shaking my arm—"you know . . . leave them alone?"

"I had fun, okay, Elle?" Chip sounded completely unconcerned. "That's all it was supposed to be about."

I dropped Max's hand and stepped forward, looking into Chip's face. His eyes were narrow, and tight wrinkles creased the skin around his mouth.

"You had fun?" I asked. "You have *got* to be kidding."

Elle stepped forward, her body moving at half speed, like she was underwater and fighting a current to stay afloat. "Tessa, I can—"

"You don't have anything better than that?" I asked, not taking my eyes from Chip's.

"It *is* kind of pathetic, Chip." Jessie snapped both hands to her hips. "I mean, you told me she was fine with all this."

"Oh, I am fine." Elle raised both hands in the air. "No one has to worry about me. And I get it, okay? He's yours." Elle pointed from Chip to Jessie and back again. "You're his. And me"—Elle stabbed her chest with her pointer finger—"I'm free."

Elle took a deep breath and shoved past me, clomping down the steps to the basement.

"Nice, Chip." Jessie shook her head. "Really nice."

"Jessie, I was trying to find the right—"

"I'm such an idiot," Jessie said. "I thought you'd actually changed." Jessie stood there looking at Chip for a minute, her bottom lip shaking as she tried to blink back the tears that filled her eyes. Then she turned, pushing past six or seven people making their way in from the garage, and disappeared.

Chip didn't even glance at me or Max as he scrambled after her, ignoring the calls from friends he passed on his way out.

When he was gone, Max wrapped his arms around my waist and kissed me. "Well," he said, "I'm done with the drama for the evening. How about you?"

"That's the understatement of the year." I sighed.

"You ready to go?"

I pulled myself from his arms and stepped to the open doorway. "Just let me go get Elle."

I took a deep breath and ignored the shaky feeling in my legs as I walked down to the basement. I found Elle behind the bar with an open bottle of Wild Turkey in her hand. Her face was stony, her eyes hard, and her glossed lips pressed against each other with so much tension they puckered. When she saw me, she shook her head and swung the bottle toward her mouth, tilting her head back so she could take a long swig.

Before I could pull up a stool and think of something to say, Nickelback's "If Today Was Your Last Day" blasted through the speakers. Elle plunked the bottle on the bar and reached for an open can of beer, grabbing the hand of the guy standing closest to her. He looked at his friends with wide eyes and a slow smirk, then turned and followed Elle to the center of the crowd without a word, some beer sloshing out of the can gripped in his free hand. Without missing a beat, he lowered himself toward Elle's body and wrapped his arms around her waist. Her eyes closed as she pressed herself against him, pushing her hands into the air and shaking her head slowly from side to side.

I took a step forward, past the rack holding the pool cues, and envisioned myself thrusting one between their grinding hips. Just as I was about to push through the mass of bodies undulating to the beat of the music in the center of the room, I felt a hand grasp my arm, pulling me back.

"Don't," Max said, the word a rock pelting me in the back.

I spun around. "What do you mean, 'don't'?"

People crowded the basement by that point. The air was smoky, and someone had dimmed the lights.

"You have to stop, Tessa. Let her live her life." He nodded in Elle's direction. "She has to figure this out for herself."

"Let go of me, Max." I hated myself, but I couldn't stop.

"No. This is supposed to be our night, Tessa." Max tried to tug me toward the staircase, gently at first, then with more force.

"I'm not going anywhere without Elle." I snapped my hand from his grasp, and he turned and shook his head.

"I don't get it," he said, enunciating the *t* sounds in a way that made me feel as if I'd been slapped. "I really don't understand why you feel like she's your responsibility. Why we can't just—"

"This isn't about me, Max!" I felt this hot wave wash through me as my voice competed with the volume of the music. He had no idea what it had been like, all that time, wondering what had happened to Elle. And now that she needed my help, following him up those steps was the last thing I would do. "And it sure as hell has nothing to do with us!"

Three girls waving their hands in the air sashayed between us, breaking whatever it was that connected Max to me.

He shook his head, saying something so soft I couldn't hear the words. Then he turned and walked away, without looking back once.

I was so angry, I didn't recognize it at first. The tightness in my chest starting off as an innocent shortness of breath. But then it began to spread. By the time I pushed into the circle of dancing bodies, my heart was pumping fast against what felt like the constriction of a clenching fist.

Then I saw the phone swaying in the air. On the little LCD screen, Elle danced, her body pumping slowly against the guy she had chosen, her eyes fluttering open and closed every few beats.

"Wonder how much *Dateline*'ll pay for this footage," a guy said to his friend. He moved in my direction as he tried to keep Elle centered.

I jumped up and snatched the phone from his hand.

"How about *nothing*, you creep?" I shouted, spitting a little in his face. I turned and ran for the bathroom near the pool table, slamming the door shut and locking it just before the guy's shoulder pounded into the wood.

"Give me my phone, bitch," he screamed through the door.

I scrambled around, pressing buttons until I found the menu that led me to his videos. When given the choice, I selected Delete All.

And then I pressed the phone to my chest and allowed myself to sink to the ground. As I slid down the side of the cabinet, I bumped into a knee-high silver trash can.

When the phone rang, I jumped, and my heart raced even faster. I couldn't catch a deep breath and thought I might pass out. As my hearing swam in and out, I chose a focal point, a technique my old therapist had taught me, and started to count to ten. On seven, I realized the scrap of paper in the trash can that was serving as my focus held a familiar pink script that flowed from one edge to the next. My breathing started to become more even, and I was able to take in deep gulps of air just thinking of what that little piece of paper could mean.

"Slow down," I told myself. "Slow down, slow down, slow down."

When the phone rang again, I sat forward, pulled the paper from the trash, and smoothed it on the knee of my jeans.

I looked at the LCD screen and saw that some guy named River was calling.

"What?" I asked.

"What? What? I want my phone, you totally freaked-out psycho. If it's not in my hand in one minute, I'm going to break down that door and take it. Do you hear me?"

"It's not smart to call the girl who's got your phone a totally freaked-out psycho. But I guess I shouldn't expect more from a complete loser."

"I can't believe this—she called me a loser. Is this really happening to—"

"Hey! Look around."

I read the little piece of paper.

Strawberry Splash Strawberry Splash Strawberry Splash.

"What?"

"Look. Around. Do you see Darcy Granger anywhere?"

"Darcy Granger? What does she have to do with anything?"

"You find her and bring her to me. Then you can have your stupid phone back."

I snapped the phone shut and stood slowly. When I looked

in the mirror, I saw streaks running down my cheeks and realized for the first time that I'd been crying. I swiped my face and looked into my eyes.

"Pull it together, Tessa."

I stood there for a few minutes calculating the chances that more than one girl at this party had an obsession with Darcy's favorite flavor of gum.

"Who's in there?" a voice asked from the other side of the door. "Is someone in there?"

I almost started crying again when I heard her. Instead, I swung the door open and pulled Darcy inside the bathroom. She looked at me with wide eyes.

"You look awful," she said.

"Thank God you're here." I felt like hugging her, but I kept my hands, and the phone, tucked behind my body.

"My phone?" With his arm outstretched, the guy stepped into the bathroom behind Darcy, his eyes wild with anger.

Darcy cut him off with a thrust of her hip. "Step back, Steven. Why'd she take it in the first place?"

"He was taking video of Elle," I said. "I heard him say something about sending the footage to *Dateline*."

Darcy turned around and crossed her arms over her chest. "I don't think your mother would like to hear about that."

"Give me a break, Darcy. There are probably thirty people out there doing exactly—"

"I'm going to watch you delete that footage. And then you're going to apologize to Tessa for acting like a stupid ape."

"I already deleted it." I held the phone in the air. Steven

snatched it from my hand and then started to turn away.

Darcy grabbed his shoulder and spun him around. "Apologize."

"Jesus. I'm sorry, okay?" He looked from me to Darcy. "You're not gonna tell my mom, are you? I'd be grounded for, like, the rest of high school."

"Just stop being such a dumb ass, Steve." Darcy pushed him out the door. "God," she said. "I'm sorry. Now, what's going on? Where's Max?"

"He left. Look, I'll tell you everything later, okay?" I pulled Darcy through the crowd of people that had gathered by the bathroom door. "We have to get Elle out of here."

I found her dancing in the middle of the crowd with the sloshy-beer guy's hands swimming all over her body. When I reached them, I pushed him away and watched as he stumbled into a couple behind him.

"Go away, Tessa!" Elle yelled.

I grabbed her arm and hauled her through the mass of sweaty bodies. She tried to pull free, but the alcohol in her system made her unsteady.

"Let me go!"

When we made it past the bar stools, I spun around and pulled her face close to mine.

"Some guy was videotaping you, Elle."

Her eyes focused on mine, and then she shook her head. "I don't care anymore."

"Well, I do. And your parents and Coop sure as hell do. That means you're getting out of here right now."

Elle didn't resist as I dragged her up the steps and through the garage. Darcy trailed behind us, her fingernails clicking a text message to whomever she was leaving behind. When we got to Darcy's car, I folded Elle into the backseat and pressed my hand to my forehead. As I looked down the street, I thought I saw the taillights of the Mustang pull away and turn the corner up ahead.

And I felt something inside me rip wide open.

Awkward

I probably hadn't talked to Drew Silver since the summer night before eighth grade when a bunch of us kids in the neighborhood had a kickball tournament. We'd been at the park, in the field between the fountain and the woods, and I remember the purplish sky taking forever to fold over us. That night, the moon was full, spilling down on our game as crickets and frogs cheered from the shadows. Elle scored the winning run, and fireflies sparked about her body as she flew, arms spread wide, from one base to the next, until finally, her feet hopped home. She'd been excited, hoping that Drew, who was about to start his sophomore year, might actually notice her. He did. She made sure of it. And they'd ended up making out until her curfew. That was just a few weeks before we lost her.

So when Drew turned around in the middle of our study

hall and slid a piece of paper off his table, fluttering it in the air between us, I wasn't sure if he was looking at me or past me.

"You freshmen eat these popularity contests up, don't you?" he asked.

I looked at him, totally confused. I guess my face was easy to read, because he plopped the paper on the table in front of me and snapped a pencil on top of it.

"Superlatives," he said. "You know: Best Looking, Athlete of the Year, Most Likely to Succeed."

"I don't get it," I said. "Why are you giving this to me?"

"Because I have more important things to do with my life than rate the self-absorbed narcissists who strut around this school like they own it." Then he turned around, balled a sweatshirt on the table in front of him, and laid his head down. Within about three minutes, his heavy breathing turned into soft snores.

"I'm a sophomore," I said quietly, looking down at the paper. There were at least twenty categories, for which I could list the name of one male and one female senior. And I wasn't going to do it. What did I care, anyway? I was about a millisecond from wadding the paper up and taking it to the nearest trash can. Until I read the third line from the top.

Best Couple.

I sat there wondering how many times I'd heard the lecture that every vote counts. My father had taken me to the polls each year of my life so that I would appreciate how this great democratic system of ours works.

So I had to vote against them. I just had to.

"Okay, Tessa." Mr. Hollon stood over my desk. "You have stretched this about as far as it will go."

I glanced at Max. He seemed to be concentrating deeply on some detail of the picture on his desk, the curls on his forehead blocking my view of his eyes. Or he was trying quite hard to ignore me. Maybe it wasn't even difficult anymore—the ignoring me, I mean. After a week of not speaking to me, maybe he just didn't care anymore.

Mr. Hollon's large hand smacked a piece of yellow paper onto my desktop.

"This is due by the end of the period," he said before turning and walking away.

I looked down and wanted to scream.

Entry Form—CHS Art Show
Name:
Grade Level:
Medium:
Theme:

Darcy turned in her chair and leaned toward me. "Have you thought about your theme?" Her silver earrings tinkled softly.

Max stood and grabbed a thumb drive sitting on top of his desk. Not that I looked at him. I only knew because I glanced from the corner of my eye. I didn't think he caught me. He certainly wasn't looking my way.

"Harsh," Darcy said under her breath as she followed him with her eyes, watching him get settled at a computer in the back of the room.

I stared at the entry form and wished I had some kind of superpower that would strike the paper into a shrieking flame. Or even better, a power that would erase someone's memory so they couldn't be angry with you anymore.

"What's your theme?" I asked Darcy. "I mean, besides the whole fashion thing."   ·

"Cycles." She pointed to the haphazard circle of her photographs on the floor. "I'm thinking of hanging them like this."

I pulled the cap off my pen and plopped it on my desk, watching as it rolled over the side and fell to the floor.

"How about you?" she asked.

I shrugged, looking down at my desk, running my fingers along the words that I should have paid attention to that first day of school.

Run, baby, run.

As I stared at the words, the letters blurred together, reminding me of a reflected image. Like my face looking back at me from a flat plane of water. Or the cool glass of a mirror. Only backward.

I scribbled two words on the entry form. Darcy looked over my shoulder and gave a little snort.

"Mirror Mirror?" she asked. "How does that make sense?"

"I dunno," I said. "But I had to think of something, right?"

"I hope you can make it work."

"Me, too, Darcy."

She knelt on the floor and folded her arms across my desktop. "What about with Max?"

I felt like pushing her, watching her fall flat on her butt. "That's different."

"How?"

"It's just not going to happen. The Elle stuff is too much for him and—"

"It's not too much for him." Darcy shook her head, and those earrings jangled even louder. "You let Elle's life eat into yours, Tessa. Max just had enough. And I don't blame him."

I looked into Darcy's brown eyes and tried to blink back tears.

"Oh, Tessa. Don't get all blubbery about it. Just do something."

"It's too late," I whispered.

"No," she said with another shake of her head, her lips parting in a soft smile. "It might be really awkward right now. But it's not too late. Trust me." Darcy patted my desktop with one hand and blew the most colossal bubble I had ever seen. Then she sucked the pink wad into her mouth, the pop reverberating through the whole room, and giggled like a little girl.

Everyone turned to stare. Even Max. And for a second, when he met my eyes, it seemed like he might wave me over or stand and walk to my side. But then he turned away. So I slumped forward in my seat and stared at the entry form for the art show, wondering how I would make my theme work. And if I would ever be able to fix things with Max.

25

I'm Glad You're So Competitive

"What're you doing out here?" I asked as I sat on the bench next to Elle. The leaves on the tree above us were budding, these fresh green tendrils stretching out toward the sun.

"Just sitting," she said, pointing to the notebook and pen at her side. "I was working on an assignment before you pulled up."

I nodded, staring into the leaping fountain, listening to the crash of the water.

"Where were you headed?" She nodded at my Jeep, which I'd parked along the side of the road.

"I was out looking for Max."

"Oh, yeah?" She raised her eyebrows and pulled her legs to her chest, wrapping her arms around her knees. "Did you find him?"

"The Mustang's parked in his driveway." I pressed my palms

into my eyes and laughed. "I drove past his house, like, three times. But I was too chicken to stop."

"It's not going to get better until you deal with it."

I pushed Elle's knees, causing her to sway to the side. "What are you, a shrink-in-training?"

"You know, as much as I hated her in the beginning, for forcing me to remember stuff I'd pushed down, for making me talk and talk and talk, and for giving me all these stupid assignments"—Elle slapped the front of the notebook, the butterfly muffling the sound—"she's actually helped."

"Well, that's good," I said. "What was your assignment this time? Something about Chip?"

"God, no. She's been all over that since the beginning. Making me delve into my reasons for choosing someone who is emotionally unavailable. Guiding me to realize that I deserve happiness, and that guys like Chip aren't going to help me attain any balance or stability in life. Crap like that." Elle plopped her feet to the thick grass covering the ground.

"Well, she sounds pretty smart."

"Yeah. But guys like Chip . . . they're just so damn hot."

I laughed, thinking that she really hadn't changed all that much.

"For this assignment, I'm supposed to list all the reasons I decided to escape. And all the things I have to look forward to now that I'm home."

"Can I read it?" I asked before I could stop myself. "I mean, not if you don't want me to. It's just one of those things I've always wondered. Why, after all that time, you risked it and got away."

"You don't need to read it," she said. "There are only two things on the first list."

I held my breath, waiting.

"I left because he said I needed a sister. And I knew that meant he was getting ready to kill me." She looked at me and shrugged. "I think I'd become a little too old for his taste."

"You say that he was going to kill you like it's nothing."

"Back then, that's how it felt. I had worked so hard to make myself numb, I was this total void inside."

"But you must have felt something, I mean, to figure out a plan and put it into motion."

"I dunno." Elle closed her eyes and tilted her face toward the sunlight trickling through the branches of the tree. "I think it was more about not letting him win."

"Well," I said, chuckling, "I'm glad you're so competitive."

"I didn't mean it like—" Elle turned and faced me. "You heard all that stuff on the news about how there had been others, right?"

I nodded, holding my hands tight, because every time I heard their names or saw their faces, I got a little shaky.

"One night, I found a bunch of pictures and some videotapes of kids about my age, maybe a little younger. I wasn't stupid. I knew that none of them had gotten away from him."

I rubbed my fingers along the wings of the blue butterfly, feeling the rise and fall of the fabric, listening to the sound of Elle's voice.

"That's what made me want to beat him. And when he started talking about a sister, I knew my time was almost up."

"You were pretty brave. I mean, you could've just left, right? But you made sure he couldn't hurt anyone ever again."

"But I couldn't have *just left*." Elle fisted one hand and pounded it on her knee, emphasizing the last two words. "That's what people don't get. He knew where I lived. He repeated my address all the time, this sneer stretching across his fat face like it was some game. My home, everything about it, was his biggest hold on me."

"How'd he know all that?" I asked. "How'd he know your name that day in the park?"

"He told me that he picked me. That I was special. And that he'd been watching me for a long time before he finally decided I was the one."

I swallowed hard, not sure what to say.

"I have no clue how he found me, how he learned all the details of my life, or why he chose me in the first place. But, after months and months trying to figure it out, I realized that it didn't matter. If someone wants to have you, they're going to be able to make it happen."

"That's why you took the risk to make sure he'd be captured? To keep your family safe? You thought he'd come after you."

"I didn't *think* it. I *knew* it. If I had just left, he would have found a way to punish me."

I took a deep breath. "I don't understand why you haven't told anyone. At least your parents."

"My parents and Coop have already been through so much." Elle swiveled her head from side to side. "They'd blame themselves. And I can't let that happen."

"What about the other list?" I asked. "The one about all the stuff you have to look forward to now that you're home."

Elle smiled and reached for the notebook. "That one's more fun," she said, flipping through the pages. She plopped the book on my lap and tapped her finger on the top of the page.

> *Sleeping alone in my bedroom.*
> *Hearing my parents' voices as they make dinner together.*
> *Fighting with Coop over the bathroom.*
> *Singing along to the radio with Tessa.*
> *Laying out in the sun. (Ah, the smell of sunscreen!)*
> *Shopping at the mall.*
> *Eating as much as I want.*
> *Falling in love.*

"That's nice," I said, my eyes tripping over the last three words, my thoughts turning to Max.

"It's perfect," Elle said. "I mean, before this, I didn't think much about the future. It's like I have to retrain my brain or something, to think ahead more than a few days."

I flipped through the last pages of the notebook, all of them blank and clear of pain. "You should fill the rest of the pages with things you want to do."

"Yeah." Elle grabbed the notebook and plucked the pen from the seat of the bench. "Like going to prom. And graduating." She scribbled the words on the blank lines below *Falling in love.*

"Making it into Ohio State," I offered.

"How could I have forgotten that one?" Elle's hand moved furiously fast. "Living in my very own apartment. Getting engaged."

I leaned back against the bench, watching as Elle remembered all of her dreams, the dimple in her left cheek coming to life once again. And like her, for the first time in a long time, I started to think about what was important to me.

The Snow Globe

I tripped over a root half buried in the muddy trail, sprawling my arms in the air to steady myself. Grandpa Lou's camera, which was slung over my shoulder, slammed into my back. I wanted to scream. Not from pain, but from overwhelming frustration.

I knew he was there. Somewhere. His car was in the parking lot. And when I'd placed my hand on the hood of the Mustang, it had been warm to the touch. My breath became all shaky in that moment, as I listened to the popping sound of the settling engine, thinking about what I had to do.

But he wasn't at the Three Sisters.

And his phone was going straight to voice mail.

My thighs burned as I fought my way up a steep hill, away from the bubbling stream that ran through the lower section of the nature reserve. My breath came in huffs, and I couldn't seem to suck in enough air. I paused against the rough bark of a tree at the top of the hill, feeling drops of sweat trickle down the back of my neck. Birds chirped overhead, and I wished I could have their view for even a few minutes. Maybe that way I could find him.

As I waited for my breathing to become more even and controlled, I noticed the entrance to a clearing ten feet away. Through thick branches, I saw the fluttering pinkish white blossoms of several cherry trees. I almost walked past them, but when I reached the grassy path to the clearing and a large gust of wind blew through, tossing handfuls of petals into the wind, I couldn't stop myself from entering.

And when I saw what was in the center of that whirlwind, I actually laughed out loud.

He turned to face me as I pressed the viewfinder to my eye. He looked confused, the wrinkles creasing his forehead muted by a passing cloud.

"Hey," I said.

He flashed me a half smile. "You scared me," he said, pushing a wave of curls from his face.

I pressed the shutter-release button and caught him as he looked at me.

"You get some good shots?" I asked, lowering my camera and taking a few steps toward him.

"I hope so," he said, looking up at the white blossoms.

Another gust of wind burst through the trees, curling up the perimeter of the clearing, whisking hundreds of delicate petals into the air. They dipped and flipped like large flakes of snow.

"It feels like we're in a snow globe," I said, flinging my hands out in the air and swirling in a slow circle. When I stopped, I noticed he hadn't moved. Not one step toward me. Not one step away. "Am I freaking you out or something?"

He pressed his lips together in a way that made me think he was trying not to smile. "Why?"

"I dunno," I said. "Something about your eyes."

He shook his head. "That's about this girl."

I took three steps toward him. "Oh, yeah?"

He nodded. "She kind of broke my heart."

"Sounds awful."

Max sat on the ground, on the blanket of petals that covered the grass, and placed his camera next to him. "It was."

I walked toward him, pulling the strap of my camera over my head. "You seem pretty nice and all."

He shrugged. "I like to think so."

I sat next to him, put my camera right next to his, and stretched out my legs. "Wanna tell me what happened?"

He raised his eyebrows and splayed his hands in the air. "She blew me off for her friend."

"Maybe," I said, squeezing his knee, "her friend needed her."

He tucked a curl behind his ear and nodded. "She did."

"So . . . you'd forgive her?" I asked. "If she apologized?"

"Dunno," he said, looking at me.

I placed a hand on his cheek, feeling the stubble on his skin. "I'm really sorry."

He smiled, the lines around his mouth marking the humor he found in the moment. "Good."

"Good?" I pulled my hand away and lay back on the grass. "That's a little harsh, isn't it?"

Max lay on his back, the heat from his body radiating toward me, reminding me of that night in his room when our skin touching had practically melted us into one. I was dizzy with the need to feel him like that again.

"No more harsh than all the times you chose her over me." There was no anger or accusation in his voice. Just simple honesty.

Above, the petals swirled in the air, falling lazily around us, fluttering across our bodies.

"Okay," I said. "That's fair."

"You think you can stop?"

"What?" I turned my head, taking in the familiar curves of his profile with my eyes.

"Putting her first."

"It's not a competition," I said with a sigh. "She's my best friend."

"I'm not talking about putting her before *me*." Max turned his head. Our noses were inches apart. "I'm talking about how you always put her before *yourself*."

I closed my eyes. Wished that I could snap my fingers and let it go. "I can try," I said.

And then his hand was on my cheek, his thumb tracing the line of my lower lip. I inched forward, and our mouths found each other, pressing together with the heat and desire that I had been craving since he'd walked away from me that night at the party.

And I wanted him.

All of him.

And I knew, as the silky petals twisted into our hair and our bodies pressed against each other, that I wouldn't let him go again.

Bare Feet

"Are you coming?" I asked, my cell phone pressed against my face.

"You're already there?" Elle sounded surprised.

"Um, yeah." I pulled at Max's arm and gently twisted his wrist, checking his watch. "I said seven. It's seven fifteen."

Max raised his eyebrows. Mouthed, *Is she coming?*

I shrugged. *She better.*

"I'm almost ready." Elle's words came out shaky, and I pictured her running down her steps.

"Well, hurry. The light's almost perfect." I glanced at three boys walking down the street. They carried a baseball bat and two gloves. One threw a ball up in the air and caught it over and over. "And this is my only chance."

"Okay, okay. Geesh!"

I flipped the phone shut and looked at Max, who was facing

away from me, pointing a digital camera toward the crystal plume of the fountain. The water glowed in the soft light of the setting sun.

I took several steps toward Max, my bare feet sinking into the cool grass, and placed my hands on his shoulders.

"Will it work?" I asked.

"If you two sit right where I put your flip-flops, it should line up just like you want."

"Cool." I turned and looked past the leafy limbs of the sweet gum to find Elle rounding the corner of her street and heading toward the park.

I was so surprised to see her riding a bike it kind of knocked the breath out of me. It wasn't that she was on the red Schwinn I found deserted all those years ago. But still. Elle and a bike just didn't go together. Not anymore.

"Why are you staring like that?" Elle asked as she rode up and hopped off the seat of the bike, her hair swinging from one shoulder to the other.

"I-I'm just surprised you got here so fast," I stammered.

Elle lowered the kickstand and let go of the handlebars. She turned into the fading sunlight, a burnt-orange tint washing over her face. "No freaking way," she said, ducking behind me. "He must've sprinted the whole way."

Max put his hand above his eyes, shielding them from the sun, and stared across the field at a tall body advancing toward us. "Isn't that your brother?"

"Yeah." Elle swung out from behind me and started waving like an overeager first grader. "He caught me."

"Elle," Coop said, his breath coming out in quick huffs. "What part of 'No, you cannot take my bike' was so hard for you to understand?" Coop swiped his bangs out of his eyes and glared at his sister.

Elle shrugged. "Sorry," she said, pointing at me. "I had to choose between Pooper's Wrath or the Fury of the Goody-Goody."

Coop crossed his arms over his chest. "And I lost out, huh?"

Elle pointed at me. "She's *way* scarier than you."

I propped a hand on my hip. "I'm not scary."

Max laughed.

"I'm not," I insisted.

"Obviously you've never kept yourself waiting," Elle said.

"Whatever, okay?" Coop said, grabbing his bike and spinning it around. "I'm late for this thing with Allie Junette."

"Ooooh," Elle and I both cooed at the same time.

"Shut up, will you?" Coop swung a leg over the crossbar of his bike and started to pedal away.

"You might want to wash off some of that cologne," Elle shouted after him. "You smell like you were attacked by a bunch of girls spraying the latest fragrance from Abercrombie."

"That sounds like fun," Coop yelled over his shoulder, flashing a huge grin.

As Coop pedaled toward the street, Max looked up at the sky, which was fading from its burnt orange to a raspberry pink.

"It's time." He wrapped an arm around my shoulders and kissed my cheek, knowing that this moment was charged with stormy emotion.

"I still don't get this," Elle said.

"You're not supposed to." I walked toward the flip-flops and listened as she followed, her feet rustling the grass behind me.

"But I'll find out next weekend?" she asked.

"If you take off your shoes," I said, sitting at the edge of the water.

A Unique Eye

"Oh, here we go again." Max stood at the table holding both our photography projects. He propped one foot on the table's leg as he looked over my shoulder, frowning.

"Should I just ignore it?" I asked. "Whatever it is."

Max leaned in and rolled his eyes. "You're not going to be able to."

I turned and with one quick glance saw enough. "Oh. My. God."

"Maybe it's not so bad."

"But," I said, "it can't be good."

Before I could say more, they were there beside us. Elle, with her hands stuffed in the pockets of her jeans, and Frankie Green, a junior whose hair always looked like he'd just stuck a fork into a light socket.

"Hey, Elle," I said, breathing in a whiff of sweet smoke that clouded around her and Frankie.

"Hey," Elle said, her bangs swooping down to shield her eyes, but not before I noticed how red and glossy they were.

"Are you stoned?" I whispered.

"Are you ever going to stop being such a goody-goody?" Elle tilted her head.

"But it's, like"—I looked at the clock on the wall—"three in the afternoon."

Elle fluttered her eyelashes.

Bitch mode, I thought. *Great.*

"I'm outta here." She turned and grabbed Frankie's hand.

"No way," I said. "You gotta see my pictures."

Elle looked at me, her eyes mere slits. "You'll stop acting like my mommy?"

I heard Max chuckle behind me. "Yes," I said. "Now look." I pointed to the center of my project. To the two large pictures that were bordered by the gingerbread house and the girls on their swings, the single sunflower and the entire field, the old couple holding hands and Coop walking through the field at the park, the Three Sisters in the summer and the Three Sisters in the winter. I pointed at the large pond, the leaping fountain, and us.

Us then.

And us now.

"Whoa," Elle said, taking a step forward. She ran her fingertips across the two pictures, feeling the slight crease where one passed over the other.

Layering the shots had been like fitting together two pieces of a puzzle. Fortunately, the center of the fountain was a straight shot toward the sky. There were only a few splashes of water that didn't quite match up. The banks in the foreground and background overlapped perfectly, creating the illusion of an entire pond when, in fact, they were two separate halves. And the girls from all those years ago, sitting on the edge of the pond dangling their feet into the water, looked like they were laughing at a joke the girls on the opposite side of the pond, the girls of the present, had just shouted around all that rushing water.

Elle stepped back, looking at the pond, the fountain, and the four laughing girls. And then she smiled. "That's creepy and cool all at the same time."

"So you like it?" I asked, trying to press down the nervous feeling that spread through my chest like fire.

"Imagine if they"—Elle pointed to the picture Max had taken the previous week—"could talk to them." Elle's finger trailed across the pond, pressing her fingertip on the body of her younger, more innocent self.

"Yeah," I said. "I wish."

Elle faced me, flicking her head so her bangs flipped out of her eyes. "Your pictures kick ass," she said.

Frankie jutted his chin toward a mass of people twenty feet away. "Lookie there," he said with a deep, smoky voice.

I swiveled, looking over the cluster of round tables centered in the commons, and found Jessie perched on Chip's lap like she was trying to keep him from flying away. I stood there wondering why Frankie had pointed them out. I didn't think it was to be mean; Frankie had always seemed too laid back to act out of spite. It could have been some kind of test. Maybe he wanted to see if Elle was really over Chip. But that didn't fit what I knew of Frankie, either. He'd never been one to get caught up in anything. Except finding his next buzz.

I glanced over my shoulder at the crazy-haired boy whom Elle had chosen as her latest conquest, and I realized, judging by the way his lips curved upward and the squint in his eyes, that he was just as disgusted by them as I had always been.

"She should just pee on him," I said.

Max laughed. "I think she's marked her territory in a much less disgusting way."

"I guess," I said as a few juniors, having finished the treats they'd bought in the bake-sale line, stood up from the table nearest to us and walked away.

"Yeah." Frankie laughed. "Winning Best Couple of the senior class. That's *got* to mean they'll get married, have three kids, and live in a two-story house bordered by a white picket fence."

"I'm sure Jessie has already picked out their china pattern," Elle said with a fake gag. Her lack of emotion impressed me. And I hoped she had really moved on.

She looked past me, her eyes darting toward Chip and away again so fast I couldn't be sure. "Well," she said, "we'd better go, huh?"

Frankie nodded, his electrified hair sizzling the air.

"We're going to that party at Johnson's tonight," Elle said. "You guys wanna meet us there?"

I looked at Max. He raised his eyebrows, waiting.

"Nah," I said with a shake of my head. "But you guys have fun."

"I'll call you tomorrow," Elle said with a shrug.

Elle and Frankie turned and made their way through the maze of tables and chairs, disappearing in a group of track kids coming in from the meet that had just ended.

"You're *dying* to go, aren't you?" Max asked, his tone playful and light. "To keep track of her. To make sure she doesn't—"

"No," I said, turning and wrapping my arms around his waist. "I'm really not." And the truth of that gave me a rush of freedom I never expected to feel.

"O! M! G!" Darcy hopped to my side and spun me around. "Honorable mention?" She popped a bubble in my face, and I caught a whiff of strawberry.

I shrugged and looked past Darcy. The white ribbon fluttered against the sky blue backdrop of my project.

"Are you kidding me?" Darcy asked. She turned and ran a finger along my title, letters I'd cut from old photographs that spelled *Mirror Mirror* at the top of my felt board. "You have nothing to say? Like 'Darcy, you were so right. I'm an awesome photographer, and I should have listened to you all along'?"

"She's too embarrassed," Max said, sliding his arm around my waist. His clean scent surrounded me, calming me with one sweet breath.

"Well, yeah." Darcy's silver earrings sparkled in the sunlight pouring through the large window beside us. "Look at all the stuff on display." Darcy swept her arm in the air, gesturing around the room. Lining the perimeter of the commons were tables showcasing various mediums of artwork. From pottery to papier-mâché, pencil sketches to acrylics, puppets to masks, the students of CHS had created pieces that were light, dark, serious, and satirical. "There are only five honorable mentions floating around this room. She was totally wrong, and now she can't argue the fact that she has talent."

"Well spoken," Mr. Hollon said from behind me. "I have two more years with you, Tessa. I'm expecting great things." He squeezed my shoulder and nodded at the focal point of my presentation. "Very creative, Tessa. How you worked the past and present into what seems to be a single shot. Even though you didn't take the pictures yourself, the way you've chosen to fulfill the digital requirement keeps you within the parameters of the art show rules."

I looked to the two photos in the center of the board, staring so hard the images of Elle and me became a little wavy.

"I'm never going to like showing off my pictures," I said.

"Get used to it." Mr. Hollon winked at me. "You've got a unique eye."

"So," I said, "you think it works?"

Mr. Hollon raised an eyebrow at me and pointed toward the ribbon, walking away just as my parents burst through the double doors from the parking lot. My mother was carrying a large gift bag with a bunch of ribbons flouncing out of its top.

"Oh, God," I said, ducking my head. "She didn't."

"She did," Darcy said with a smile. "And I helped."

"Tell me you're kidding." I looked up at Darcy as she popped another bubble.

"You're gonna love it!" She clapped her hands together as my parents made their way through the crowd.

"Tessa," my father said, rubbing the top of his head as he looked at my photographs. "These are great."

My mother reached out and squeezed her arms around my shoulders. "You got a ribbon," she said. "Grandpa Lou would be so proud."

Max stepped forward with a hand extended toward my father. "Hey, Mr. McMullen," he said with a smile.

"Hello, Max," my father said, clasping Max's hand and giving it a solid shake.

My mother caught my eye and mouthed, *So cute*, scrunching her shoulders up to her ears like a fifth grader. I tried not to roll my eyes.

"You're totally embarrassing," I said, looking from my mother to my father.

"He didn't see," my mother whispered into my ear. "And so what if he did? He's adorable."

"The gift," I said, pulling away from my mother. "I mean, really?"

"It's your first public showing. Look at everyone." My mother swooped her hand in a large circle, pointing out all the people. "And you need this."

"Truly, you do." Darcy nodded. "But don't freak out, okay?"

"Yeah," Max nodded. "Just go with it."

I grabbed the bag from my mother's hand and set it on the ground in front of my display board. I swear I pulled out a tree's worth of tissue paper before getting to the box inside.

When I saw it, I sucked in a breath. It was a new Nikon. Digital. Top of the line.

I looked at my mother. And then my father. Opened my mouth to say something, but no words came out. Darcy bent down and lifted the box out of the gift bag, opening it and pulling the camera from its dark compartment.

"We know how you feel about your grandpa Lou's camera," my father said, wrinkles of concern creasing his forehead. "But trust me, if he'd been able to take pictures with this, he would have."

"Yeah," Darcy said as she flipped one of the camera's many switches and pulled off the lens cap. "This thing is sweet. And it's not like you have to get rid of your other one."

Max ran a hand through his hair, and several curls popped out between his fingers. "Change can be good, Tessa."

I took a deep breath and looked at my large purse, which slumped sideways on the floor, holding the only camera I had ever wanted. But my thoughts of rejecting the gift fluttered away as I remembered my grandfather, standing at the base of a tree in the woods, pointing his camera into the twisting branches where I, in my sundress and pigtails, struck a pose for him to shoot.

You gotta take lots and lots of shots, he'd said, *to get the right one.*

"Thanks," I said, knowing that they were right. Grandpa Lou would have loved everything about this new digital camera. "It's really nice."

"Okay, you two," Darcy said, shoving me toward Max. "Step in front of the redbrick wall. That's the best backdrop."

"I'm sure it has to be charged first," I said. "You'll have to wait—"

"Darcy told me to charge it ahead of time," my mother said, tilting forward on her toes. "It's ready."

I leaned into Max as Darcy's fingers fluttered over the camera's settings, choosing the best for indoor lighting.

"Hey," Max whispered in my ear as Darcy knelt in front of us. "This is the first photo of us together."

"That's a lot of pressure," I said, looking over my shoulder. "What should we do?"

Max tilted his head to the side. "I could sweep you off your feet."

I shook my head. "Way too cheesy."

"We could gaze into each other's eyes. Go for one of those introspective shots."

"Only if we want to give my father a heart attack."

"Okay. That's out." Max laughed, his eyes gleaming. "I've been told I rock at making a fish face."

"You've been holding out on me?" I asked, stepping away from him.

"It's just wrong to show all your talents right up front."

"So there's more I don't know about you?"

"Much, much more." Max's face took on this serious look, and then he sucked in his cheeks and plumped his lips, pulsing them up and down like a freakish-looking fish.

I laughed so hard that when Darcy snapped the shot, I wasn't even looking at the camera.

Acknowledgments

The creation of this book would not have been possible without the guidance and support of some very special people. It seems insufficient to offer you only two pages, considering the fact that without you, my book would not be. I sincerely hope that the following words relay your importance in my life.

First, I must mention my amazing family and all of my extraordinary friends. I'm fortunate that there are *way* too many of you to name— you know who you are. I appreciate your constant reminders that I just needed to keep writing, and that I really could turn my dreams into reality. Your inspiration and encouragement kept me going during the most challenging times.

Jimmy Chesire, the only official writing teacher I have ever had, deserves a distinguished recognition. Your gentle critiques always nudged me in the right direction. Without our discussion on synchronicity, I might never have given this a real try.

My earliest readers were my loving and supportive parents, Diana Dermody and Keith McBride, and my talented writer friends, Mara Purnhagen and Janet Irvin. Thanks for struggling through those initial drafts and offering spot-on revision suggestions. Mara earns a gold star for helping me navigate the most difficult aspect of becoming published; your guidance during my search for an agent was truly invaluable.

The entire crew of children's librarians at the Washington Centerville

Public Library has been so uplifting. What fun it has been to share all my book news with you!

I am extremely fortunate to be working with Regina Griffin, Nico Medina, Alison Weiss, Mary Albi, Greg Stadnyk, and the rest of the gifted team at Egmont USA. I appreciate all of you for believing in this book, for fighting for it, and for treating it with such care.

My two children are the real reason this book came to be. You gave me an excuse to quit teaching and take a chance on myself. I love you for your giggles and hugs. And the fact that you are such nappy-nappersons.

Eric, my husband and best friend, where do I begin? If not for you, none of this would be happening. Thanks for taking that leap of faith with me, for supporting me in my decision to dive headfirst into my writing. It was scary, right? I've hardly caught my breath. But look, it worked!

I give the highest praise to my agent, Alyssa Eisner Henkin, to whom I will never be able to express the depth of my gratitude. Thanks for propelling me from one draft to the next, for all the hours of brainstorming, and for not settling until this thing was in top shape. You are incredibly talented, and I am still reeling with excitement that you plucked me out of your slush pile and offered me representation!

Thanks to all of you for believing in me, and for helping me believe in myself. Much love.

KRISTINA McBRIDE, a former high-school English teacher and yearbook advisor, wrote *The Tension of Opposites* in response to the safe return of a child who was kidnapped while riding his bike to a friend's house. She lives in Ohio with her husband and two young children. This is her first novel. Visit her online at www.kristinamcbride.com.

LAKE COUNTY PUBLIC LIBRARY

3 3113 02913 8346

Ex-Library: Friends of
Lake County Public Library

X MCBR
McBride, Kristina.
The tension of opposites

LAKE COUNTY PUBLIC LIBRARY
INDIANA

JUL   '10

AD	FF	MU
AV	GR	SJ
BO	HI	CNL
CL	HO	
DS	LS	

Some materials may be renewable by phone or in person if there are
no reserves or fines due. www.lakeco.lib.in.us   LCP#0390